HEALING THE WHOLE MAN HANDBOOK

Effective Prayers
for the Body, Soul, and Spirit

by
Joan Hunter
and
Michael Hinson

Unless otherwise indicated, all Scripture references used in this book are from the New International Version of the Bible from "PC Study Bible" (version 3.1 for windows) from BibleSoft. More info can be found at www.biblesoft.com

Medical information came from: A.D.A.M.'s Health Illustrated Medical Encyclopedia at: http://www.nlm.nih.gov/medlineplus/encyclopedia.html

A.D.A.M. is an encyclopedic dictionary recommended by NLM. It contains 4,000 articles about diseases, tests, symptoms, injuries, nutrition, and surgeries. It is also illustrated with medical photographs and illustrations. This resource was written by professionals in laymen's terms.

First Printing 9/2005
Second Printing 11/2005
Third Printing 01/27/06

Healing the Whole Man: published 2005 by Joan Hunter Ministries, 526 Kingwood Dr. Suite 333, Kingwood, TX 77339

ISBN # 0-9770971-0-2

This Book is dedicated to all the believers who have been faithfully doing the works of Jesus throughout the years. It is also dedicated to the believers who will catch the vision contained in this book and run with it.

We would like to make it understood that we are in no way associated with the medical or physiological profession. We do not claim to treat or diagnose any disease or illness. We do not offer the information included in this book as a substitute for medical advice or treatment. It is for your general knowledge only. We also do not take responsibility for any individual's disease or illness nor are we responsible for their healing. We offer no guarantee that anyone will be healed or that any disease or illness will be prevented.

We do however believe that we are spirit beings who have a soul and live in a body according to I Thessalonians 5:23. We also believe that most problems that manifest in the soul and body have a spiritual root and that Jesus paid the price for our healing (Isaiah 53:5, I Peter 2:24).

We do believe God heals today because He is the same yesterday, today and tomorrow.

Acknowledgements:

Naida Johnson, RN, CWS, FCCWS for her devotion to this book and the many hours she has spent in the editing of this book.

Table of Contents

Introduction

by

Joan Hunter

Ephesians 1:17-19 states: *that the God of our Lord Jesus Christ, the Father of glory, may give to you the spirit of wisdom and revelation in the knowledge of Him, the eyes of your understanding being enlightened; that you may know what is the hope of His calling, what are the riches of the glory of His inheritance in the saints, and what is the exceeding greatness of His power toward us who believe, according to the working of His mighty power* (NKJV).

It is God's plan that your eyes be opened to everything that He has for you in ministry as well as every other area of life. It is His plan that the eyes of your understanding be enlightened to those you should be ministering to as well. It is essential we understand what God has called us to say and do each and every day.

The book of Mark says that those who believe will lay hands on the sick and "upon occasion" they may recover. No, it states …*they will lay hands on the sick, and they will recover* (Mark 16:18c).

Most Christians believe that God can heal, no matter what denomination they belong to or what church they attend. So why aren't people being healed within the church around the world? Why aren't

Christians laying hands on the sick and seeing them recover?

The scripture says "those who believe." It could be interpreted as those who believe that God will actually use them, those who believe God's Word is for them personally and those who believe that God will move through them as they obey His Word. Those who believe the Word understand the hope of the calling on their lives and know that God will move through them to accomplish the miraculous.

I remember the day I realized God could use me, not because I was Charles and Frances Hunter's daughter, not because I went to ORU (Oral Roberts University), or because of any ability of my own. I knew He could use me because I believed His Word was true and at that point the possibilities for my life became limitless through faith in God.

If God can use me; He can use you, too. If God can heal me from the top of my head to the soles of my feet, He can heal you. If He can restore my broken heart and wounded spirit, He can heal yours as well. God can do through you what He has done through me and even more. Don't put limits on what God can do for you or through you because of your particular circumstances. Instead, believe that you have a limitless God, that His Word is true and that it is His plan to use you to change lives.

Chapter 1

Why am I Sick?

Why am I sick? This question is asked by everyone including professionals, housewives and even pastors. There is only one answer: sin! Think about it. Was there sickness in the Garden of Eden? Sin causes sickness. However, it does not have to be your personal sin. Hebrews 11:4 tells us that Abel was a righteous man, but we know he died because of his brother's sin. According to the Word of God, the sins of the fathers are passed down to the third and fourth generations (Exodus 34:7).

When Jesus spoke to the crippled man who was healed, He confirmed that sin causes sickness. Afterward Jesus found him in the temple, and said to him, *See, you are well again. Stop sinning or something worse may happen to you* (John 5:14). Paul confirmed this also when he was talking to Christians about the way they took communion: *That is why many among you are weak and sick, and a number of you have fallen asleep* (1 Corinthians 11:30).

There are some who believe that sin is not the culprit and quote John: *As he went along, he saw a man blind from birth. His disciples asked him, "Rabbi, who sinned, this man or his parents, that he was born blind?" "Neither this man nor his parents sinned," said*

Jesus, "but this happened so that the work of God might be displayed in his life" (John 9 1-3).

The disciples had been taught that sin caused sickness and that is why they asked the question. Jesus never denied that sin causes sickness. He just stated that in this particular case neither the afflicted man nor his parents sinned, but this blindness existed so the work of God might be displayed.

Some people have been taught that their sickness is from God and it somehow brings glory to God. If you hold onto this distorted thinking, then would it not bring Him more glory if you were even sicker? This way of thinking is contrary to Jesus' teaching and would contradict Jesus' commissioning of His disciples. *He called his twelve disciples to him and gave them authority to drive out evil spirits and to heal every disease and sickness* (Matthew 10:1). The word "every" means "all" diseases and sicknesses, excluding none.

Some Christians have been taught that the healing ministry of the church ceased when the last of the original twelve disciples died. We count ourselves among His disciples and we agree with the early church. We believe Jesus still heals today. We have seen countless types of disease and illness healed in the name of Jesus and we know that the healing power of God is as real an experience today as during the lives of the apostles. We believe the Acts of the Holy Spirit still occur today wherever the Kingdom of God is being preached and the people believe. *When Jesus had called the Twelve together, he gave them power and authority to drive out all demons and to cure diseases, and he sent them out to preach the kingdom of God and to heal the sick* (Luke 9:2).

Finally, there is a group of people who believe that God still heals today, but do not believe that God wants to heal them or use them to minister healing to others. They believe this for any number of reasons, all of which are not true. The truth is God is willing to heal anyone who believes, as Jesus showed in Matthew: *Jesus reached out his hand and touched the man. "I am willing" he said. "Be clean!" Immediately he was cured of his leprosy* (Matthew 8:3).

Sin causes sickness but Jesus came to heal, and He still heals today. Jesus will not only heal you, He will also use you to minister healing to others by faith.

Chapter 2

The Call On Your Life

In the next few chapters of this book you will see terms like your "call" or "calling", your "vision" or your "gifting". The call or calling on your life refers to the purposes and destiny that God placed within you when you were born. Your "calling" exists in both the past and present tenses and will be referred to in that manner. Your "call" is alive and makes up part of your identity whether you are currently fulfilling it or whether it is still hidden within your heart.

Your "vision", as referred to in this book, is the present and future tense fulfillment of the call on your life. It is the potential that will happen when your calling becomes reality. It is also God-given and thus carries His life in it.

And finally your "giftings" are your God-given abilities, both natural and supernatural through Jesus to fulfill the vision He has given you. These gifts exist in the past, present and future tense and will grow in both strength and number to insure the fulfillment of your vision.

Before you begin to minister healing to others through the prayers in this book, it is important to remember that God wants us to know the hope of His calling (Ephesians 1:18). God has a purpose for each believer's life. The passion you feel for ministry was put there by God. We believe that you are reading this book now to help fulfill God's call on your life. You may not answer God's call through full-time ministry in a Christian organization, but God has given you a ministry (2 Corinthians 5:18).

So our question to you is, "Do you know the call that God has given you?" You should be able to answer the question, "What is God's purpose for your life?" without doubt or hesitation. Think about your purpose, about what God has called you to accomplish, about His plan for your life. Unless that purpose is alive in your heart and becomes the central motivation of your daily walk, how can you be sure you are accomplishing God's will?

If you are unaware of your calling and purpose, you may be in danger of picking up the calling of someone else. Ask yourself these questions: Have you ever envied someone else's calling? Do you want what someone else has?

We meet people everywhere who are seeking the calling of others and have missed their own. We have actually met people who want to be a Frances Hunter. They try to do everything just like she did because they want to have her calling.

We have friends who have mimicked the mannerisms of Christian leaders right down to their hand motions. Some have gone so far as to copy Billy Graham's North Carolina accent, the way he holds his Bible and many of his phrases. God's plan, however, was to make us each unique members of the same Body of Christ (I Corinthians 12:12-14; Ephesians 4:16). He does not tell us to conform to each other, but rather to be conformed to the image of His Son (Romans 8:29). We are not to have the mind of

Frances Hunter or Billy Graham. We are to have the mind of Jesus Christ (I Corinthians 2:16).

Be who God intended you to be and do what God made you to do (I Corinthians 12:4-12; Romans 12:3-8). Don't become a living Xeroxed copy of someone else's calling. Wouldn't it be sad to get to heaven and discover you spent your life doing something other than what God had called you to do? It is possible.

We know a man who had such an experience and his story is life-changing. While this man was in law school, the Lord called him and his new bride to be missionaries in Africa. They said, "Yes, Lord, we'll go!" and began raising the necessary funds. Just as they were ready to leave for the mission field, they discovered she was pregnant. Knowing that the area to which they were called was a remote jungle, friends and family advised them to have the baby in the United States and then move to Africa.

They delayed their departure. Their blessing from God, a son, needed six months of medical care after his birth. Since the medical expenses used up their savings, the man accepted a job in a law firm in order to pay the bills. He became a very successful Christian business-man and led many people to a relationship with the Lord wherever he went. When he received the Baptism of the Holy Spirit, he became on fire for God! As one of the leaders in Florida's Full Gospel Businessmen, he led thousands of people to the Lord, went on many missionary trips, funded and planted many churches and raised all of his sons into ministry. In addition to all of that, each year he sent tens of thousands of dollars to missionaries in Africa, because it was always on his heart.

After he had retired, he was rocking on the porch of his large home overlooking the river, thanking the Lord for His blessings and for the great things God had done through him. Suddenly, God interrupted his train of thought. Clearly the voice of the Lord said, "I never called you to do any of this. I called you to be a missionary in Africa. No one would have known you, but you would have done what I called you to do. If you had obeyed me, it would not have been the same. Your son would not have become ill and you would not have gone through these trials. I called you to be a missionary in Africa."

This man had always known that something was missing in his life and at that moment he realized exactly what it was. It so profoundly touched him that wherever he goes, he tells everyone who will listen: "Answer the call that God places on your life."

Yes, God does have a specific purpose and plan for your life. He wants you to fulfill what He called you to do. When you hear *"Well done, good and faithful servant"* (Matthew 25:21), it will be because you accomplished what God wanted you to, not because you did what you thought or hoped He wanted you to.

God's purpose for your life is for you alone and nobody else on earth can accomplish it in the way that you can. God made each of us for a specific purpose. *For we are God's workmanship, created in Christ Jesus to do good works, which God prepared in advance for us to do* (Ephesians 2:10).

If God calls you to something that you don't feel you have the ability to accomplish, don't let that keep you from answering His call. For example, if you had to choose between Peter and Paul as the apostle to the Jews and the Gentiles, which would you pick? Wouldn't it have made more sense to send Paul to the Jews?

He was a Hebrew of Hebrews and an educated Pharisee who could talk with them intelligently. In the same respect, wouldn't it make more sense to send Peter, the uneducated fisherman, to the Gentiles?

But God is not limited to man's wisdom (James 3:14-18; I Corinthians, 2:4). God sent Paul to the Gentiles and Peter to the Jews. God called Peter and Paul according to His purpose and His plan, so that they would accomplish the tasks set before them by His power and by His grace alone.

You can help identify the true call on your life by looking at the goals you have set in your heart. If your goals are to promote yourself, make money, have a place of leadership, arrive at a level of notoriety, or gain importance and prestige before men, then those goals are not from God (Acts 8:9-24). Goals that flow out of a selfish, self-centered mindset can't be aligned with the eternal purposes of God. Your goals should be designed for the benefit of others. God-given goals will focus on the eternal destiny of souls and the complete fulfillment of God's purposes in the lives of others.

Ministry goals won't be about you if they come from God. Jesus was offered the whole world and turned it down. He was offered a high position and refused it (Matthew 4:1-11). He came for people, and He specifically came for those who were lost, hurting and in need. Our Lord Jesus emptied himself and took on the form of a bondservant (Philippians 2:7).

If God put the desire in your heart to reach people and change lives, then you will find yourself following Jesus' example of sacrificial service (John 13:14; Matthew 19:16-22). If your calling is truly humble in appearance and it doesn't exalt you, then it may very well be from God (Matthew 7:13-14).

We have had the privilege to sit across the table from many successful Christian leaders who have told us to consistently choose the road that is the most selfless. If you take the road that seems most likely to promote your own interests, you will find it leads to places other than where God intended you to go. You will be going around the mountain one more time to find God's will for your life. There is a way to avoid this trip. Die!

The price to be paid to avoid these mistakes in direction is the death of "self". To walk in the fullness of the anointing, which is the empowerment of your calling, your natural "fleshly" man must go to the cross and die. The resurrection power of God can't continually flow through uncrucified flesh (Philippians 3:9-11).

We often meet people who are ready for every part of ministry except death to self. They believe they have already died. They do not fully understand what it means to live for God rather than for self (Galatians 2:19-20). Simply put, it means that your "self" does not live anymore. *For where you have envy and selfish ambition, there you find disorder and every evil practice* (James 3:16).

If you live each day by your own selfish will and natural desires, you will bring disorder and evil works with you wherever you go. You may say, "But I'm anointed, I'm powerful. I lay hands on the sick and they recover. I prophesy. I cast out demons." *Many will say to me on that day, 'Lord, Lord, did we not prophesy in your name, and in your name drive out demons and perform many miracles? Then I will tell them plainly, 'I never knew you. Away from me, you evildoers!'* (Mathew 7:22).

Are your motives for yourself or for His sheep? When Jesus appeared to Peter before His crucifixion, He told them to feed and take care of His sheep (John 21:15-17). He wanted them to understand that whatever they did for His sheep, it was as if they did it for Him. It is true for us also. When we minister to His sheep, we are ministering to Him (Matthew 25:40).

If you are unsure of the call on your life, seek God for it. God did not make you and then leave you without direction and purpose. He is placed your calling within your heart when He formed you and placed you in your mother's womb (Psalms 139:13-16). He had a purpose for your life from the beginning. Even the hairs on your head are numbered and God has a wonderful plan for your future (Luke 12:7; Jeremiah 29:11). All you have to do is ask God to reveal to you what He has already placed in your heart. If you are unsure, ask Him now!

Our own desires and plans, which tend to capture our attention and affection, often compete with His plan and purpose for our lives. Your heart may need to be circumcised from fleshly plans before you can truly see God's plan for your life. The only thing keeping you from doing what He called you to do is your "self". As you die to yourself and live for others, His plan for you will unfold rapidly. You will know in your spirit that you are on the right course and your life will take on a different motivation and value. Many of the desires in your heart for service to others will line up with God's purposes; and contentment will begin to fill your soul.

A Christian attorney in South Carolina was elected to the state House of Representatives. She was a conservative female candidate in a region where no conservative or woman had ever been elected in the history of the district. Her desire was to become a state judge. After a fair amount of politicking in the state's political circles, she became a judge. She won her race.

Because of her conservative views, she was given many high profile cases. She had to judge criminal cases where the death penalty was sometimes involved. She suddenly found that she had to make life and death rulings.

Unaware she was wrestling with the burdens of her position, her brother awoke in the middle of the night with an urgency to call her. He told her that the Lord had put something on his heart that he needed to share with her. He said, "It was the Lord's plan for you to be a judge. He is the one who opened the doors for you to have that position. He is the one who put the desire in your heart to be a judge, because He wanted a righteous judge that would ask Him what to do before dropping the gavel."

She started to cry as she said, "That's what I do. I was worried that it may have been out of my own desires that I became a judge and now people's lives are in my hands." This message was a confirmation that God had indeed called her to be a judge.

God gives you the desires of your heart because it is He who places those desires in your heart to start with.

Chapter 3

Your Gifts and His Supply

Most believers are familiar with the scripture that says *for God's gifts and his call are irrevocable* (Romans 11:29). Do you know what that means? If you believe it has to do with your spiritual gifts and God's call on your life, you have been taught improperly by people who have taken this scripture out of context. This scripture has nothing to do with the spiritual gifts or the call of God on your life. One of the most dangerous things that you can do with scripture is to separate the writings of Paul from the teachings of Jesus. This separation can tear the Word of God apart. The belief that this passage is about your gifts and calling is contrary to Jesus' parable of the talents.

This is the story of the Master who gave talents to his workers. Two of them took what was given to them and produced more, but one buried his talent and didn't do anything with it. In this parable the workers who produced more were given more, but the one who did nothing with his talent had it taken away from him (Matthew 25:14-30). This teaching of Jesus lines up with what we know about life.

We have seen through life experiences that people who have been given gifts and callings and don't use them, lose them. Take the time to read all of Romans 11 and you will see that this chapter is about salvation and the limited time that the Gentiles have for repentance. Romans 11:29 could read for God's gifts (of salvation) and his call (for repentance to the Jews) are irrevocable.

Do not deceive yourself by believing that you can choose to ignore God's call on your life and His spiritual gifts to you indefinitely before you act on them. The truth is, if you do not use them, you can lose them. *From everyone who has been given much, much will be demanded; and from the one who has been entrusted with much, much more will be asked* (Luke 12:48b). If you have a call from God, don't wait to act on it unless He tells you to wait. You might be burying the talents God has given you to accomplish His plans.

With that understanding, consider what the Bible says: *And my God will meet all your needs according to his glorious riches in Christ Jesus* (Philippians 4:18-19). If He is going to supply all your needs according to His riches in Christ Jesus, just what does that mean to you?

During the first Gulf War President Bush sent General Schwarzkopf overseas to free Kuwait from the invading Iraqis. President Bush told him, “Anything you need, just let me know.”

Schwarzkopf could have called the President back and said “You know, I would like a condo in Vail and I've always wanted to own a red corvette. Two tickets to Disney World would also be nice to have when this is all over so my family and I can spend some quality time together.”

President Bush would have responded with, “What in the world are you talking about? Didn't you understand that I was referring to anything you needed to get the job done that I sent you to do? All you have to do is just ask me, and I will make sure you have it".

You will not be able to get to heaven and say, "Oh God! If You had just given me $10,000,000, I would have been able to do so much more for You. Or, if You had just given me this or that, then I would have accomplished so much more."

You already have what you need to accomplish the task He has called you to do, or He will supply it as you request it. If you don't have what you need to complete the task, then either you are not doing what God sent you to do, you have not asked Him for His help, or it is not His timing.

It is, however, not uncommon for a person to have to live outside their own abilities or comfort zone before His supply becomes a reality. No matter what your circumstances are like, do not limit God to your own abilities or by your own thinking. Ephesians says: *Now to him who is able to do immeasurably more than all we ask or imagine, according to his power that is at work within us* (Ephesians 3:20).

When God establishes a vision, His provision will always be there to accomplish what He has planned. He can and will supply all that you need to fulfill the call on your life.

Chapter 4

Vision and the Motivations of the Heart

When a long distance runner runs a race, he knows his purpose is to cross the finish line. He knows the finish line is there when he starts the race. He also knows it is there while he is running the race, but he can't see it because it is many miles away. The finish line is always in his sight even though it is not immediately visible.

This may best describe God's vision for your own life. Your vision is the present and future tense fulfillment of God's call on your life. True visions are God-inspired and are full of His life. They come to pass through our spoken words and subsequent actions. These visions are essential to our very existence.

Where there is no vision, the people perish (Proverbs 29:18 KJV). We have found through life experiences that sharing your God-given vision is an important way to ensure your calling is fulfilled. It is His purpose and plan for you to share the vision with others (Habakkuk 2:2). If you are married, God will give you a vision that He wants you to share with your spouse.

We know a pastor in Africa who was called to be a missionary in the United States. He told his wife over and over that God had called him to be a missionary and establish a ministry in the USA. For months his wife repeatedly said “No, no, no! I don't feel that we are called to go there.” But he kept sharing the vision with her until one day she said, “I know we are supposed to go to the U.S.!" She began to repeat the vision back to him because now it was alive in her heart also.

Share the vision that God has given you with others. If it is from God, it will stand. If it is not from God, it will not stand. But share your vision.

By now you should be aware of the call of God on your life or be seeking Him for the vision if you don’t already have one. At this point we must ask you to examine your heart and ask yourself these questions. What really drives you? What is in your heart of hearts? Do you understand the implications of this question? If God gave you a heart for souls and you are waiting to collect enough money to go overseas, but you don't have enough compassion to go across the street to minister to the lost, is your drive really for souls or is it for a mission overseas?

Here is a different way of expressing the same concept. If you cannot go to your local grocery store and use the gift God has given you, then what qualifies you to use it in the church? If it is not in your heart to touch people and see them healed in your local neighborhood, why should God open the door to greater opportunities?

Before you minister to others, it is essential that your heart’s motivation be right before God. The Bible states in many places that when Jesus saw the crowds, He had compassion on them because they were like sheep without a shepherd (Matthew 9:36, 14:14, 20:34; Mark 1:41, Luke 713). Compassion is a driving force to ministry and is often misunderstood to be a soft mushy "sympathy" as described in Webster's Dictionary.

However, true compassion is an intense combination of both love and hate. Jesus had that kind of compassion. He loved the people with an uncompromised love and at the same time He hated the condition in which they were trapped. The word compassion in the Greek actually means to be stirred so strongly inside that your bowels are moved. The combination of great love and hatred creates an intense inner stirring. One empowers your spirit and the other motivates your soul into action.

It is important to understand the components of compassion and why we should be motivated in the same manner as our Lord. We don't feel that it is necessary to explain the nature of hate or what it feels like because everyone has experienced it. However, we have found that many have misunderstandings about the nature of love.

Some people have a misconception that the love that is in their heart is from themselves and that they have the ability to produce more. But this is not a reality. The truth is that the love we have did not come from us, it came from God. It was in the beginning, and it will be in the end. God is, so love is. *God is love* (1 John 4:16b).

Paul's prayer to the Ephesians was *And I pray that you, being rooted and established in love, may have power, together with all the saints, to grasp how wide and long and high and deep is the love of Christ, and to know this love* (by experience) *that surpasses knowledge-that you may be filled to the measure of all the fullness of God* (Ephesians 3:17-19).

We believe it will take an eternity to fully comprehend all that love encompasses. Each day of our lives, we gain a greater understanding of who God is; and as we do, we will experience His love with more intensity and purity.

This passage of scripture is all about love: *If I speak in the tongues of men and of angels, but have not love, I am only a resounding gong or a clanging cymbal. If I have the gift of prophecy and can fathom all mysteries and all knowledge, and if I have a faith that can move mountains, but have not love, I am nothing. If I give all I possess to the poor and surrender my body to the flames, but have not love, I gain nothing.*

Love is patient, love is kind. It does not envy, it does not boast, it is not proud. It is not rude, it is not self-seeking, it is not easily angered, it keeps no record of wrongs. Love does not delight in evil but rejoices with the truth. It always protects, always trusts, always hopes, always perseveres. Love never fails (1 Corinthians 13:4-8a).

If you do not have this passage memorized, we suggest you do so now. Read it until you can quote it anywhere at anytime. You can read it and know all the words, but when these words become a revelation within your heart, they will change your life.

Unfortunately, it is possible to do all of the amazing things in I Corinthians 13:1-3 without a motivation of love. This apparently is what has happened to some members of the church. Some parts of the modern church may have drifted away from the lifestyle of love as it was exhibited by the early church. The first act of the New Testament church was to sell all of their excess property and give the proceeds to the poor.

When hurricane Ivan came through Florida, it destroyed some churches and tore the roofs off of many others west of Tallahassee. Several churches located east of Tallahassee gave their building funds to the congregations of the damaged churches when they heard the church insurance policies would not cover the cost of the repairs. These churches were not concerned about denominational lines or doctrinal differences. They wanted to reach out to mend hearts and aid churches that were in need. They gave up the building funds they had accumulated over several years so others could have a building in which to worship God.

The Bible says that the world would know that we are Christians because of our love (John 13:35). Most people in the United States know enough about God's Word to be saved. However, they also know some questionable Christians and do not want to be like them. There are many things we could say about this subject but if you get nothing else out of this chapter, please remember this: love never fails. Love never fails. *Love never fails* (I Corinthians 13:8a).

When you do minister to someone and you have done nothing but love them, then....Love never fails. You may pray for someone who is not instantly healed. Remember that love never fails. God's call on your life will always be driven by a spirit of compassion. Love them and believe that love never fails. God is love. God never fails. Love never fails.

And now these three remain faith, hope, and love, and the greatest of these is love (I Corinthians 13:13).

Chapter 5

It's All About Relationships

Jesus came that we might have life and have it more abundantly (John 10:10).

Life is not about places or things, however it is about our relationship and service to God as well as our relationships and service to His people. To confirm this fact in your own life, assume that at midnight tonight you knew you were going home to be with the Lord. What would you do differently between now and then? More than likely, places and things would lose their value and you would spend your remaining time with those people who mean the most to you.

When we become alienated in our relationships, our lives reflect the strain and our hearts can harden. This alienation can infiltrate slowly, but surely into every area of our lives, family, friends, church, God. It is quite obvious that the most important relationship we have is with our Father.

In our travels we are quite surprised to see so many believers who have lost the intimacy between themselves and God. We are equally surprised to see so many believers in the church who have never known this intimacy at all. It is defined by a *love that surpasses mere knowledge* (Ephesians 3:19).

Christians who don't have an understanding of intimacy with God are frequently reading Christian books and going to Christian conferences searching for what is missing in their lives. There is nothing wrong with Christian books or conferences; but if you feel like there is something missing in your walk with God, maybe what is needed is an alignment to His heart and His unconditional love. Then the Christian books and conferences will add to your walk instead of trying to replace what you feel is missing.

There are many reasons why we separate ourselves from God. Sin, unbelief, and disobedience are the most common reasons and they are all easily rectified by repentance so we will not go into great detail about them at this time. There is another reason that is less talked about, but seems to be very common. It is a separation through time by slowly hardening your heart toward God because He did not perform as you would have if you were God. You have been hurt or even angry with God so you hold unwritten things against Him while waiting for Him to correct them.

This may be best explained using the marriage relationship. It is not uncommon for us to minister to men and women who don't have the love for their spouses they once had. Over time the spouse did things wrong or did not meet expectations. Small hurts slowly add up. Eventually their heart hardened toward their spouse and they no longer feel the love that once was the cornerstone of their marriage. The intimacy was gone.

Our response to these people is always the same. What could your spouse do to win back your love? We get many responses from "I am not quite sure", to a list of things that would fill a ream of paper.

To this our response is again the same. Release your spouse of their debt!

The spouse most likely does not deserve to be released and has not done enough to win you back, but simply release them from what you are holding against them. Lay down the conditions that you have set in your heart for your spouse to meet on the Altar of God and simply love your spouse. Then make the declaration to give 100% of your heart back to your spouse. You do it just like this:

Prayer to Release Spouse

"I willingly lay down all the conditions that I am expecting my spouse to meet on the Altar of God. I (your full Christian name) choose to give 100% of my heart to (your spouse's full Christian name) from this day forth."

We have watched many people do this very thing and the love they once had for their mates filled their hearts again. It is so interesting to hear the testimonies of the amazing changes that took place in their relationships when they got home.

Unconditional love is what God has called you to. If you have anything other than unconditional love, then you are in contradiction to who He is and who He made you to be.

Many Christians do the same thing to God that they did in their relationships even though they know in their heart they don't have the right to hold anything against God. Yet many times we still do. We prayed and He did not answer our prayers the way we wanted or someone we loved died and we didn't understand why.

There are many reasons why we separate ourselves from God, however He will never separate Himself from us. *"Never will I leave you; never will I forsake you"* (Hebrews 13:5). Jesus came that we might be reconciled to God. *All this is from God, who reconciled us to himself through Christ and gave us the ministry of reconciliation: that God was reconciling the world to himself in Christ, not counting men's sins against them. And he has committed to us the message of reconciliation* (2 Corinthians 5:18-19).

When you are ministering to others, you may need to lead them in this simple prayer of restoration. You yourself may need to say this same prayer. We have seen countless numbers of people say this prayer and a love for God filled their hearts again.

Prayer for Restoration

"Father, I willingly lay down on Your Altar all the conditions that I was expecting You to meet. I (<u>your full Christian name</u>) choose to give 100% of my heart to You from this day forth. I will be Your servant and you will be my God in Jesus' name."

The other factors of sin, disobedience and unbelief are easily corrected. For you to be healed, sin must be confessed and not hidden in your heart. God set a pattern for how often He is willing to forgive us our sins. *If we confess our sins, he is faithful and just and will forgive us our sins and purify us from all unrighteousness* (1 John 1:9).

Then Peter came to Him and said, "Lord, how often shall my brother sin against me, and I forgive him? Up to seven times?" Jesus said to him, "I do not say to you, up to seven times, but up to seventy times seven (Matthew 18:21-22 NKJV). In the Greek this passage can be interpreted "not seven times but seventy-seven times for the same sin in the same day." It is God's nature to forgive us without measure.

However, there is a condition to forgiveness. God will only forgive us with the measure that we forgive others. *For if you forgive men when they sin against you, your heavenly Father will also forgive you. But if you do not forgive men their sins, your Father will not forgive your sins* (Matthew 6:14-15). If you hold any unforgiveness towards anyone, then you cannot be forgiven.

Jesus explained it like this: *"Therefore, the kingdom of heaven is like a king who wanted to settle accounts with his servants. As he began the settlement, a man who owed him ten thousand talents was brought to him. Since he was not able to pay, the master ordered that he and his wife and his children and all that he had be sold to repay the debt. The servant fell on his knees before him. 'Be patient with me,' he begged, 'and I will pay back everything.' The servant's master took pity on him, canceled the debt and let him go.*

"But when that servant went out, he found one of his fellow servants who owed him a hundred denarii. He grabbed him and began to choke him. 'Pay back what you owe me!' he demanded. His fellow servant fell to his knees and begged him, 'Be patient with me, and I will pay you back.' "But he refused. Instead, he went off and had the man thrown into prison until he could pay the debt.

When the other servants saw what had happened, they were greatly distressed and went and told their master everything that had happened. "Then the master called the servant in. 'You wicked servant,' he said, 'I canceled all that debt of yours because you begged me to. Shouldn't you have had mercy on your fellow servant just as I had on you?'

In anger his master turned him over to the jailers to be tortured, until he should pay back all he owed. "This is how my heavenly Father will treat each of you unless you forgive your brother from your heart" (Matthew 18:23-35).

You have been forgiven everything but if you can't forgive others who have sinned against you, then you are acting contrary to God's nature and will be separated from God. This is the prayer to confess sins:

Prayer to Confess Sin

"Father, I have sinned. I confess my sin(s) of (insert the sin(s) you committed). I repent and turn from this. Forgive me of this sin. I chose to forgive those who have sinned against me. Father, I choose to forgive (name of person who sinned against you). What they did was sin. Take this sin from them and place it on the cross of Jesus and on the Day of Judgment I will not hold this sin against them. Even now they are free. Father, bless them."

Unbelief is another form of sin that separates us from God. The opposite of unbelief is faith. Each man on earth has been given a measure of faith according to the Word of God (Romans 12:3). You already have faith and you use it every day. If you are sitting down while you are reading this, then you applied your faith. You had faith the chair would hold you when you sat down.

Faith pleases God. Faith is believing. The things of God are just that simple. *And without faith it is impossible to please God, because anyone who comes to him must believe that he exists and that he rewards those who earnestly seek him* (Hebrews 11:6).

Prayer to Confess Unbelief.

"Father, I have not applied the faith You have given me. I have allowed doubt and unbelief to enter in. I confess this as sin and choose to turn back to You. Forgive me this sin in Jesus' name."

Disobedience is another form of sin that also separates us from God. When God was calling Moses to lead the children of Israel out of Egypt, He allowed Moses to express his doubts and inabilities and He answered them all. However, when Moses said, "Send someone else", *the Lord's anger burned against Moses* (Exodus 4:14).

God put up with Moses' doubt and inabilities but He would not allow disobedience. He does not allow it today. He will correct you because He loves you. *The Lord disciplines those He loves* (Hebrews 12:6). Understand that if God has called you to accomplish something, you must do it. To run from it will separate you from God, and your life will reflect the emptiness that is found in the children of disobedience.

There was a man at a church in Indiana who was in constant pain from a back injury caused by an auto accident twelve years before. He had received prayer many times with only limited results. After a few questions, we determined he was running from the call of God on his life. In fact, he had had the accident right after he told the Lord, "No." We led him in the prayer of repentance for disobedience and he was instantly healed.

Prayer for Disobedience:

"Father, I have disobeyed Your Word and Your plan for my life. I repent and turn back to serving You alone. Forgive me this sin and place it on the cross of Jesus Christ. I am Your servant from this day forth."

Most believers know of the first and greatest commandment but do you know the second? *Jesus replied: "Love the Lord your God with all your heart and with all your soul and with all your mind. This is the first and greatest commandment. And the second is like it: Love your neighbor as yourself"* (Matthew 22:37-39).

Jesus was not telling us that the second commandment was similar to the first, but was like it as seen from a different perspective. If you don't love your neighbor as yourself, you are deceived when you say you love God. When Peter asked Jesus, *"And who is my neighbor?"* Jesus responded with the story of the Good Samaritan (Luke 10:30-37).

John confirmed this when he said: *For anyone who does not love his brother, whom he has seen, cannot love God, whom he has not seen. And he has given us this command: Whoever loves God must also love his brother* (1 John 4:20b-21).

We are called to love everyone unconditionally. Jesus said: *If you love those who love you, what reward will you get? Are not even the tax collectors doing that*? (Matthew 5:46).

The tax collectors would sit by the gates of the wall that surrounded Jerusalem. If your taxes were not paid, the tax collectors would not allow you to enter the city to worship God or make offerings at the temple.

We sometimes hold debts that others owe us and we will not let them past the walls of our heart unless that debt is paid. Jesus told people who did that, that they were no different than the tax collectors.

"If you love those who love you, what credit is that to you? Even 'sinners' love those who love them. And if you do good to those who are good to you, what credit is that to you? Even 'sinners' do that. And if you lend to those from whom you expect repayment, what credit is that to you? Even 'sinners' lend to 'sinners,' expecting to be repaid in full.

But love your enemies, do good to them, and lend to them without expecting to get anything back. Then your reward will be great, and you will be sons of the Most High, because he is kind to the ungrateful and wicked. Be merciful, just as your Father is merciful. Do not judge, and you will not be judged. Do not condemn, and you will not be condemned. Forgive, and you will be forgiven. Give, and it will be given to you. A good measure, pressed down, shaken together and running over, will be poured into your lap. For with the measure you use, it will be measured to you" (Luke 6:32-38).

God frees us from judgment and condemnation and He forgives us with the same measure we use towards others. If there is anyone in your life that you have been holding anything against, release them and be free. This is also true when you are praying for others. Lead them in repentance so that they may be free as well.

Matthew states you are to *Love your neighbor as yourself* (Matthew 22:39). We are surprised at the number of Christians who don't love themselves. Not only do some Christians not love themselves, but we have met people who even hated themselves. This is definitely a contradiction to who you are and who you are called to be. Self-hatred will eventually affect all relationships, including the one with your heavenly Father. Whether it came in through sin, disobedience, or just believing lies about you, the fruit of hate is always the same. Devastation!

When you act contrary to who God made you to be, you will not like the fruit of your labor and will eventually not like yourself. If these ungodly actions continue over a period of time without repentance; you will not only hate your actions, you will hate yourself for continuing in them.

Your self-hatred may be brought on by your own sins, however, in some cases, it could be brought on by the sins of others. For example, if you grew up in an ungodly household where there was yelling, back-biting, condemnation and constant criticism; as an adult you may exhibit many of these same characteristics. If you continue these same behaviors, you will have a very hard time loving yourself.

Some people were abused as children. They may be able to forgive their abuser, but they often take on the false belief that they were the cause of the abuse. They believe that there was something wrong or different about them that caused them to feel responsible for what happened. We have even ministered to people in their late seventies who did not like themselves because they believed they were somehow responsible for the abuse they received sixty-five years before. Believing such a lie is very common among victims of abuse and will keep people from loving themselves and will make it difficult for them to truly give their heart fully to others.

The answer to these problems is always the same. It is the cross of Jesus Christ. All healing takes place at the cross. Whether it is because of sin, disobedience, ungodly habits or believing a lie, the answer is always the same. The way to change from hating yourself to loving yourself is simply repentance. Repentance means change, to turn the other way. It means to no longer act contrary to who you are in your heart and to take your previous actions to the cross.

Prayer of Repentance

"Father, I have not acted in accordance to Your nature and I am upset with myself for these actions. They are sin. I repent and I will no longer continue to act this way. Father, take this sin from me, place it on the cross of Jesus Christ and separate it from me. Forgive me of this sin and forgive my fathers of this same sin as well in Jesus' name."

There are some who teach that you need to forgive yourself. You will not find this teaching anywhere in the Bible. It is an "I" centered thinking that is contrary to the cross. It turns you inward to forgive yourself instead of turning you to the cross where you accept God's forgiveness of your sins through Jesus Christ. Once you repent, you become free of these sins and don't need to forgive yourself as if you really could.

The Bible says to cast your cares upon Jesus because *He cares for you* (1 Peter 5:7). It is not uncommon to find people who are carrying the cares of their life and their own circumstances on their own shoulders. This is a simple but effective prayer to free you from the burden of these things:

Prayer to Cast Cares on the Altar

"Father, I am carrying the burdens of my relationships and circumstances. I choose to lay all my cares, all my worries, all my fears, all things I cannot change on Your altar. Father, I lay my spouse on Your altar. Father, I lay my children on Your altar. Father, I lay my job, my finances on Your altar. Father, I lay (<u>name the circumstances that you can't change</u>) on Your altar. You are my supply and You alone can move in my circumstances. I give these to You and trust You with them in Jesus' name."

We have countless testimonies of people whose heavy hearts became lighter or who felt the weight of the world leave their shoulders after repeating this prayer. We quite often use this prayer for people who have upper back or shoulder pain.

Finally, remember when you are ministering to people, you are called to a ministry of reconciliation which is all about relationships.

Chapter 6

Steps in Ministering

When ministering to people, what do you do first?

Step One: Ask the person what they want. The Bible says, to *give to the one who asks you* (Matthew. 5:42). Don't start praying for the person before you talk with them. Ask them what they want. The question isn't "What do you want me to do for you?" It is "What do you need Jesus to do for you?" or "What are you expecting from God?"

Jesus had been ministering all day when a blind man called out to Him. What did Jesus say? *"What do you want me to do for you?"* (Mark 10:51). Why did Jesus ask him what he wanted? Wasn't it obvious that a blind man would want his sight restored?

A.B. was a man in Florida who had been in the healing ministry exactly one day. He had been praying for people and seeing them healed, when a man comes rolling up in a wheelchair. His legs were atrophied. They were very thin and obviously very weak. It was obvious that he had not walked in a long time, if at all. A.B. was really taken back and did not know how to pray for the crippled man. A.B. was willing, but in the back of his mind he thought, "I'm going to pray for this guy, Lord, and if he does not get out of this wheelchair, one of us is going to be really embarrassed and I am quite sure that person will be me."

Before A.B. could do anything, the man in the wheelchair asked, "Can you lead me into the baptism of the Holy Spirit?"

A.B. said, "Yes, I can do that." If the man in the wheelchair hadn't spoken up, A.B. would not have known what he wanted. A.B. would have started praying for his legs.

Step two: Ask the person how long they have had the problem. A woman who had a bad back for over four years came to us for ministry. She had received prayer from many other people without being healed. When we asked what happened four years before, she explained that her husband had left her for his secretary. She was still very hurt and bitter about it. She was led in a prayer of forgiveness; she put her hurt feelings on the cross and she was healed instantly. In the book of Mark, *Jesus asked the boy's father, "How long has he been like this?"* (Mark 9:21).

Step three: Look. You asked them what they wanted, but now you need to look them in the eyes. It is really that simple. *"The eye is the lamp of the body. If your eyes are good, your whole body will be full of light. But if your eyes are bad, your whole body will be full of darkness"* (Matthew 6:22-23a).

Always look the person in the eye and be sure they look back at you. Peter and John did this. *Peter looked straight at him, as did John. Then Peter said, "Look at us!" So the man gave them his attention, expecting to get something from them* (Acts 3:4-5). If the person you are ministering to closes their eyes, ask them to open them. If they turn their head away from you or will not look you in the eye, they might be afraid.

If you see fear, step back until they relax. Some people become uncomfortable if you stand closer than an arm's length away, as if that space is a 'trust zone' which you have trespassed or "trust-passed". Also, be sure you are not standing between the person and an aisle-way or a door, their way out. Whether it's a man or a woman, if you still see fear, try getting down on one or both knees to minister. In this position you should no longer be a threat.

If you do not detect fear, but the person still will not look you in the eye, it may be that they have unconfessed sin. They may be in a dispute with the Lord or with His representatives (pastors, lay ministers, etc.) and may be holding judgments in their heart against them. *Therefore confess your sins to each other and pray for each other so that you may be healed. The prayer of a righteous man is powerful and effective* (James 5:16).

If they do not repent of the sin or release the judgment against the other person, what will happen while you are ministering to them? Most likely nothing unless they repent! Help bring them to repentance. And remember, never break trust with someone who confesses sin. If you do, you can cause them great pain and can bring judgment upon yourself.

Also look for outward signs of internal conditions. People communicate with body language as well as with their words. Are their arms crossed in front of them? Are they overly nervous or lethargic? Are there any other outward signs? Pray for whatever they request; but as a responsible representative of Jesus Christ, stay alert to other possible problems also (Matthew. 24:42-43).

Step four: Listen. When you ask the person what they want, listen carefully to what they are saying. Many times, the first words that come out of a person's mouth will tell you the root problem. But also listen for complaints, gripes, or words that reveal attitudes against someone. Listen for signs of unforgiveness, judgments and bitterness (unfulfilled revenge).

See to it that no one misses the grace of God and that no bitter root grows up to cause trouble and defile many (Hebrew 12:15). However, do not let them go into detail about their situation. It can weigh you down and may take you off track or in a direction that will not lead to healing.

You may find that many of the problems, which they claim were caused by other people, are the very problems that now live within themselves. This is especially true when they are in judgment of others. The only way you can set yourself up as the judge of someone is to be over them. We tend to become angry and less patient with others when sin exists within us. Otherwise, you would have compassion on them and hurt for them. When the Jewish men were about to stone a woman caught in adultery Jesus said, *If any one of you is without sin, let him be the first to throw a stone at her* (John 8:7).

This doesn't mean that your judgment about them was inaccurate, but if your conclusion caused any emotion other than compassion; you may have things within you that you need to crucify such as anger, bitterness, unforgiveness, selfishness or other sins.

Listen for what they are truly seeking. Is there something which they are not saying? Many men have no idea what they are feeling at the time, much less how to communicate it.

We ministered to a man whose wife had committed adultery and he was looking for help. He truly didn't know what he wanted. He was full of anger. He did not understand the hurt and mixture of emotions that he was going through. He just wanted to get rid of her. He had already seen an attorney and was ready for a divorce. That wasn't what he wanted because he really loved the woman. He just wanted the hurt to go away. He wanted somebody to help him through the pain so he could get back to a place of peace.

Three hours after receiving ministry he had his wife under his arm and said to her, "I love you and we will get through this together. No one will dishonor you while I am your husband. We will get through this."

Step five: Relax. You and the person you are ministering to need to relax. Whether it is the first time you have prayed for someone or the thousandth time, you need to be relaxed. Take a deep breath. You can't make it happen in your own power. If you aren't at peace, it will be hard to minister peace to someone else.

There are several things you can do to help people relax before they receive ministry. Tell them to: "Take a deep breath and relax" or "Relax like you are in your easy chair at home." If they tell you that they have a serious disease or illness like breast cancer, you should always say, "That is easy". You will be amazed at how often people relax after they hear those three simple words.

Some Christians will start speaking in tongues, raising their hands, singing or praising God while you try to minister to them. Stop them and ask them to put their hands down at their sides. This is not the time for them to pray or even thank God. They will thank Him later. Some people believe that by doing all of these things, they will somehow motivate God to act on their behalf while others have been taught that this is the “spiritual” thing to do.

We are not saying you should not raise your hands in church or praise and worship God. However, when someone is receiving prayer, we have found much better results when the person gets out of God’s way and allows Him to work. After they have received ministry, then encourage them to thank Jesus and to praise God for their healing. God wants to heal everyone. People need to relax and receive His touch.

Step six: Wait on the Lord. When you wait on the Holy Spirit, three minutes can seem like a long time and five minutes may feel like forever. This is when most Christians in the healing ministry miss God. They take it on themselves to do all they can think of to do rather than wait on the leading of the Holy Spirit.

There have been occasions when we have waited on the Holy Spirit for what seemed like a very long time. He may not always show up immediately, but He always shows up. Sometimes we don’t know what we are waiting for Him to do, but we know that the Lord will accomplish His will when we wait on Him. If you are praying for people in a church service, you probably cannot wait fifteen to twenty minutes, but you can meet with them later when you have more time. You should take all the time they need. Don’t try to rush God or the person receiving ministry.

We believe that the person we are praying for is the most important person in our lives during that time. If there is one person or a hundred more people waiting for prayer, we give the person in front of us all of our time and attention as the Spirit directs.

Final Step: Don't quit. If you pray for people who don't get instantly healed, don't quit. Jesus prayed more than once for people. He prayed twice for a blind man before he was totally healed (Mark 8:22-25). So don't quit. If someone does not get healed the first time you pray for them, pray again. Keep praying and asking God what to do next. And remember, God's timing is perfect.

You should be familiar with the story in Acts: *One day Peter and John were going up to the temple at the time of prayer--at three in the afternoon. Now a man crippled from birth was being carried to the temple gate called Beautiful, where he was put every day to beg from those going into the temple courts. When he saw Peter and John about to enter, he asked them for money. Peter looked straight at him, as did John. Then Peter said, "Look at us". So the man gave them his attention, expecting to get something from them.*

Then Peter said, "Silver or gold I do not have, but what I have I give you. In the name of Jesus Christ of Nazareth, walk." Taking him by the right hand, he helped him up, and instantly the man's feet and ankles became strong. He jumped to his feet and began to walk. Then he went with them into the temple courts, walking and jumping, and praising God. When all the people saw him walking and praising God, they recognized him as the same man who used to sit begging at the temple gate called Beautiful, and they were filled with wonder and amazement at what had happened to him (Acts 3:1-10).

Peter and John met this man when they were going into the temple courts. Did Jesus ever go into the temple courts? The four Gospels record that He went quite often. It says, *Now a man crippled from birth was being carried to the gate Beautiful where he was placed every day* (Acts 3:2). If he sat begging at the temple gate every day, why didn't Jesus heal him? If Jesus walked by this man, why didn't He heal him?

There is timing and purpose for everything in God. *There is a time for everything, and a season for every activity under heaven* (Ecclesiastes 3:1). And a time to heal.

That particular day was God's chosen day for a miracle. Peter and John were there and they followed God's plan. The crippled man got healed and many came to the Lord because of his testimony. There is a perfect time for each healing and that timing will always bring glory to God.

This is all very simple. It is easy. These are basics steps that you need to practice when ministering healing to people. Don't be afraid to use the common sense and good judgment the Lord gave you, but always be led by the Holy Spirit and remember that "Love Never Fails."

Chapter 7

Practical Applications of Prayer

In the chapter, "How to Pray for Various Conditions", you will see many references to the practical things you should do when praying for others. This chapter will explain these things.

Growing Out Legs

Chiropractors can often tell if a person has a back problem by measuring their legs. He measures the legs by asking the person to sit in a chair with their back firmly against the back of the chair. The chiropractor stands in front of the person holding their legs up at the ankles with his thumbs on the side of the ankle bones and his hands over the top of the feet. If there is a difference in the leg length, it will be obvious by the displacement of his thumbs. They will not be adjacent to one another, indicating that one leg appears to be longer than the other.

We have yet to meet anyone with a serious back problem who had legs that measured the same length. This does not mean that the length of one leg is actually shorter than the other. (This only happens if there is bone loss from injury or a birth defect that left one leg shorter than the other. People with this condition will often be wearing a lift in their shoe to compensate for the short leg.) However, this does mean that the back is out of alignment, and that the spine, pelvis, muscles, tendons or ligaments have moved to compensate for the problem, causing one leg to extend a shorter distance than the other. One leg appears to be shorter than the other.

We check the lengths of the legs in the same manner as a chiropractor. Following this example with your hands over their ankles and your thumbs on their ankle bones, command the back to line up.

Prayer to Adjust the Legs

"I command the brain stem and the spinal column to be in perfect alignment. I command the muscles, tendons and ligaments to go back to their normal length and strength. I speak in new discs and vertebrae (when necessary). I command the pain to go and the legs to return to their normal position in Jesus' name."

Under no circumstances do you ever pull on the legs. Pray and wait until the ankles line up by the power of the Holy Spirit. Usually the legs will adjust quickly, but occasionally it may take several minutes.

Are there other ways to heal backs besides “growing out” legs? Our answer is absolutely “yes”. However, when you minister this way, you will see the power of God at work and so will the person for whom you are praying. Tell the person you are praying for as well as anyone else watching nearby, to keep their eyes open and watch what God is doing. They don’t want to miss their miracle. We have been ministering healing this way for over thirty years and have seen countless numbers of backs successfully healed by "growing out" legs.

Pelvis Adjustment

The pelvis is the foundation of the spine. If the back is out of alignment, the pelvis needs to shift to keep the body as upright as possible. When it is out of alignment, it can cause problems ranging from duck feet to PMS. To minister healing to an individual, you simply place your hands loosely on the top of their hipbones. If you are ministering to someone of the opposite sex, ask them to place their hands on their hipbones and then you place your hands loosely over theirs. You repeat the prayer and then wait as the Holy Spirit does the adjustment. You may need to allow a few minutes for the adjustment to occur.

Prayer to Adjust the Pelvis

"I command the pelvis to rotate into its normal position. I command all the organs to go back into place and muscles, tendons and ligaments to go back to their normal length and strength in Jesus' name."

Do not move the pelvis yourself. Wait on the Holy Spirit. What happens next is often astounding. The pelvis will often rotate back and forth and the people will many times feel their ligaments, organs or pelvis move. When praying for a woman's PMS symptoms, command the ligaments to lengthen and the pelvis to open to alleviate pressure. For a quick and easy birth, command the pelvis to open for an easy delivery. If they have duck feet, command the pelvis to close. If they are pigeon-toed, command the pelvis to open.

Middle Back Adjustment

Through experience, we have found that many aliments caused by a curvature of the spine or pain in the region of the upper chest or back can be healed by commanding the ribs to rotate back into their normal position. We use this prayer when ministering healing to people with scoliosis and have seen many healed. Place your hand on the back of the spine in the center of the back and repeat this prayer:

Prayer for Adjustment of the Middle Back

"In the name of Jesus, I command the ribs to rotate and go back into place. I command the vertebrae and discs in the spine to line up. And I command all muscles, ligaments and tendons to go back to their normal length and strength in Jesus' name."

Growing out Arms

Chiropractors can often tell if a person has an upper back problem by measuring their arms. The doctor does this by having them stand with their feet pointing forward, toes even, and asking them to extend their arms straight forward to their fully outstretched length. They instruct them to keep the hands apart about one quarter of an inch. When the arms are fully outstretched, the doctor tells the client to put their hands together, bend their elbows and look at their hands. If the upper back is out of alignment, it will be reflected in the position of the hands.

It is not uncommon for someone with an upper back problem to have their arms appear to be different lengths. Unless there was a birth defect or bone loss at some time in their lives, the arms are not actually different lengths. Bones are positioned by ligaments, tendons and muscles. Changes in their control affect the positioning and action of our skeletal structure, our bones, including our arms, legs, back, pelvis and neck.

We minister to people with upper back problems in the same way. Ask the person to stand with their feet forward and stretch out their arms as far as they can with their hands facing each other about one quarter inch apart. Instruct them to put their hands together, bend their elbows and look at the difference in their arm length. Instruct them to keep their eyes open to watch what God is going to do, to stretch out their arms again about one quarter inch apart, place your hand on the center of their upper back and repeat this prayer:

Prayer to Adjust Arm Length

"In the name of Jesus I command the upper back to go back into place and the brain stem to line up with the spinal column. I command the muscles, tendons, and ligaments to go back to their normal length and strength. I speak in a new disc and vertebra (if necessary). I also command the arms to grow and the pain to go in Jesus' name."

Under no circumstances do you ever push on the back or pull the arms. Pray and wait until the length of the arms line up by the power of the Holy Spirit. Usually, they will adjust quickly but occasionally the process may take several minutes.

Are there other ways to heal upper backs besides growing out arms? Our answer is absolutely "yes". However, when you minister this way you can see the power of God at work. As long as the person that you are praying for keeps their eyes open, they will see what God is doing. Anyone nearby can also easily see the changes as they occur. During the thirty years we have been ministering healing by growing out arms, we have seen countless upper backs healed.

Adjusting the Neck

If the head or the neck is out of alignment, the muscles of the neck will tighten to compensate for the problem. This can be the cause of many problems from headaches to back spasms and even numbness in the extremities. Injuries caused by falls or whiplash can do major damage to the discs, vertebrae, muscles, tendons and ligaments in the neck and upper back. To minister healing, stand in front of the person, place one hand on each side of the neck with your fingertips on the back of the neck directly over the spine and repeat the following prayer.

Prayer to Adjust the Neck and Spine

"In the name Jesus, I command the brain stem and the spinal column to come back into alignment. I command all the muscles, tendons and ligaments to return to their normal length and strength. I speak in new discs and vertebrae (if necessary). I command the pain to go and the neck to go back into alignment in the name of Jesus."

Do not lift on the neck or turn it in any direction. After you have ministered, have them turn their head and do something they could not do before.

Practical Things to Remember

1. You are ministering all healing in the name of Jesus. Always use His name with each command such as "I command (type of healing) in the name of Jesus."

2. After praying for someone, tell them to say "Thank you, Jesus." Always thank Him first.

3. Next, have them put their faith into action. Instruct them to do something that they could not do before (especially if they had restricted movement).

4. If their symptoms are still present, pray again. Don't give up. Instruct them to expect their healing (the absence of symptoms, etc.) not the pain, while they are thanking God for the improvement and the eventual completion of the healing.

5. Never tell anyone to stop taking medication even when all the symptoms have disappeared. Tell them they must check with their doctors for instructions regarding any change in their medications.

6. A relationship with Jesus is what everyone needs most. If they are not born again, lead them in the prayer of salvation.

Chapter 8

God Gets the Glory

By this time you should be prepared to pray for people to be healed and blessed by God. It is not uncommon at the end of a ministry session for people who received their healing to say, "Oh, thank you! Thank you!"

In return, most believers who are ministering will respond by saying, "Thank Jesus, not me," to turn the attention away from them and give the glory to God where it is due. Here is another way to deal with this same situation.

When people who were healed say "Oh thank you! Thank you!" just respond by saying, "I just watched God answer your prayers. That's what happened here." That response removes you from the situation completely. It gives all the credit to God and makes you an observer of God's power rather than the source of that power. This will allow you to avoid that awkward moment when you have to deflect the glory from you to God. By telling them you watched God answer their prayers, you are saying God did it and He could have done it without you. It takes all the glory away from you and gives it to God where it belongs.

Wait on the Holy Spirit. He will move through you. It is not a function of your ability, but of your availability. The more mature you become in the Lord, the more you realize it never was by or through your ability that anyone was healed. Be aware of the words that come out of your mouth after you pray for someone. Are you rejoicing that they were touched and freed or are you talking about how you prayed for someone and how they got healed? Is it about you? Or is it about what God did for them?

It is after the fact that you can clearly see the motivation of your heart by the words that come out of your mouth. *For out of the overflow of the heart the mouth speaks* (Matthew 12:34b). Your words will confirm whether your motivation is to see people set free or to elevate yourself by letting others know that when you pray for people, they are healed.

It is not uncommon to be excited when someone is healed. We believe that you should be very excited. We get excited every time someone is healed. However, who gets the glory? Can you tell others about the healing without mentioning your participation in it at all? Is the ministry about you and your gifting or is it about God?

If you find that you have been self-centered in ministry, then this is the perfect time to repent. *But if you harbor bitter envy and selfish ambition in your hearts, do not boast about it or deny the truth. Such "wisdom" does not come down from heaven but is earthly, unspiritual, of the devil. For where you have envy and selfish ambition, there you find disorder and every evil practice* (James 3:14-16).

If you have been selfish and your motives are for yourself, repent. Don't stop ministering to others, just do it with God's motives and not your own. It is not uncommon to meet powerfully gifted people who believe they are serving God with their gifts, but who may, in reality, be serving themselves. *Many will say to me on that day, 'Lord, Lord, did we not prophesy in your name, and in your name drive out demons and perform many miracles?' Then I will tell them plainly, 'I never knew you. Away from me, you evildoers!'* (Matthew 7:22-23).

Be sure to always give God the glory.

Chapter 9

Ministry to Children

When you are ministering to children, always position yourself at eye level with them. Get on your knees or sit down in a chair. Always ask, "What is your name?" Don't talk about them or ask them personal questions when you first meet. Talk about your own children or some of your experiences as a child until they start to join in or until you know they are relaxed enough for you to minister to them.

Most children don't come running up to the front of the church for prayer. They are dragged to the altar by their parents. Parents often say things like, "Can you change this kid's habits and help them? We have tried everything." Or "He has had this medical problem or that problem since he was born." Take the time and talk to the child on their level. Don't speak to them in baby talk, talk to them like an adult, because they are in front of an adult seeking help.

Take extra time if the child has not hit the age of accountability. For a girl, the age of accountability begins when she starts menstruation (around twelve years of age) and for a boy it begins when he can grow hair on his face (around the age of thirteen). These events essentially mean that they have entered puberty. The age of accountability is a Jewish custom that marks the time when children become (young) adults and they then stand before God for their own actions.

Mistakes prior to this age are not necessarily childish; however, responsibility for the consequences in Jewish law falls upon the parents, not the child. It is understood that the child may be fully aware of what he is doing and the consequences. However, prior to this time, the child has not reached the age of accountability and is accountable only through the parents.

We have found that in many cases we don't need to pray for the child unless they specifically ask for prayer. We have found the greatest success by praying for the parents.

For the unbelieving husband has been sanctified through his wife, and the unbelieving wife has been sanctified through her believing husband. Otherwise your children would be unclean, but as it is, they are holy (I Corinthians 7:14).

There is a Christian child psychologist in Florida who has had great success ministering to disturbed children with Attention Deficient Disorder (ADD) as well as other problems. He ministered only to the believing parents. Never once did he see the child. He met with the mom and dad, prayed with them and instructed them on how to handle their child. Many times he would not only counsel them, but he would also give them homework assignments that had to be completed before he would meet with them again. All of the children changed in just a short period of time after he ministered to their parents.

The sins of the fathers are carried down to the third and fourth generations. No one can avoid this spiritual law. Until someone repents (changes), this law remains in effect. The curse stops when somebody repents and stands in for his fathers and says, “No more, this sin stops here and now. I repent for my sins and the sins of my fathers."

We were at a large church in Chicago when a mom started screaming in the back of the room. Running to the back, we found a young boy turning blue from a severe asthma attack. The parents had sent someone to the car to get his asthma medicine, but the church was packed and the car was parked a long distance from the church.

After asking the Lord what to do, we clearly heard Him say, “Pray for the mom.” We took the hysterical mother to a quiet corner and led her in a prayer of repentance for adultery. She immediately repented and when she did, she felt something tangible leave her. At the same moment, the boy started breathing deeply. He was fine. The mother’s repentance and the boy’s recovery happened simultaneously. We never touched the boy or laid hands on him, yet he was healed.

We are not telling you that asthma is caused by adultery, but rather that it is caused by the sins of the fathers (a parent or an ancestor). In this case, there was a particular situation involving sin. The asthma and this sinful situation started at the same time and repentance brought healing to both at the same time.

The Bible has a great deal to say about the effects of the sins of the fathers (Exodus 34:5-7; Leviticus 26:39-42; Numbers 14:18).

You shall not bow down to them or worship them; for I, the LORD your God, am a jealous God, punishing the children for the sin of the fathers to the third and fourth generation of those who hate me (Exodus 20:5).

Jesus also spoke about the sins of the fathers. He told the Pharisees that they were doing the same things their fathers did. *"Abraham is our father," they answered. "If you were Abraham's children," said Jesus, "then you would do the things Abraham did. As it is, you are determined to kill me, a man who has told you the truth that I heard from God. Abraham did not do such things. You are doing the things your own father does"* (John 8:39-41).

When you lead people in prayers of repentance, it is important to have them repent for the sins of their fathers (parents, grandparents, ancestors) as well. Then tell them to put all these sins on the Cross of Jesus Christ. (See Chapter 11 for specific prayers.)

Chapter 10

Deliverance

Ministering deliverance is not hard or complicated. It is as easy as praying for the sick. It does, however, require an understanding of God's Word and a comprehension of God's authority. Deliverance was one third of Jesus' ministry. If you are going to lay hands on the sick and see them recover, then it will also be a part of your ministry.

What is a demonic being? It is an evil spirit that is looking for a body to inhabit and needs a doorway in which to enter. Can Christians have demons? Our answer is always the same: Do Christians have bodies? Remember that the cause of sickness is sin and sin is also the doorway that many demonic spirits use to move into a person's life. Demons can't inhabit your spirit; but given the right into your life, they can affect your body and your soul, which is your mind, your will and your emotions. You will not find demons behind every doorknob or rose bush, but they do exist and they can reap havoc on God's people.

If you are not familiar with the scriptures that show that demons exist and how they operate, you need to read and re-read them again. Begin with the healing ministry of Jesus. Jesus cast seven demons out of Mary Magdalene and went on to cast demons out of many others also (Mark 16:9; Matthew 8:16, 28-

32; 10:8, Mark 1:32-34, 39; Luke 8:2; 27-33;11:14 as well as many other scripture verses).

Demons (or devils) are not the cause of every problem in life. However, if they are the cause of the problem in the person coming to you for ministry, you need to know how to minister deliverance (freedom) according to God's Word.

How do we deal with these spirit entities? First of all, you need to know you have authority over demons. This authority is God given to all believers without exception. *And these signs will accompany those who believe: In my name they will drive out demons* (Mark 16:17). He gave us this authority, just as He gave it to his disciples. He called his twelve disciples to Him and gave them authority to drive out evil spirits and to heal every disease and sickness. Jesus gave His followers the authority to deliver others from demons. If you are a follower of Jesus, then you have the same authority (Matthew 10:1; Mark 3:14-15; 6:7-13; 16:17; Luke 9:1; 10:17-19). It is interesting to consider that His followers ministered healing and cast out demons both before and after Jesus died as well as before and after they received the Holy Ghost in the book of Acts.

Along with being fully persuaded that you have this authority, you must also have an understanding of how it functions. This authority is yours when you understand your position in Christ and not just your power or abilities in Him. It may be best explained this way: You are driving down the highway at night and a big man on a large motorcycle tries to get you to pull off the road. There is no doubt you would resist him. However, if a police officer on a patrol motorcycle tries to pull you over, you know you have stop. He is no stronger than the other man but he is operating within a higher authority and counts on that power to back him up. He knows and understands his authority.

It is not what you can do to the demon that gets them to obey, but it is who you are in Christ that they have to submit to. The seventy-two returned with joy and said, *Lord, even the demons submit to us in your name* (Luke 10:17).

How do you know which demons or evil spirits are causing a problem? In general, they are described by their function, meaning how these spiritual beings manifest in the natural realm. The Word of God mentions many types such as a spirit of infirmity (Luke 7:21; 8:2; 13:11 KJV), deaf and dumb spirits (Mark 7:32, 37; 9:25), the spirit of heaviness (Isaiah 61:3 KJV), the spirit of haughtiness or pride (Proverbs 16:18), a spirit of bondage (Romans 8:15 KJV) etc. Many of these manifestations are listed in the prayer section of this book, along with how to minister freedom from each.

We have found through life experiences that demons are singular in their purpose. There are many types of evil spirits or demons and each one has its own manifestation. For example, a spirit of anger can only manifest as anger. A spirit of infirmity can only manifest as sickness. And a spirit of perversion is always perverse and has no other traits.

Setting people free from demons is very easy because demons must obey believers acting under the authority of God using the name of Jesus. However there is this one caution: as in any ministry make sure you are led by the Spirit and not by your own desires to see someone free. Jesus clearly explains that if we cast a spirit out of someone but neglect to deal with the cause (doorway) in which the spirit came in, we could be doing more harm than good. *When an evil spirit comes out of a man, it goes through arid places seeking rest and does not find it. Then it says, 'I will return to the house I left.' When it arrives, it finds the house swept clean and put in order. Then it goes and takes seven other spirits more wicked than itself, and they go in and live there. And the final condition of that man is worse than the first"* (Luke 11:24-26).

It is very important that the root cause is dealt with and that there is repentance from this cause. There are two very important questions to ask in order to find the root cause:

1. How long have you had the problem? (When did it start?)
2. What happened just before or when this started? (Identify the doorway.)

Fear, unforgiveness, bitterness, pride, lust, greed, generational sins, curses and any participation in the occult are just a few of the root causes.

We prayed for a woman in Iowa who had been in pain for four years. She had been in an auto accident and her back had never healed though she had received much prayer. There had been an ugly insurance lawsuit and she had been falsely accused. She was still angry at both the person who hit her and their attorney. When we prayed for her, she forgave them both and was instantly healed. As she forgave them she could feel the anger, bitterness and pain leave her body.

We could have ministered to her by just casting out the spirit of pain. However, if we had not led her in repentance for the anger and unforgiveness, she may have had even more problems if the spirit of pain returned (Luke 11:24-26).

Setting people free is easy. When you are ministering, don't look for the darkness that may be residing in people. Look for the light that is in them and the light will expose any darkness. We also want to point out that there is no record in the Bible where Jesus ever yelled at the demons or repeated Himself over and over again. He simply drove them out with a word. *When evening came, many who were demon-possessed were brought to him, and he drove out the spirits with a word and healed all the sick* (Matthew 8:16).

Also, you must remember that when the demons are driven out, they can't go into you, your family members or even your house. The word confirms that they go to the dry and arid places. *When an evil spirit comes out of a man, it goes through arid places seeking rest and does not find it* (Luke 11:24). The dry and arid places are places without the water of life (Revelation 22:1).

Although evil spirits still exist, are still evil and still have power, always remember they all have to submit to the name that is above every name, the name of Jesus Christ. *At the name of Jesus every knee should bow, in heaven and on earth and under the earth* (Philippians 2:10).

The demons do not have to submit to your will, but they have to submit to God's will through the name of Jesus. So, always walk according to God's truth as revealed in His Word, be led by the peace of God, and follow the leading of the Holy Spirit.

Chapter 11

Prayers of Repentance

This is a collection of effective prayers that you will use in the "How to Pray for Various Conditions" section of this book. Learn them. They are very effective in healing.

Prayer of Salvation

"Father, I know that Jesus came that we may have life and that life more abundantly. (John 10:10) The Word of God confirms that he who follows Jesus must be a servant of the Lord. As that servant, he would lose the life he knows and would receive a new life in Christ (Mark 10:43; Romans 6:4). I am willing to die to my old life and pick up this new life as a servant of the Lord Jesus Christ.

"Father, I confess I have been living for myself. The path I have chosen has not produced life-giving fruit that lasts. I am willing to give my whole life to you and confess with my mouth that Jesus is Lord and that I am now the servant of the Lord. No longer will I live for myself, but I will live for Christ from this day forth. I confess my sins and ask that they be removed from me and put on the cross of Jesus Christ. (Take the time needed to confess these sins.) I know this is the beginning of a journey that will continue through eternity. I (Insert full Christian name) give you 100% of my heart and confirm my covenant with Jesus who is raised from the dead and now lives in my heart."

Prayer for Forgiveness

"Father, I understand that You do not forgive sin but You do forgive people who sin (Matthew 6:12). I understand that You separate the sins from those who confess and repent of those sins. The Word of God confirms that Jesus bore my confessed sins on the cross and that He no longer holds them against me (1 Peter 2:24). I also understand that no one but Jesus deserved forgiveness and that You will forgive me of my sins with the same measure that I choose to forgive others (Matthew 6:14-15).

"Father, I choose to forgive (<u>insert name</u>). What they did to me is sin. Take this sin from them and put it on the cross. And on the Day of Judgment when I stand before Your Throne, I will hold no accusation against them. Father, I ask you to bless them in Jesus' name."

Repentance for Judgment and Condemnation

"Father, I understand Your Word says You will judge me with the same measure I use to judge others. I also know by Your Word that I will be condemned with the same measure that I use to condemn others (Luke 6:37-38; 1 Corinthians 5:12). I know it is correct to judge things as right and wrong according to your Word, but only You know the motives and intent of another's heart (Hebrews 4:12).

"Father, I have judged others and have condemned them. This is sin, and I repent of this sin and ask You to separate this sin from me in Jesus' name and put it on the cross of Jesus Christ."

Prayer to Break Word Curses

"Father, I know Your Word says to say things that edify, build up, correct and confirm (1 Thessalonians 5:11; 2 Timothy 4:2). Words of condemnation, slander, complaining, griping and gossip or accusation are not of You. They are sin (James 5:9).

"Father, people have said words about and against me that were sin. I choose to forgive them of this sin and on the Day of Judgment I will hold no accusations against them. Even now they are free and I bless them in Jesus' name. And Father, I have said words about (insert name) that did not edify, did not correct, and did not confirm. I take responsibility for these words. They are sin. I choose to repent of them and only say words that bless (insert name) from this day forth. I take responsibility for those words. I renounce those words in the name of Jesus and I ask You to separate me from this sin in Jesus' name and to put it on the cross of Jesus."

Prayer to Break Generational Curses

"Father, I know Your Word says that if we confess our iniquity (sins) and the iniquity (sins) of our fathers that you will heal us (James 5:16; Leviticus 26:40-42).

"Father, I take responsibility for my sins. I ask You to forgive me of my sins, separate them from me and place them on the cross of Jesus Christ. I also ask you to forgive my fathers of this same sin, separate their sins from them, put them on the cross as well and thus break the curse off of me and my family in Jesus' name."

Prayer to Break Ungodly Covenants

"Father, I understand that sexual intercourse is the sign of the marriage covenant and that you call the marriage covenant holy (Matthew 19:6). I know your Word states that sex outside of marriage is sin (Matthew 15:19-20). I also understand that I have entered into covenant with every person with whom I have had sexual relations.

"Father, I renounce the ungodly covenant I made with (insert name). This was sin and I renounce it as such. Separate this sin from me, place it on the cross of Jesus, and break this covenant I made off of me and my household. I also renounce any other ungodly covenants I have made as well, in Jesus' name.

Chapter 12

The Immune System and Electrical and Magnetic Frequencies, Prions and pH Balance

The immune system is a complex system of organs--highly specialized cells and circulatory system separate from blood vessels--all of which work together to clear infection from the body.

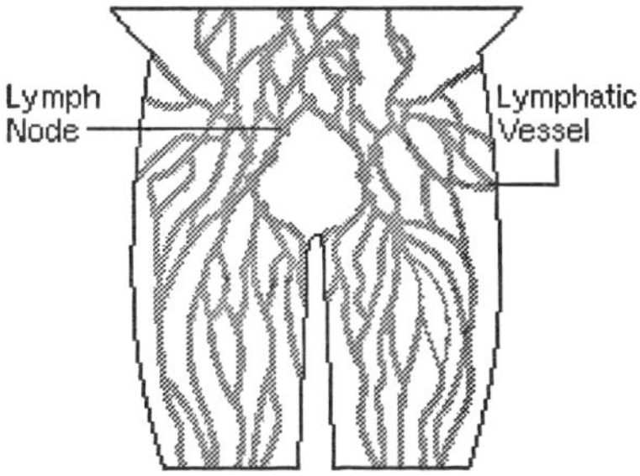

The Lymph Circulatory System

Lymphatic vessels form a circulatory system that operates in close partnership with blood circulation. Lymphatic vessels and lymph nodes are the parts of the special circulatory system that carries lymph, a transparent fluid containing white blood cells, chiefly lymphocytes.

The organs of the immune system, positioned throughout the body, are called lymphoid organs. The word "lymph" in Greek means a pure, clear stream--an appropriate description considering its appearance and purpose.

Pockets of lymphoid tissue are in many other locations throughout the body, such as the bone marrow and thymus. Tonsils, adenoids, Peyer's patches, and the appendix are also lymphoid tissues.

Lymph fluid bathes the tissues of the body, and the lymphatic vessels collect and move this fluid eventually back into the blood circulation. Lymph nodes dot the network of lymphatic vessels and provide meeting grounds for the immune system cells that defend against invaders. The spleen, at the upper left of the abdomen, is also a staging ground, a place where immune system cells confront foreign microbes.

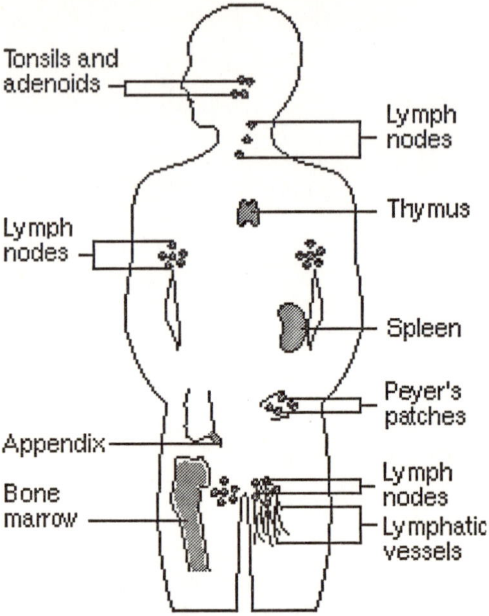

Organs and tissues of the immune system dot the body in a protective network of barriers to infection.

Both immune cells and foreign molecules enter the lymph nodes via blood vessels or lymphatic vessels. All immune cells exit the lymphatic system and eventually return to the bloodstream. Once in the bloodstream, lymphocytes are transported to tissues throughout the body, where they act as sentries on the lookout for foreign antigens.

Most diseases start when the immune system is destroyed or low. The immune system is the gatekeeper, the system that admits sickness, or the deficiency that opens the door for sickness, into the body. Add this command wherever applicable:

Prayer to Restore the Immune System

"I command the immune system to be restored. I command it to be effective in stopping diseases, germs and viruses from inflicting this body, in Jesus' name."

Electrical and Magnetic Frequencies

The human body is made up of trillions of cells that are constantly performing chemical reactions that produce energy for our life functions. Part of the energy released from these reactions is electrical energy that has its own magnetic frequency. Modern science is now able to measure these electrical and magnetic frequencies.

Science has found that in bodies where sickness such as cancer exists, the electrical and magnetic frequencies are altered from their natural state (out of harmony and balance). There are studies that suggest that that cancer ceases to grow when the magnetic frequencies are returned to their natural state. We have found by our own experiences that commanding the body to return to its natural electrical and magnetic frequencies has produced healing in dealing with many diseases.

Prayer to Normalize Electrical and Magnetic Frequencies

“In the name of Jesus I command all of the electrical and magnetic frequencies in this body to return to normal harmony and balance.”

Prions

Prions are molecules of a normal body protein that have changed their configuration. They are unique in their ability to reproduce on their own and become infectious. Unlike normal proteins, prions are insoluble in all but the strongest solvents and are highly resistant to digestion by proteases (the enzyme that dissolves protein to be absorbed back into the body). These prions have mutated and now bind together forming protein aggregates (clumps).

It is not yet clear to medical science if these aggregates are themselves the cause of the cell damage or are simply a side effect of the underlying disease process. However they tend to exist where disease is present. We have seen people healed of various diseases by simply commanding the prions to dissolve and be discarded by into the body.

Prayer to Remove Prions

"I command all the prions to completely dissolve and be discarded from the body and I command healing to every cell affected by these prions, in Jesus' name."

pH Balance

The pH balance or levels (acid - alkaline measurement) of our body fluids affects every cell in our bodies. pH imbalances over a long period of time can cause multiple problems.

With the same rigid manner the body regulates its internal temperature, so it also manages to preserve a very narrow pH range; especially in the blood. To maintain a normal blood pH, it will even create stress on other tissues or body systems.

Chronic acidification will interfere with all cellular activities and functions. When the pH of the body gets too acidic, we may experience low energy, fatigue, excess weight, poor digestion, headaches and other pains, and can experience even more serious disorders. The causes often are from poor diet, toxicity and improper elimination & neutralization of acids.

Prayer to Normalize the pH Balance

"I command, the pH balance of this body to normalize. I command healing to every cell affected by any abnormal levels, in Jesus' name."

Chapter 13

PRAYERS FOR VARIOUS CONDITIONS

ABUSE

Abuse may be physical, sexual, emotional, verbal, or a combination of any of these experienced at any age. If parents don't take care of the basic needs of the children, that can be considered abuse as well. You are required by law to report any ongoing sexual abuse of a minor. If you have been informed of such abuse and don't report it to the proper authorities, you can be prosecuted as well as the perpetrator of the crime. The victims often believe that they are in some way responsible for the abusive treatment. They believe a lie.

How to Minister: (All commands done in Jesus' name).

1. Instruct victims of ongoing physical abuse to go to a safe house.
2. Lead them in the prayer of forgiveness towards the abuser.
3. Rebuke the lies they have believed.
4. Speak the peace of God upon them

ACNE

Acne is a skin condition characterized by whiteheads, blackheads, and inflamed red pimples or "zits." Acne is caused when tiny holes on the surface of the skin, called pores, become clogged. Each pore is an opening to a canal called a follicle, which contains a hair and an oil gland. Normally, the oil glands help keep the skin lubricated and help remove old skin cells. When glands produce too much oil, the pores can become blocked, accumulating dirt, debris, and bacteria. The bacteria can become infection causing repeated skin eruptions which can leave serious scarring. Usually seen on the face, Acne can also affect other areas of the body such as the back.

How to Minister: (All commands done in Jesus' name).
1. Rebuke the infection and command it to go.
2. Lay hands on their head, commanding the skin pores to open and to drain normally.
3. Command glands to produce a normal amount of oil.

ADDICTION (Alcohol, Cigarette, Drugs, or Food).

An Addiction is a physical and or a psychological dependence on a substance, for example: alcohol, nicotine in cigarettes, or drugs (such as tranquilizers, cocaine, marijuana, heroin etc.). People can also be addicted to eating food (also called Gluttony).

The root cause is most often rebellion. This rebellion generally occurs at or just after the age of accountability (puberty) and sets the stage for an addictive spirit which is a symptom of rebellion. This symptom follows a person their whole life until they repent. Many are able to get free of substance abuse but must fight with the addictive spirit until they repent of rebellion.

How to Minister: (All commands done in Jesus' name).
1. Confirm their desire to be free from the addiction.
2. Have them repent for their rebellion.
3. Have them renounce the words spoken in rebellion
4. Speak a replacement for any damaged parts of their body, for example a new brain, liver, etc.
5. Speak peace to them.

ADDISON'S DISEASE (Also called Adrenal Insufficiency).

Addison's Disease is an endocrine or hormonal disorder that occurs in all age groups and afflicts men and women equally. The disease is characterized by weight loss, muscle weakness, fatigue, low blood pressure, and sometimes darkening of the skin.

Addison's Disease occurs when the adrenal glands do not produce enough hormones. The disease is also called Adrenal Insufficiency. Addison's Disease may be due to a genetic abnormality of the adrenal glands. Most cases are caused by the gradual destruction of the outer layer of the adrenal glands by the body's own immune system. About seventy percent of reported cases of Addison's Disease are caused by autoimmune disorders, in which the immune system makes antibodies that attack the body's own tissues or organs and slowly destroy them.

How to Minister: (All commands done in Jesus' name).

1. Lead them in the prayer of repentance for the sins of their fathers.
2. Command the electrical frequencies and chemical balance to be in order.
3. Command a creative miracle---a new pair of Adrenal Glands.
4. Command the hormones from the Adrenal Gland to maintain normal levels.

ADHESIONS (See SCARS, KELOIDS, and ADHESIONS).

ADRENAL GLANDS (Also see Addison's Disease).

The Adrenal Glands are located on top of both kidneys. The inner part of the adrenal glands secretes hormones such as adrenalin that affect blood pressure, heart rate and sweating. The outer portion secretes many different hormones that control the use of fats, proteins and carbohydrates in the body. This area also secretes male sex hormones as well as mineral corticoids that control blood pressure and the levels of salt and potassium in the body. The hypothalamus or pituitary glands could fail to produce hormones that control the adrenal glands and cause a problem with the adrenal glands. Abnormal production of hormones or disease or infection inside or around the adrenal gland could cause problems as well.

People with this disorder are commonly found to be stressed, constantly worried or overworked with little or no rest.

How to Minister: (All commands done in Jesus' name).

1. Rebuke any infection and command the adrenal glands to function properly.
2. Command the hormones to return to normal levels.
3. Lead in a prayer of repentance for worry (lay worry on the Altar of God), stress (give problems to Jesus) or not resting (God requires a Sabbath day's rest).

ADRENAL INSUFFICIENCY (See Addison's Disease).

AGORAPHOBIA (Panic Disorder)

A Panic Disorder is a condition in which a person has episodes of intense fear or anxiety that occur suddenly (often without warning). These episodes could last from a few minutes to several hours. The typical age of onset is between adolescence and the mid-thirties. Women are two to three times more likely than men to be affected with a Panic Disorder.

The cause for these attacks is generally not known and can vary between people, but they seem to be more common with people who have gone through divorce or separation or have experienced a troubled family history.

How to Minister: (All commands done in Jesus' name).

1. If they are having a Panic Attack, call them by their full Christian name. When you have their attention, say, "Peace, in the name of Jesus".
2. Ask when Panic Attacks started. Find out what happened to them just before the first occurrence.
3. Lead them in repentance or forgiveness to correct the situation.
4. Command the spirit of fear and or anxiety to leave.
5. Speak peace to them.

AIDS/HIV

HIV (human immunodeficiency virus) is the virus that causes AIDS. This virus may be passed from one person to another when infected blood, semen, or vaginal secretions come in contact with an uninfected person's broken skin or mucous membranes (mouth, eyes, nose, vagina, rectum, and opening of the penis). In addition, infected pregnant women can pass HIV to their baby during pregnancy or delivery as well as through breast-feeding. It can also be passed by sharing infected needles or through blood transfusions.

People with HIV have what is called HIV infection. Some of these people will develop AIDS as a result of their HIV infection. AIDS stands for Acquired Immunodeficiency Syndrome. Acquired – means that the disease is not hereditary, but develops after birth from contact with a disease causing agent (in this case, HIV). Immunodeficiency – means that the disease is characterized by a weakening of the immune system.

Syndrome – refers to a group of symptoms that collectively indicate or characterize a disease. In the case of AIDS this can include the development of certain infections and/or cancers, as well as a decrease in the number of certain cells in a person's immune system. A diagnosis of AIDS is made by a physician using specific clinical or laboratory standards.

How to Minister: (All commands done in Jesus' name).
1. Lead in repentance when necessary.
2. Rebuke the spirit of HIV.
3. Speak in a new immune and blood system.
4. Command the electrical and magnetic frequencies to be in harmony and return to normal balance.
5. Command all prions to completely dissolve and leave the body.
6. Command the blood to come into proper pH balance.

ALLERGIES

Allergic reactions are inappropriate immune responses to a normally harmless substance. The immune system—which includes antibodies, white blood cells, mast cells, and other substances—defends the body against foreign substances called antigens. However, in susceptible people, the immune system can overreact to certain antigens (also called allergens), which are harmless in most people. The result is an allergic reaction.

About one third of the people in the United States have an allergy. Allergens may cause an allergic reaction when they land on the skin or in the eye, are inhaled, eaten, or injected. A seasonal allergy (such as hay fever) is caused by exposure to such substances as grass or ragweed pollen. Or an allergic reaction can be triggered by taking a drug, eating certain foods, breathing in dust or animal dander or changes in physical conditions such as walking into a cold room or bright light. It is common for a person with allergies to have a family history from one or both parents.

How to Minister: (All commands done in Jesus' name).

1. Lead them in a prayer of repentance for generational curses.
2. Lay hands on the head, commanding the immune system to return to normal, and all the tissues and organs to be healed and function normally.
3. If not an inherited trait, find out what happened just before symptoms began and lead in a prayer for repentance or forgiveness.

ALOPECIA (See BALDNESS).

ALZHEIMER'S DISEASE

Alzheimer's Disease is a progressive, relentless loss of mental function, characterized by degeneration of brain tissue, including loss of nerve cells. In Alzheimer's Disease, parts of the brain degenerate, destroying nerve cells and reducing the transmission of signals in the brain. Abnormalities develop to some degree in all people as they age but are much more numerous in people with Alzheimer's.

What causes Alzheimer's is unknown, but genetic factors do play a role: The disease seems to run in some families and is caused or influenced by several genetic abnormalities. In the United States, about four million people have Alzheimer's Disease. Higher than normal concentrations of aluminum have been found in the brain of some people diagnosed with Alzheimer's Disease. Some patients have been misdiagnosed and found to have excessive spinal fluid that exerts pressure on the brain and imitates the symptoms of Alzheimer's Disease.

How to Minister: (All commands done in Jesus' name).

1. Lead them in a prayer of repentance for generational curses.

2. Command the metallic levels in the blood and the brain to return to normal.
3. Command the excessive spinal fluid to return to normal.
4. Speak a creative miracle and command a new brain.

AMBLYOPIA (Also called Lazy Eye).

Amblyopia is loss of visual acuity in one eye caused by lack of use of that eye in early childhood. Vision loss is usually caused by the abnormal functioning of the brain, not of the eye. Amblyopia is the most common cause of vision loss in children and develops only during childhood. Amblyopia should be suspected in a child if any of the following are seen: eyes that turn in or out, eyes that do not appear to work together or if they show a lack of depth perception.

Strabismus (crossed eyes), different refractive errors (farsightedness, nearsightedness, astigmatism) in the two eyes, and childhood cataracts are common causes of Amblyopia. The preferred eye becomes dominant and has normal vision. The non-favored eye is ignored by the brain to avoid a clash between the two different images from the eyes. As a result, the visual system in the brain for the non-favored eye fails to develop properly. Between ages 5 and 10, the brain stops growing and the condition becomes permanent.

How to Minister: (All commands done in Jesus' name).

1. Command the eyes to send complete signals to the brain.
2. Command the brain to read the messages from both eyes and function normally.
3. Command the eye muscles to be of equal length and strength and the nerves to function normally.
4. Command the eye to be healed and vision to be normal.

5. Lead them in a prayer of repentance for generational curses.

AMYOTROPHIC LATERAL SCLEROSIS (ALS)

Also known as "Lou Gehrig's disease" or "ALS", Amyotrophic Lateral Sclerosis is characterized by progressive loss of motor nerve function in the spinal cord and brain. In about ten percent of cases, ALS is caused by a genetic defect. In other cases, the cause of the nerve deterioration is unknown.

How to Minister: (All commands done in Jesus' name).

1. Lead them in a prayer of repentance for generational curses.
2. Command the spirit of ALS to leave.
3. Command a new nervous system and a new brain.
4. Command that all systems will be totally healed and function normally.

ANEMIA (See also Sickle Cell Anemia).

Red blood cells contain hemoglobin, a protein that enables the cells to carry oxygen from the lungs and deliver it to all parts of the body. When the number of red blood cells is reduced or the amount of hemoglobin is low, the blood cannot carry an adequate supply of oxygen. An inadequate supply of oxygen in the tissues produces the symptoms of Anemia and without enough oxygen the organs of the body do not function effectively. This can be caused by a lack of vitamin B-12. Vitamin B-12 is essential for normal nervous system function and blood cell production. The main sources of vitamin B-12 include meat, eggs, and dairy products. It can also be caused by a slow loss of blood within the body.

How to Minister: (All commands done in Jesus' name).

1. Command the gastrointestinal tract to be healed and to properly absorb and utilize necessary vitamins and minerals especially Vitamin B-12.
2. Command the bone marrow to function normally and to manufacture normal amounts of healthy red blood cells.
3. Command any area of bleeding to be healed and function normally.
4. Command the blood to come into proper pH balance.

ANEURYSM

An Aneurysm is a bulge (dilation) in the wall of an artery, usually the aorta, but can develop in other arteries of the body as well such as within the brain. The bulge usually occurs in a weak area of the artery wall. The pressure of blood inside the artery forces the weak area to balloon outward. If untreated, an Aneurysm may rupture, resulting in serious internal bleeding.

The most common cause of aortic aneurysms is atherosclerosis, which weakens the wall of the aorta. Less common causes include injuries, inflammatory diseases of the blood vessel and some infectious diseases such as syphilis. In older people, almost all Aneurysms are associated with atherosclerosis. High blood pressure, which is common among older people, and cigarette smoking increase the risk of an Aneurysm.

How to Minister: (All commands done in Jesus' name).

1. Lay hands on the affected area, commanding a creative miracle -- new arteries with good strong walls.
2. Command restoration of normal blood flow.

ANGINA

Angina is a specific type of chest pain caused by inadequate blood flow through the blood vessels (coronary vessels) of the heart muscle. Angina is not a heart attack, but may be a symptom of heart disease and, if untreated, can lead to a heart attack.

How to Minister: (All commands done in Jesus' name).

1. Command the coronary arteries to open up completely and allow sufficient blood flow to the heart muscle.
2. Speak in a new heart.

ANOREXIA NERVOSA

Anorexia Nervosa is characterized by a distorted body image, an extreme fear of obesity, refusal to maintain a minimally normal body weight, and, in women, the absence of menstrual periods. Hereditary factors have been shown to play a role in the development of Anorexia Nervosa. Social factors are also important. The desire to be thin pervades Western society, and obesity is considered unattractive, unhealthy, and undesirable.

Even before adolescence, children are aware of these attitudes, and two thirds of all adolescent girls will diet or use other measures to control their weight. It has been estimated to affect about one percent of girls aged twelve to eighteen. The disorder usually begins in adolescence, occasionally earlier, and less commonly in adulthood. We have found the primary cause to be rebellion as stated in the Psalms. This generally starts with words of rebellion stated during or right after puberty.

Some became fools through their rebellious ways and suffered affliction because of their iniquities. They loathed all food and drew near the gates of death (Psalms 107:17-18).

How to Minister: (All commands done in Jesus' name).
1. Have them repent of their rebellion at adolescence.
2. Have them renounce the words spoken in rebellion.
3. Cast out the spirit of death and speak in life.

ANXIETY (See also Fear, Panic Disorder).

Anxiety is a feeling of apprehension or fear. The source of this uneasiness is not always known or recognized, which can add to the distress a person feels. The most effective solution is to identify and address the source of the stress, fear or anxiety. Unfortunately, this is not always possible. Ask what the person thinks might be making them "stress out". Is something constantly on their mind? What do they worry about most? Does anything in particular make them sad or depressed?

How to Minister: (All commands done in Jesus' name).
1. Lead them in a prayer to lay all worry, stress and care on the Altar of God.
2. Lead them in a prayer of repentance when necessary.
3. Speak peace to them.

APPESTAT (see Obesity)

The appestat is the brain's control center for the appetite (or desire for food).

ARMS AND HANDS

Numbness, tingling, and pain usually caused by a neck problem.

How to Minister: (All commands done in Jesus' name).
1. Grow out the arms.
2. Command the neck to be adjusted.

3. Command the nerves to be restored to normal structure and function.
4. Command numbness, tingling and pain to go
5. Lead them in a prayer to lay all worry, stress and care on the Altar of God.

ARTERIOSCLEROSIS (Atherosclerosis)

Arteriosclerosis is a condition in which patchy deposits of fatty material develop in the walls of medium-sized and large arteries, leading to reduced or blocked blood flow.

Atherosclerosis can affect the arteries of the brain, heart, kidneys, other vital organs, and legs. It is the most important and most common type of arteriosclerosis, a general term for several diseases in which the wall of an artery becomes thicker and less elastic.

There are two main theories about why atherosclerosis develops: High levels of cholesterol in the blood injure the artery lining, causing an inflammatory reaction and enabling cholesterol and other fatty materials to accumulate at the affected site. Or, repeated injury to the artery wall may occur through various mechanisms involving the immune system or through direct toxicity.

How to Minister: (All commands done in Jesus' name).
1. Command the neck to be adjusted.
2. Command all the arteries to be cleansed of all cholesterol deposits and elasticity to return to normal.
3. Command all blockages to disappear and blood to flow to every area of the body normally.

ARTHRITIS (Also see Osteoarthritis and Rheumatoid Arthritis)

Arthritis involves inflammation of one or more joints and the breakdown of cartilage. Cartilage normally protects the joints, allowing for smooth movement. Cartilage also absorbs shock when pressure is placed on the joint when you walk or otherwise bear weight. Without the usual amount of cartilage, the bones rub together, causing pain, swelling, and stiffness in hips, knees or feet. It can develop in any joint of the body including the hands, arms, shoulders, neck and back.

How to Minister: (All commands done in Jesus' name).
1. Cast out the spirit of arthritis.
2. Command all inflammation and swelling to be healed and pain to go.
3. Command the cartilage to be restored.
4. Lead in the prayer of forgiveness.

ASTHMA (Also see COPD).

Asthma is a disease in which inflammation of the airways restricts airflow into and out of the lungs. When an Asthma attack occurs, the muscles of the bronchial airways tighten and the lining of the air passages swells, reducing airflow and producing a characteristic wheezing sound. Mucus production is increased. Most people with Asthma have occasional wheezing attacks separated by symptom-free periods. Some asthmatics have chronic mild shortness of breath with periodic episodes of increased shortness of breath. Other asthmatics may have a cough as their predominant symptom. Asthma attacks can last from minutes to days, and can become life threatening if the airflow becomes severely restricted.

How to Minister: (All commands done in Jesus' name).
1. Lead in repentance for the sins of the fathers.
2. Cast out the spirit of asthma.
3. Speak healing to all the tissues of the respiratory system.

4. Grow out the arms.
5. Speak the peace of God into their life.

ASTIGMATISM

Astigmatism is a common condition in which the cornea of the eye is asymmetrically curved, causing out-of-focus vision. The cause of astigmatism is unknown. It is usually present from birth, and often occurs together with nearsightedness or farsightedness. A minor degree of astigmatism is considered normal and does not require correction.

How to Minister: (All commands done in Jesus' name).
1. Command the spirit of astigmatism to go.
2. Command the eye(s) to return to the proper shape and vision to return to normal.

ATTENTION DEFICIT DISORDER (A.D.D.) ATTENTION DEFICIT HYPERACTIVITY DISORDER (A.D.H.D.)

ADD and ADHD both include problems with inattentiveness, over-activity, impulsivity, or a combination of these. For these conditions to be diagnosed as ADHD, they must be out of the normal range for the child's age and development. ADHD affects school performance and relationships with others. Parents of children with ADHD are often exhausted and frustrated. Advanced scientific studies have shown that the brains of children with ADHD are different from those of other children. These children handle neurotransmitters (including dopamine, serotonin, and adrenalin) differently from their peers. ADHD is often genetic. Whatever the specific cause may be, it seems to be set in motion early in life as the brain is developing.

Depression, sleep deprivation, learning disabilities, tic disorders, and behavior problems may be confused with, or appear along with, ADHD. Every child suspected of having ADHD deserves a careful evaluation to sort out exactly what is contributing to the concerning behaviors.

Attention Deficit Disorder (ADD) is the most commonly diagnosed behavioral disorder of childhood, affecting an estimated three to five percent of school aged children. It is diagnosed much more often in boys than in girls.

How to Minister: (All commands done in Jesus' name).

1. Lead them in a prayer of repentance for the sins of the fathers.
2. Command silence to all the abnormal noises in the head.
3. Command the spirit of ADD/ADHD to go.
4. Speak in a new brain, if necessary.
5. Command the hormones to be in balance and the neurotransmitters to work properly
6. Command peace to the family and the home.
7. Suggest a change in diet where applicable.

AUTISM

Autism is a complex developmental disorder that appears in the first three years of life, although it is sometimes diagnosed much later. It affects the brain's normal development of social and communication skills and encompasses a wide range of behavior. The common features include impaired social interactions, impaired verbal and nonverbal communication, and restricted and repetitive patterns of behavior.

How to Minister: (All commands done in Jesus' name).

1. Gently and with a quiet attitude, hold the person if possible.
2. Speaking softly but firmly, command the spirit of Autism to go.

3. Lay on hands and command a new brain and the total restoration of the nervous system.
4. Speak the peace of God into their heart and soul.

BACK PROBLEMS (See also DISC PROBLEMS).

Back pain is one of the most common complaints treated by physicians. Nearly four out of five people will experience back pain at some time in their lives. The vast majority of these cases do not have a definable cause for the pain.

Back pain can develop in association with a number of causes including but not limited to muscle strain, injury to the back, overuse, muscle disorders, pressure on a nerve root, poor posture, ruptured discs, or fractures of the spine. Pregnant women, smokers, construction workers, and people who perform repetitive lifting are at increased risk for back problems resulting in chronic pain.

How to Minister: (All commands done in Jesus' name). Pinpoint the problem when possible. (for example, ask: What is the doctor's diagnosis? What do you know specifically about what is wrong? Do you have pain? Were you in an accident? Have you had surgery?)

1. For lower back problems, grow out the legs.
2. For middle of the back pain, grow out the arms.
3. For upper back pain, command the neck to come into proper alignment.
4. Command the pelvis to rotate into the perfect position for the spine to line up perfectly.
5. Do any or all of these as needed and repeat, if necessary.
6. Command the discs, vertebrae, muscles, ligaments, and tendons to be healed and adjusted. Be specific when possible.

7. Speak a new disc or vertebrae into the back, if necessary.
8. Command all pain to go.

BALANCE, LOSS of (See also Dizziness).

Loss of Balance may be described as lightheadedness, feeling faint, being unsteady, dizziness or vertigo (the room seems to be spinning or moving). Lightheadedness or Loss of Balance can occur when there is not enough blood getting to the brain. This can happen if there is a sudden drop in your blood pressure or you are dehydrated from vomiting, diarrhea, fever, or other causes. Older people can experience this feeling if they get up too quickly from a lying or seated position. Lightheadedness often accompanies the flu, common cold, or allergies. It can also be a side effect of some medications, such as blood pressure pills. Balance is also affected by problems in the inner ear. (Also see Meniere's disease.)

How to Minister: (All commands done in Jesus' name).

1. Rebuke the cause of the imbalance (for example, infection, disease, loss of sleep, etc.).
2. Command the neck to come into alignment.
3. Grow out the arms.
4. Command the balance center in the inner ear to be healed and the temporal bones to rotate back into position.

BALDNESS (Also called Alopecia).

Partial or complete loss of hair is called Alopecia. Hair loss usually develops gradually and may be patchy or diffuse (all over). Roughly one hundred hairs are lost from your head every day. The average scalp contains about 100,000 hairs. Each individual hair survives for an average of 4 1/2 years, during which time it grows about half an inch a month. Usually in its fifth year, the hair falls out and is replaced by a new one within six months. Genetic Baldness is caused by the body's failure to produce new hairs and not by excessive hair loss.

Both men and women tend to lose hair thickness and amount as they age. Inherited or "pattern baldness" affects many more men than women. About 25% of men begin to bald by the time they are thirty years old, and about two-thirds are either bald or have a balding pattern by age sixty. The most common type of baldness is called Male Pattern Baldness. Common Baldness cannot occur without the presence of specific inherited genes. These genes can be passed on by either parent.

How to Minister: (All commands done in Jesus' name).

1. Command healing to the hair follicles and the blood to flow normally.
2. Command the hair to be restored to normal amount.
3. Lead them in a prayer of repentance for generational curses.

BARRENNESS (See Infertility).

BED-WETTING

Involuntary urination in children over five to six years of age is called Bed-wetting and usually occurs at night. Children develop complete control over their bladders at different ages. Nighttime dryness is usually the last stage of toilet training. When children wet the bed more than twice per month after age five or six, we call it Bed-wetting or enuresis.

Children who were dry for at least six months and then started wetting again have secondary enuresis. The key here is to find what changed. It might be physical, emotional, or just a change in sleep patterns. When the child has never been dry, the condition is called primary enuresis. While the child is in a deep sleep, their body is producing more urine than the bladder can hold. The child's brain has not learned to respond to the signal that the bladder is full during the night. It is not the child's or the parent's fault. You will find that a bedwetter will very likely have a short leg.

How to Minister: (All commands done in Jesus' name).
1. Grow out the legs.
2. Command the pelvis to come into alignment.
3. Command the vertebrae in the lower back to be adjusted, the nerves to the bladder to be released, the bladder to be healed and function properly.
4. Command the brain to awaken the child when the bladder is full.

BELL'S PALSY

Bell's Palsy is a disorder caused by damage to a cranial nerve and is characterized by a sudden facial drooping and a decreased ability to move some facial muscles. The disorder involves the seventh cranial nerve, the nerve that controls movement of the facial muscles. The cause is often not clear, although herpes infections may be involved.

The disorder is presumed to be associated with inflammation of the facial nerve where it travels through the bones of the skull. Other conditions, such as Sarcoidosis, Diabetes, and Lyme disease, are associated with Bell's Palsy. Increased stress seems to aggravate this condition.

How to Minister: (All commands done in Jesus' name).
1. Cast out the spirit of Bell's Palsy.
2. Command the pain to go.

3. Lay hands gently on the face, commanding the nerves to be regenerated and restored to perfect function.

BIPOLAR DISORDER (Also known as Manic-Depressive)

Bipolar Disorder (BD) is a brain disorder that causes unpredictable mood swings. People with BD go from an emotional high (known as Mania) to a low (known as Depression). The disease cycles between these highs and lows.

BD affects approximately 1% of the population (about 1 in every 100 people). Women and men are equally as likely to develop the condition which usually appears between the ages of twenty and forty.

Women typically spend more time in the depressed phase, while men may be manic more often. Up to 33% of people with BD have symptoms their entire lives. These symptoms can interfere with work and make relationships difficult. In mania, people may risk harm to themselves or to others, acting on impulse and not realizing how dangerous their actions might be.

How to Minister: (All commands done in Jesus' name).

1. Lead them in a prayer of repentance for generational curses.
2. Lead them in a prayer of forgiveness from traumas suffered at a younger age.
3. Cast out the spirit of Bipolar Disorder.
4. Command the electrical and magnetic frequencies to be in harmony and balance.

BIRTH

Pray for an easy delivery and a normal child.

How to Minister: (All commands done in Jesus' name).

1. Speak a blessing over a healthy, normal baby in the womb with the power of the Holy Spirit.

2. Lead parents in prayer to dedicate the child to God.
3. Command the pelvis to rotate in the perfect position for delivery.

BLADDER PROBLEMS (See Incontinence).

BLADDER INFECTIONS (See Urinary Tract Infections)

BLINDNESS

Blindness is a loss of vision not correctable with lenses. Blindness can be partial, with loss of only part of the vision. It can also be complete, in which case there is no perception of light. People with vision worse than 20/200 or a field of vision of less than 20 degrees in the better eye are considered legally blind.

Blindness has many causes. In the United States, the leading causes are diabetes, glaucoma, macular degeneration, and accidents (such as chemical burns or injuries from bungee cords, fishing hooks, fireworks, racket balls, and similar objects). Worldwide, the leading causes of blindness are cataracts, onchocerciasis ("river blindness"), trachoma, leprosy, and vitamin A deficiency.

How to Minister: (All commands done in Jesus' name).

1. If the cause is known, address it specifically (such as glaucoma, cataracts, infection, detached retina, etc.).
2. Cast out the spirit of blindness.
3. Command healing to the eyes and perfect sight to be restored.
4. Command a creative miracle to the nerves, eye structures, and brain.

BLOOD PRESSURE PROBLEMS (Hypertension),

Blood pressure is a measurement of the force applied to the walls of the arteries as the heart pumps blood through the body. The pressure is determined by the force and amount of blood pumped, and the size and flexibility of the arteries. Blood pressure is continually changing depending on activity, posture, temperature, diet, emotional state, physical state, and medication use.

Problems are caused by numerous dysfunctions of the body organs. Ask if the doctor has diagnosed any possible underlying causes (such as diabetes, heart disease, arteriosclerosis, kidney problems, etc.).

Hypertension means blood pressure is higher than normal levels. Hypotension indicates low blood pressure.

How to Minister: (All commands done in Jesus' name).

1. Command the heart to be healed, the arteries and vessels to be opened and function normally with proper elasticity.
2. Lead in a prayer of repentance if diet was a cause.
3. Grow out the arms.
4. Command the muscles and nerves to be normal and allow blood to flow properly.
5. Lead them in a prayer of repentance for generational curses.

BOWLEGGED

Knees and hips swing outward, giving person a "cowboy" look.

How to Minister: (All commands done in Jesus' name).

1. Command the pelvis to come into alignment.
2. Grow out the legs.
3. Command the legs to straighten.

BPH (BENIGN PROSTATE HYPERTROPHY)

(See Prostate Problems).

BRAIN DAMAGE

The brain can be damaged either at birth, from illness, injury, accident or disease (such as a stroke or tumor). Such injury to brain tissue and the nerves it controls causes loss of function such as decreased mentation (retardation, confusion, and memory loss), inability to control bodily functions or mobility of limbs, loss of speech or inability to swallow safely.

How to Minister: (All commands done in Jesus' name).

1. Lay hands on the head commanding a creative miracle - "a new brain".
2. Command all the nerves to function normally and any memory loss to be restored.
3. If caused by a stroke, command the spirit of death to go.

BREAST CANCER

Breast Cancer is the second most common cancer (after lung cancer) affecting women in the United States. Although it is much more common in women, men can also develop this disease.

An abnormal mass or group of cells in the breast is usually called a lump (or tumor). The presence of a lump, however, does not always mean cancer. A benign (harmless) tumor is not cancerous. It usually does not spread and may be easily removed. A malignant tumor, however, is able to spread to other parts of the body, causes damage to surrounding tissues, and develops into what is known as cancer or a malignancy.

How to Minister: (All commands done in Jesus' name).

1. Curse and cast out the spirit of cancer.
2. Lead them in prayer of repentance for generational curses.

3. Lead them in prayer of repentance for bitterness or unforgiveness, if necessary.
4. Command electrical and magnetic frequencies to come into harmony and balance.
5. Curse any prions and command them to dissolve and be absorbed by the body.
6. Command all damaged tissue be restored to normal healthy cells.

BROKEN BONES

If more pressure is put on a bone than it can stand, it will split or break. A break of any size is called a fracture. If the broken bone punctures the skin, it is called an open fracture (compound fracture). A stress fracture is a hairline crack in the bone that develops because of repeated or prolonged forces against the bone and are often seen in people with osteoporosis.

How to Minister: (All commands done in Jesus' name).

1. Command the affected bones to come together in normal alignment and strength and be healed.
2. Command all muscles, tendons, nerves, and ligaments to line up with the healed bones and strength restored.
3. Rebuke trauma and command the pain to go.

BRONCHITIS

Bronchitis is an inflammation of the main air passages to the lungs. Bronchitis may be sudden (acute) and short-lived, or chronic, meaning that it lasts a long time and often recurs. To be classified as chronic, you must have a cough with mucus most days of the month for three months out of the year.

How to Minister: (All commands done in Jesus' name).

1. Rebuke the infection.

2. Lay hands on the upper chest and throat, commanding the tissues in the bronchial tubes and lungs to be healed and function normally.
3. Lead them in the prayer of repentance for any ungodly words spoken, if necessary.

BULIMIA

Bulimia is an illness defined by food binges, or recurrent episodes of significant overeating, that are accompanied by a sense of loss of control. The affected person then uses various methods -- such as vomiting or laxative abuse -- to prevent weight gain.

Many, but not all, people with bulimia may also suffer from Anorexia Nervosa, an eating disorder involving severe, chronic weight loss that can lead to starvation.

How to Minister: (All commands done in Jesus' name).

1. Lead them in prayer of repentance for their rebellion at adolescence.
2. Have them renounce the words spoken in rebellion.
3. Speak healing to areas of the body damaged by their abnormal eating behaviors.

BUNIONS

Bunions are often caused by narrow-toed, high-heeled shoes. The pressure compresses the big toe and pushes it toward the second toe. This causes a marked protrusion at the base of the big toe. The condition may become painful as extra bone and a fluid-filled sac grow at the base of the big toe. This leads to swelling and pain. Bunions occur more frequently in women and sometimes run in families.

How to Minister: (All commands done in Jesus' name).

1. Lead them in a prayer of repentance for generational curses.

2. Rebuke the inflammation.
3. Grow out the legs.
4. Command the toe and bones to go back into place and the ligaments to strengthen, for the foot to be normal.

BURSITIS

Bursitis is an inflammation of the fluid-filled sac (bursa) that lies between a tendon and skin, or between a tendon and bone. The condition may be acute or chronic. Bursa are fluid-filled cavities near joints where tendons or muscles pass over boney projections. They assist movement and reduce friction between moving parts. Bursitis can be caused by chronic overuse, trauma, rheumatoid arthritis, gout, or infection. Sometimes the cause cannot be determined. Bursitis commonly occurs in the shoulder, knee, elbow, and hip. Other areas that may be affected include the Achilles tendon and the foot.

How to Minister: (All commands done in Jesus' name).
1. Cast out the spirit of bursitis.
2. Lead them in a prayer of forgiveness, if necessary.
3. Lay hands on the area and command all inflammation and pain to go.
4. Command the tissues to be healed, and normal fluid be produced for painless movements of the joints.

CANCER (Also see Breast Cancer).

Cancer involves the uncontrolled growth of abnormal cells that have mutated from normal tissues. This growth can kill when these cells prevent normal function of vital organs or spread throughout the body, damaging essential systems.

Cancer arises out of normal cells in the body, and can develop in almost any organ or tissue, such as the lung, colon, breast, skin, bones, or nerve tissue. In general, cancer appears to be caused by abnormal regulation of cell division. Cancers can occur when cells divide too rapidly or when cells "forget" how to die.

A benign (harmless) tumor is not cancerous. It is a form of lump that usually does not spread and may be easily removed.

A malignant tumor or a malignancy is able to spread to other parts of the body and cause damage to surrounding tissues, and this is what is known as cancer.

How to Minister: (All commands done in Jesus' name).

1. Curse the root of the cancer cells and cast out the spirit of cancer.
2. Lead them in a prayer of repentance for generational curses.
3. Lead them in prayer of repentance for bitterness or unforgiveness, if necessary.
4. Command electrical and magnetic frequencies to come into harmony and balance.
5. Curse any prions and command them to dissolve and be absorbed by the body.
6. Command the body's defensive "killer" cells to multiply and attack all cancer cells.

CANDIDA ALBICANS (Also called Yeast Infection).

Yeast is an important part of the digestive process within the body. However, under certain circumstances, it can overgrow and cause problems. It then is considered a form of infection. A fungal (yeast) infection that affects the mucous membranes of the body is generally the cause of vaginal infections. It is aggravated by sugar intake and is the cause of thrush (a form of Candida) in newborns. It is aggravated or exacerbated by antibiotic and / or steroid usage. It can occur on areas of the skin that are dark (hidden to light), warm and moist. Usually found in women, it can also affect men.

How to Minister: (All commands done in Jesus' name).
1. Rebuke the infection.
2. Command the body's system to be restored to normal function.
3. Lead them in a prayer of repentance to break word curses.

CANKER SORES

Canker sores are NOT contagious and can appear as a single pale or yellow ulcer with a red outer ring, or as a cluster of such lesions. The cause of Canker Sores is not entirely clear, but may be related to a virus, a temporary weakness in your immune system (for example, from cold or flu), hormonal changes, mechanical irritation, stress or low levels of vitamin B-12.

For unknown reasons, women seem to get Canker Sores more often than men. This may be related to hormonal changes. Less commonly, mouth sores can be a sign of an underlying illness, tumor, or reaction to a medication.

How to Minister: (All commands done in Jesus' name).
1. Rebuke any infection or virus and curse the root of it.
2. Command the immune system to be strengthened and to function properly.
3. Command the electrical and magnetic frequencies to be in harmony and balance.
4. Command all pain and discomfort to disappear.
5. Command all affected tissues to be healed and function normally.

CARPAL TUNNEL SYNDROME

Carpal Tunnel Syndrome is a compression of the median nerve at the wrist, which may result in numbness, tingling, weakness, or muscle atrophy in the hand and fingers. This syndrome is common in people who perform repetitive motions of the hand and wrist, such as typing. When the wrist is poorly positioned, there isn't enough space for the median nerve to travel to the hand.

It is generally caused by pressure exerted on the median nerve at the point where it passes through the wrist. The median nerve supplies sensation to the thumb-side of the palm, and to the thumb, index finger, middle finger, and the thumb-side of the ring finger. It also supplies movement to part of the hand.

The nerve enters the hand between the wrist bones (called the carpal bones) and the tough membrane that holds the bones together (the transverse carpal ligament). This space is called the carpal tunnel. Since the passageway is rigid, any swelling in this area can cause compression of the nerve (this is also called entrapment of the nerve).

The condition occurs most often in people thirty to sixty years old, and is five times more common in women than men. Some of the conditions associated with carpal tunnel syndrome include pregnancy, premenstrual syndrome (PMS), and menopause. This is probably because of hormonal changes that cause fluid retention and swelling of the tissues.

How to Minister: (All commands done in Jesus' name).

1. Lay hands on the wrist area and command the tissues, tendons, and ligaments in the wrist to be healed and relaxed.
2. Command the "tunnel" to open up and pressure on the nerves to be released.

3. Command normal circulation and strength to be restored.
4. Command any numbness and tingling to leave and the wrist to be healed and to function normally.

CATARACTS

The lens of an eye is normally clear. If the lens becomes cloudy, the condition is known as a Cataract. Rarely, Cataracts may be present at or shortly after birth. These are called congenital Cataracts.

Adult Cataracts usually develop with advancing age and may run in families. Cataracts are accelerated by environmental factors, such as smoking or exposure to other toxic substances, or they may develop at any time after an eye injury. Metabolic diseases such as diabetes also greatly increase the risk for Cataracts. Certain medications, such as cortisone, can also accelerate Cataract formation.

Congenital Cataracts may be inherited. The gene for such Cataracts is dominant which means that the defective gene will cause the condition even if only one parent passes it along. Approximately 50% of children in such families will be affected.

How to Minister: (All commands done in Jesus' name).

1. Lay hands on eyes and command the cataracts to dissolve.
2. Command the blood and fluid to flow through the eye layers normally.
3. Lead them in a prayer of repentance for generational curses.

CEREBRAL PALSY (Also called CP).

Cerebral Palsy, or CP, is a group of disorders characterized by loss of movement or loss of other nerve functions. These disorders are caused by injuries to the largest portion of the brain that is involved with higher mental faculties, sensations, and voluntary muscle activities. The injury usually occurs during fetal development or near the time of birth.

Initially, Cerebral Palsy was thought to be related to birth asphyxia (strangulation during birth, which leads to lack of oxygen to the brain) and trauma, but in a study of 45,000 births it was shown that birth asphyxia is an uncommon cause of Cerebral Palsy. Affected brain areas receive lower levels of oxygen (hypoxia) at some point, but it is not known why this occurs.

Researchers suspect that certain factors or events during the development of the fetus may make it more susceptible to any hypoxia that occurs, and this may be why some infants are affected while others can suffer low oxygen levels but not lasting brain damage. Premature infants have a slightly higher incidence of Cerebral Palsy. Cerebral Palsy may also occur during early infancy as a result of illnesses.

How to Minister: (All commands done in Jesus' name).
1. Cast out the spirit of Cerebral Palsy.
2. Speak a new brain into the body.
3. Command normal communication from the brain to the other body parts.
4. Command the muscles, tendons, and nerves to function properly.
5. Lead them in a prayer of repentance for generational curses.

CHOLESTEROL, HIGH (Also called Hyperlipidemia).

Cholesterol is a soft, waxy substance found in all parts of the body tissues of both humans and animals. Called a lipid (blood fat), it is manufactured in the liver for normal body functions including the production of hormones, bile acid, and vitamin D. It is transported in the blood to be used by all parts of the body. More than half of the adult population has blood cholesterol levels higher than the "desirable" range. High cholesterol levels often begin in childhood. Some children may be at a higher risk due to a family history of high cholesterol.

In general, you want your total cholesterol to be less than 200 mg/dl, because that level carries the least risk of heart disease. When the level is above 200 mg/dl, the risk for heart disease is increased.

Foods from animal sources (such as eggs, meat, poultry and dairy products) contain cholesterol, but plant-derived foods do not. Sufficient cholesterol is made by the liver for the body's needs. Consuming excessive amounts of fats, particularly saturated fats in the form of cholesterol, can damage one's health. The main risk of this condition is atherosclerosis which can contribute to disorders such as stroke and heart attack. (Also see Arteriosclerosis).

How to Minister: (All commands done in Jesus' name).

1. Lead them in pray of repentance for improper diet, if necessary.
2. Command the cholesterol level to return to normal and the body to retain only the necessary amounts.
3. Lay hands on the person's head, commanding all potentially damaged parts of the body (arteries, heart, etc.) to be healed and to be normal.

CHRONIC OBSTRUCTIVE PULMONARY DISEASE

Chronic Obstructive Pulmonary Disease (COPD) is a group of lung diseases with limited airflow and varying degrees of air sac enlargement, airway inflammation, and lung tissue destruction. Emphysema and chronic bronchitis are the most common forms of COPD.

The leading cause of COPD is smoking, which can lead to the two most common forms of this disease: emphysema and chronic bronchitis. Prolonged tobacco use causes lung inflammation and variable degrees of air sac destruction. This leads to inflamed and narrowed airways (chronic bronchitis) or permanently enlarged air sacs of the lung with reduced lung elasticity (emphysema). Between 15% and 20% of long-term smokers will develop COPD.

Other risk factors for COPD are passive smoking (exposure of non-smokers to secondary cigarette smoke from others), male gender, and working in a polluted environment. Occupational Lung Disease (Asbestosis, Silicosis, and Coal Miner's disease) are other forms of COPD. The degree of airway obstruction and the amount of tissue damage in the airways themselves determine the severity of the illness.

How to Minister: (All commands done in Jesus' name).

1. Curse the root of the disease.
2. Lead them in a prayer of repentance, if necessary. (For smoking, see Addictions)
3. Command total healing to all damaged tissues of the respiratory system.
4. Command new lungs, if necessary.

CIGARETTES (See Addictions).

CLEFT LIP / CLEFT PALATE

Cleft Lip and/or Cleft Palate are congenital (present from before birth) abnormalities that affect the upper lip and the hard and soft palate of the mouth (the top of the mouth). Severity of the abnormalities may range from a small notch in the lip to a complete opening extending into the roof of the mouth and nose. These features may occur separately or together.

Cleft Lip and Cleft Palate may occur in association with other syndromes or birth defects. There are numerous causes for these birth defects, including mutant genes inherited from one or both parents; or drugs, viruses, or other toxins that can cause abnormalities in a developing fetus. As well as being disfiguring, these abnormalities can cause feeding difficulties, problems with speech development, and ear infections.

How to Minister: (All commands done in Jesus' name).

1. Lead them in a prayer of repentance for generational curses.
2. Lay hands on the mouth, commanding a creative miracle; all the tissues and structures to be normal.
3. Command any pain to go.

COLD SORES (See Herpes).

COLDS (See also Sore Throat, Influenza, Croup, and Laryngitis).

A common Cold is an infection of your upper respiratory tract. It includes symptoms of runny nose, sore throat and a cough, watery eyes, sneezing, miserable congestion and a fever less than 102 degrees F. Any one of more than 200 viruses can cause a common cold and symptoms tend to vary greatly. Most adults are likely to have a common cold two to four times a year. Children, especially preschoolers, may have a common cold as many as eight to ten times annually.

The most common complication of common colds in children is an acute ear infection (Otitis Media), which occurs when bacteria infiltrate the space behind the eardrum. Unlike a common Cold, ear infections may require treatment with antibiotics.

In adults or children, a common Cold that doesn't resolve may lead to Sinusitis, Croup or Laryngitis. Other secondary infections that may develop following a common Cold include Strep Throat, Chronic Bronchitis, and/or Pneumonia. A Cold may also be referred to as an Upper Respiratory Infection.

Croup is an inflammation of the voice box (larynx) and the airway just beneath it. Your child may have a common cold for several days and then one night unexpectedly develop a loud, barking cough. The swelling and narrowing of the airway may make breathing difficult. One of the cold viruses is typically the cause. Croup primarily affects children younger than five years old because their small airways are more susceptible to narrowing when swollen.

Adults may simply have a Cold with Laryngitis, but children may develop Croup.

How to Minister: (All commands done in Jesus' name).

1. Rebuke the infection and curse the root of it.
2. Command the immune system to be strengthened and to function properly.
3. Command the electrical and magnetic frequencies to be in harmony and balance.
4. Command all pain and discomfort to disappear.
5. Command all affected tissues to be healed and function normally.

COLITIS

Colitis is an inflammation of the large intestine that is caused by many different disease processes, including acute and chronic infections, primary inflammatory disorders (ulcerative colitis, Crohn's colitis, lymphocytic and collagenous colitis), lack of blood flow, and history of radiation to the large bowel.

How to Minister: (All commands done in Jesus' name).

1. Grow out the legs (Do the leg adjustment).
2. Command the nerves controlling the colon to function normally.
3. Command all inflammation to leave and the colon to be healed.
4. Lead them in a prayer to lay all cares, stress and worries on the Altar of God.

COLORECTAL CANCER

The colon and rectum are part of the large intestine (large bowel). Colon and rectal cancers, which are sometimes referred to together as "colorectal cancer," develop from the lining of the large intestine. When cancer arises from the lining of an organ like the large intestine, it is called a carcinoma.

Other types of colon cancer are rare, and include lymphoma, carcinoid tumors, melanoma, and sarcomas. Colorectal cancer is the second leading cause of cancer deaths. In almost all cases, however, this disease is entirely treatable if caught early by colonoscopy.

There is no single cause for colon cancer. However, almost all colon cancers begin as benign polyps which, over a period of many years, develop into cancers. Factors that increase the risk of colon cancer are colorectal polyps, cancer elsewhere in the body, a family history of colon cancer, and ulcerative colitis.

How to Minister: (All commands done in Jesus' name).

1. Curse the root of the cancer cells and cast out the spirit of cancer.
2. Lead them in a prayer of repentance for generational curses.

3. Lead them in a prayer for repentance for bitterness or unforgiveness, if necessary.
4. Command electrical and magnetic frequencies to come into harmony and balance.
5. Curse any prions and command them to dissolve and be discarded by the body.
6. Command the body's defensive "killer" cells to multiply, attack and destroy all cancer cells.
7. Command all damaged tissues to be healed and to function normally.

COMA

Decreased consciousness refers to diminished alertness or awareness. A Coma is a state of deep unconsciousness. This may result from a multitude of conditions including intoxication (drug, alcohol, or toxin), metabolic abnormalities, seizure activity (epilepsy), central nervous system diseases and conditions, head trauma, shock, decreased oxygen (hypoxia), and low blood pressure (hypotension).

Decreased consciousness, unconsciousness, and Coma require medical evaluation (with the possible exception of alcohol intoxication, simple fainting, or a previously recognized seizure disorder).

How to Minister: (All commands done in Jesus' name).
1. Cast out the spirit of death of brain cells.
2. Lay hands on the head, commanding the brain to be healed
3. Command a creative miracle to any damaged brain tissue (brain tissue will not regenerate on its own).
4. Command the body and all its organs to operate normally and consciousness to return.

CONGESTIVE HEART FAILURE (CHF) (See Heart).

CONSTIPATION

Constipation refers to passing infrequent or hard bowel movements. Constipation may involve pain during the passage of a bowel movement, inability to pass a bowel movement after straining or pushing for more than ten minutes, or no bowel movements after more than three days. Infants who are exclusively breastfed may go seven days without a stool.

Constipation is most often caused by a low-fiber diet, lack of physical activity, not drinking enough water, or delay in going to the bathroom when the urge is felt. Stress and travel can also contribute to constipation or changes in bowel habits. Other times, diseases of the bowel (such as irritable bowel syndrome), pregnancy, certain medical conditions, mental health problems, neurological diseases, high stress, or medications may contribute to constipation.

How to Minister: (All commands done in Jesus' name).

1. Command the colon to function normally.
2. Lead them in a prayer of repentance, if necessary.
3. Lead them in a prayer of repentance for improper diet, if necessary.
4. Lead them in prayer to lay all cares, stress, fears and worries on the Altar of God.

CORNS and CALLUSES

Corns and Calluses are thickened layers of skin caused by repeated pressure or friction. A Corn is thickened skin on the top or side of a toe, usually from shoes that do not fit properly. Corns can be very painful.

A Callus is thickened skin on your hands or the soles of your feet. The thickening of the skin is a protective reaction. For example, farmers and rowers get callused hands that prevent them from getting painful blisters. People with bunions often develop a Callus over the bunion because it rubs against the shoe. Both Calluses and Corns can be removed by a qualified Podiatrist, but can recur.

How to Minister: (All commands done in Jesus' name).

1. Lay hands on the affected area, commanding the Corns and Calluses to fall off and not return.
2. Command the Callus be replaced by healthy tissue.

CROHN'S DISEASE

Crohn's disease is a chronic autoimmune disease that can affect any part of the gastrointestinal tract but most commonly occurs in the ileum (the area where the small and large intestine meet). Autoimmune disorders occur when the immune system attacks the body's own cells. In Crohn's disease, these rogue immune cells attack the gastrointestinal system. The cause is unknown, but genetic factors seem to play a role.

Inflammation frequently occurs at the end of the small intestine that joins the large intestine, but the condition may affect any area of the digestive tract. As a result of the immune attack, the intestinal wall becomes thick, and deep ulcers may form.

The disease may occur at any age, but adolescence and early adulthood are the periods of highest risk. The only known risk factors include a family history of Crohn's disease, Jewish ancestry, and smoking.

How to Minister: (All commands done in Jesus' name).

1. Cast out the spirit of Crohn's disease.
2. Rebuke the infection.
3. Command the bowel tissue to be healed and function normally.

4. Lead them in a prayer of repentance for generational curses.
5. Command the immune system to function normally.

CROSS-EYED or WALLEYED (Also called Strabismus).

Strabismus involves a deviation of the alignment of one eye in relation to the other. Strabismus is caused by a lack of coordination between the eyes or uneven development of one or more of the six small muscles that control eye movements. As a result, the eyes look in different directions and do not focus simultaneously on a single point. In most cases of Strabismus in children, the cause is unknown. In more than half of these cases, the problem is present at or shortly after birth.

When the two eyes fail to focus on the same image, the brain may learn to ignore the input from one eye. If this is allowed to continue, the eye that the brain ignores will never function well. When the eyes look outward, it is called Walleyed. When they look inward, it is called Cross-eyed.

How to Minister: (All commands done in Jesus' name).

1. Place your hands over the eyes and command the muscles, ligaments, and tissues to be healed and return to normal strength and length.
2. Lead them in a prayer of repentance for generational curses.
3. Command the brain to function normally and process the input from both eyes.
4. Command any scar tissue to be removed.

CROUP (See Cold).

CUSHING'S SYNDROME

Cushing's Syndrome is a metabolic disorder that has several possible causes. Cushing's Syndrome is caused by elevated levels of cortisol, an important glucocorticoid hormone, over an extended period of time. The growth of a tumor on one of the two adrenal glands causes about 15% of all cases of Cushing's Syndrome. Adrenal tumors secrete cortisol and may be benign or malignant.

Other causes of Cushing's Syndrome are secretion of ACTH by a pituitary tumor, by another organ of the body, or regular use of corticosteroids such as prednisone, commonly used to treat chronic conditions such as rheumatoid arthritis and asthma.

Although they may develop in anyone at any age, adrenal tumors are more common in adults -- 70% of all adrenal tumors occur in adults. They are found in women more often than men and are relatively rare, occurring in six out of every one million people.

How to Minister: (All commands done in Jesus' name).

1. Cast out the spirit of Cushing's Syndrome.
2. Lay hands on the kidney area of the back (approximately at waist level) commanding the adrenal glands to function properly.
3. Lead them in a prayer of repentance, if necessary.

CVA or Cardiovascular Accident (See Stroke).

CYSTIC DISEASE

This condition affects women, usually near or at menopause; and is characterized by a rapid development of cysts in a breast. It is also called fibrocystic disease or cystic mastitis.

How to Minister: (All commands done in Jesus' name).

1. Cast out the spirit of fibrocystic disease.
2. Lay hands on chest, commanding all the cysts to dissolve. (Have the person lay their hands on their chest first, then lay your hands on top of theirs).

3. Command all the cells and tissues of the breast to be healed and normal, and a creative miracle for any damaged parts.

CYSTIC FIBROSIS

Cystic Fibrosis is an inherited disease that affects sodium channels in the body. It causes breathing and digestive problems. Cystic Fibrosis affects the mucus and sweat glands of the body and is caused by a defective gene. Thick mucus is formed in the breathing passages of the lungs and this predisposes the person to chronic lung infections.

Many pancreatic enzymes involved in the breakdown and absorption of fats in the intestine are absent, causing malabsorption (inadequate absorption of nutrients from the intestinal tract) and malnutrition.

It is the most common fatal hereditary disorder affecting Caucasians in the United States. It is most common among Caucasians of Northern or Central European descent and is much less common in other ethnic groups. Risk factors include a family history of cystic fibrosis or unexplained infant death. Even though most patients are diagnosed by their first birthday, a small number are not diagnosed until age eighteen or older. These patients usually have a milder form of the disease.

How to Minister: (All commands done in Jesus' name).

1. Lead them in a prayer of repentance for generational curses.
2. Cast out the spirit of Cystic Fibrosis.
3. Lay hands on the area of the pancreas and liver, commanding the glands of the body to secrete normally.
4. Command the lungs, pancreas, and liver to be healed and function normally.

DEAF-MUTE

This description indicates the person can neither hear nor speak.

How to Minister: (All commands done in Jesus' name).
1. Cast out the deaf and dumb spirit.
2. Continue with the instructions for Deafness.
3. Lead them in a prayer of repentance for generational curses.

DEAFNESS

Hearing loss is the total or partial inability to hear sound in one or both ears. Minor decreases in hearing are normal after age twenty. Some deafness related to nerve damage affects one out of five people by age fifty-five. It usually comes on gradually, and it rarely ends in complete deafness. Alzheimer's disease or other neurological problems may sometimes be falsely suspected in older people because they have hearing problems. There are many causes of hearing loss. They can be divided into two categories:

Conductive loss occurs because of some mechanical problem, such as fluid in the ear. The three tiny bones of the ear may fail to conduct sound to the cochlea or the eardrum may fail to vibrate in response to sound. Nerve loss occurs when the nerve is injured physically or by some other means. Conductive loss is often medically reversible -- nerve loss is not.

Ear infections are the most common cause of temporary hearing loss in children. Fluid can linger in the ear following an ear infection. Although this fluid can go unnoticed, it can cause significant hearing problems in children.

How to Minister: (All commands done in Jesus' name).
1. Cast out the spirit of Deafness.

2. Put your fingers gently in the person's ears and command the deafness to go and hearing to be restored.
3. Grow out their arms (do the arm adjustment).
4. Command a new eardrum and bone structures, if needed.
5. Command the nerves and muscles to relax, releasing the nerves to the ears and allowing the blood to flow normally into the area. Command the hair-like nerves to the inner ear to function normally.
6. Place the hands on the sides of the skull and command the temporal bones to rotate back into position.
7. Test the person's hearing and repeat the above steps, if necessary.

DEEP VEIN THROMBOSIS (Also called DVT).

Deep Venous Thrombosis indicates there is a blood clot in a large vein located deep within a limb. It mainly affects the veins in the lower leg and thigh. The formation of a blood clot (thrombus) in these larger veins may interfere with circulation of the area. It may also break off and travel through the blood stream (embolize) until it lodges in the brain, lungs, heart, or other area, causing severe damage to that organ (e.g. stroke, pulmonary embolus, or heart attack).

Thrombophlebitis is another term used in this category although it can occur in small veins also. Usually occurring in the calf of the legs, it can cause severe pain to the area as well as swelling and warmth.

Risks include prolonged sitting, bed rest or immobilization (such as long plane or car trips), recent surgery or trauma (especially hip, knee or gynecological surgery), fractures, childbirth within the last six months and the use of medications such as estrogen or birth control pills. Risks also include a history of abnormal levels of blood clotting factors making the blood more likely to clot abnormally. This condition is more commonly seen in adults over age sixty, but can occur in any age group.

How to Minister: (All commands done in Jesus' name).

1. Command the blood clot to dissolve.
2. Command the blood to flow properly and all damaged tissues to be healed.
3. Lead them in a prayer of repentance for generational curses.

DEGENERATIVE JOINT DISEASE (See Osteoarthritis).

DEPRESSION (See also Postpartum Depression).

Depression may be described as feeling sad, blue, unhappy, miserable, or "down in the dumps". Most of us feel this way at one time or another for short periods. But true clinical Depression is a mood disorder in which feelings of sadness, loss, anger, or frustration interfere with everyday life for an extended time.

Depression is generally ranked in terms of severity -- mild, moderate, or severe. The degree of Depression influences how the condition will be treated. Symptoms of depression include:

- Trouble sleeping or excessive sleeping
- A dramatic change in appetite, often with weight gain or loss
- Fatigue and lack of energy
- Feelings of worthlessness, self-hate or inappropriate guilt
- Extreme difficulty concentrating
- Agitation, restlessness, and irritability
- Inactivity and withdrawal from usual activities
- Feelings of hopelessness and helplessness
- Recurring thoughts of death or suicide

Low self esteem is common with Depression. So are sudden bursts of anger and lack of pleasure from activities that normally make you happy.

Depressed children may not have the classic symptoms of adult Depression. Watch especially for changes in school performance, sleep, and behavior. If you suspect your child might be depressed, bring it to a doctor's attention.

Depression is more common in women than men and is especially common during the teen years. Men seem to seek help for feelings of Depression less often than women. Therefore, women may only have more documented cases of Depression.

Depression often runs in families. This may be from heredity, learned behavior, or both. Even with a genetic predisposition, it is usually a stressful or unhappy life event that triggers the onset of a depressive episode.

Depression may be brought on by:

- Disappointment at home, work, or school (in teens, this may be breaking up with a boyfriend or girlfriend, failing a class, or divorce of parents)
- Death / separation from a friend or relative
- Prolonged pain or having a major illness
- Medical conditions such as hypothyroidism (under active thyroid), cancer, or hepatitis
- Drugs such as sedatives or high blood pressure medications
- Alcohol or drug abuse
- Chronic stress
- Childhood events such as abuse or neglect
- Social isolation (common in the elderly)
- Nutritional deficiencies (such as folate and omega-3 fatty acids)
- Sleeping problems

How to Minister: (All commands done in Jesus' name).

1. Take your time and love them with the love of the Lord.
2. If possible, identify the cause and when it started.
3. Lead them in a prayer of repentance or forgiveness, if necessary.
4. Command the electrical and magnetic frequencies to be in harmony and balance.
5. With your hand on their heart, command the spirit of Depression to go.

DERMATITIS (Also see Eczema).

Dermatitis is an inflammation of the skin.

How to Minister: (All commands done in Jesus' name).

1. Rebuke the infection or irritation.
2. Command the itching to stop.
3. Command cells that manufacture skin to create new and healthy tissue.

DETACHED RETINA

Retinal Detachment is a separation of the light-sensitive membrane in the back of the eye (the retina) from its supporting layers. The retina is a transparent membrane at the back of the eye which processes the images that are focused on it by the cornea and the lens. Retinal detachments are often associated with a tear or hole in the retina through which the internal fluids of the eye may leak. This causes separation of the retina from the underlying tissues.

Retinal Detachment may be caused by trauma, the aging process, severe diabetes, or an inflammatory disorder, but it frequently occurs spontaneously. In pre-term babies, Retinal Detachment can be caused by abnormalities of the retina associated with premature birth.

During a detachment, bleeding from small retinal blood vessels may cloud the interior of the eye, which is normally filled with clear vitreous fluid. Central vision becomes severely affected if the macula, the part of the retina responsible for fine vision, becomes detached. It can lead to irreversible blindness.

How to Minister: (All commands done in Jesus' name).
1. Lay hands on the eye(s) and command the retina and its nerve endings to reconnect to the eye and be healed.
2. Command the eye to function normally and eyesight to be restored to normal.

DIABETES

Diabetes is a life-long disease marked by high levels of sugar in the blood. It can be caused by too little insulin (a hormone produced by the pancreas to regulate blood sugar), resistance to insulin, or both.

To understand diabetes, it is important to first understand the normal process of food metabolism. Several things happen when food is digested:

- Glucose is a source of fuel for the body. It is a form of sugar provided through nutrients ingested with food and fluids. It is absorbed into the blood stream to be delivered to all the cells of the body.
- An organ called the pancreas makes insulin. The role of insulin is to regulate the amount of glucose in the bloodstream.

People with diabetes have high uncontrolled blood glucose. Their pancreas either does not produce enough insulin to metabolize the sugar or their muscle, fat, and liver cells do not respond to insulin normally, or both. Left uncontrolled, Diabetes can contribute to blindness, kidney disease, neuropathy (numbness and pain in all extremities), and circulation problems.

How to Minister: (All commands done in Jesus' name).

1. Cast out the spirit of diabetes.
2. Lead them in a prayer of repentance for generational curses.
3. Command a new pancreas into the body that will produce enough insulin to control and use blood sugar normally.
4. Command any damaged body parts (from excess sugar) to be healed and made whole.

DIARRHEA

Diarrhea is frequent passing of loose, watery bowel movements. Diarrhea is considered chronic (ongoing or prolonged) when you have had loose or frequent stools for longer than four weeks.

The most common cause of diarrhea is a mild viral infection that resolves on its own within a few days. This is called viral gastroenteritis or "stomach flu." Viral gastroenteritis often appears in mini-epidemics in schools, neighborhoods or families. It is often passed from person to person. Hand washing after toileting can diminish the risk.

Uncontrolled diarrhea can lead to severe dehydration, metabolic imbalances and rectal bleeding. Uncontrolled diarrhea in small children can be fatal.

How to Minister: (All commands done in Jesus' name).

1. Command the pelvis to come into alignment.
2. Command digestive system to be healed and to function normally.
3. Rebuke any possible infection.

DISC PROBLEMS (Also see Back Problems).

This is commonly called "slipped disc." The disc (or cushion) between two vertebrae (bones in your back) has either deteriorated or is bulging out, pressing on a nerve and causing discomfort and pain.

How to Minister: (All commands done in Jesus' name).

1. Minister as you would for Back Pain and command the disc to be restored and be healed, recreated if necessary; all pressure on the nerves to be released and all inflammation and swelling to go.
2. Command the vertebrae to be healed, rotated back into place, bones to come together if fractured, ribs to be healed and go back into place and all pain to leave.

DIVERTICULOSIS/DIVERTICULITIS

Diverticulitis is inflammation of an abnormal pouch (diverticulum) in the intestinal wall, usually found in the large intestine (colon). Small protruding sacs of the inner lining of the intestine (Diverticulosis) can develop in any part of the intestine. They are most common in the colon, specifically the sigmoid colon. These sacs, called diverticula, occur with increasing frequency after the age of forty.

Diverticula are thought to develop as a result of high pressure or abnormal pressure distribution within the colon. High pressure exerted against the colon wall causes pouches of the intestinal lining to bulge outwards through small defects in the colon wall.

Diverticulosis is very common, being found in more than half of Americans over the age of sixty. Only a small percentage of these people will develop the complication of Diverticulitis. Diverticulitis is caused by inflammation or (sometimes) a small perforation within a diverticulum. If the perforation is large, stool in the colon can spill into the abdominal cavity, causing an abscess or peritonitis which is very serious.

How to Minister: (All commands done in Jesus' name).
1. Command the pelvis to come into proper alignment.
2. Command the sacs to disappear and the bowel wall to return to normal strength and function.
3. Lead them in a prayer of repentance and place all their stress, worries and cares on the Altar of God.
4. Command infection to go and tissues to be totally healed.

DIZZINESS (Also see Vertigo).

Dizziness is a common neurological symptom encountered in medical practice. The most common form of severe Dizziness is known as vertigo. This term describes a sensation of motion when there is no motion or an exaggerated sense of motion in response to certain body movements.

Vertigo and Dizziness are symptoms linked to a variety of inner ear disturbances and other systemic illnesses. The sensation of Dizziness is frequently accompanied by other symptoms, such as unsteadiness, lightheadedness, anxiety, loss of balance etc. The causes range from infections to fatigue to allergies.

How to Minister: (All commands done in Jesus' name).
1. Command the electrical and magnetic frequencies to be in harmony and in balance.
2. Command the fluid in the inner ear to return to normal.
3. Command normal balance to return.

DJD (Degenerative Joint Disease. See Osteoarthritis).

DOWN SYNDROME

Down Syndrome is a chromosome abnormality, usually due to an extra copy of the 21st chromosome. This syndrome can result in mental retardation along with other abnormal conditions. It is the most common single cause of human birth defects, with an occurrence in 1 out of every 660 births.

Children with Down Syndrome have a widely recognized and characteristic appearance. The head may be smaller than normal and abnormally shaped. Prominent facial features include a flattened nose, protruding tongue, and upward slanting eyes. The inner corner of the eyes may have a rounded fold of skin rather than coming to a point. The hands are short and broad with short fingers and often have a single crease in the palm. Retardation of normal growth and development is typical and most affected children do not reach average adult height.

How to Minister: (All commands done in Jesus' name).

1. Cast out the spirit of Down Syndrome.
2. Lay hands on the person's head and command a new brain.
3. Command the cells to revert to the correct number of chromosomes and for the extra chromosome to go.
4. Command the body to be healed and function normally.
5. Command the facial features to be normal.

DROWNING

Drowning is death by suffocation from being submerged in water. If a person has been rescued from a near drowning situation, first aid and medical attention is critical. Immediate action and first aid can prevent death.

- 6,000 to 8,000 people drown in the U.S. each year. Most drowning occurs within a short distance of safety.
- A person who is drowning usually can NOT shout for help. Be alert for signs of drowning.

- Suspect an accident if you see someone in the water fully clothed. Watch for uneven swimming motions, which indicate a swimmer is getting tired. Often the body sinks and only the head shows above the water.
- Children can drown in a few inches of water.
- It may be possible to revive a drowning victim even after a prolonged period of submersion, especially if the person was in very cold water.

How to Minister: (All commands done in Jesus' name).

1. Cast out the spirit of death.
2. Command the water to come out of the lungs.
3. Command life to reenter the body.
4. Command the brain and body to function normally and be totally healed.

DRY EYES

Dry Eyes are caused by a lack of tears. Tears are necessary for the normal lubrication of your eyes and to wash away particles and foreign bodies. If you have Dry Eyes, you will feel a burning, scratching, or stinging sensation. You may also have strained or tired eyes after reading, even for short periods of time. If you wear contacts, they will likely feel uncomfortable. Having Dry Eyes for a while can lead to tiny abrasions on the surface of your eyes. Common causes of Dry Eyes include:

- Aging
- Dry environment (wind, air conditioning)
- Sun exposure
- Smoking or second-hand smoke exposure
- Cold or allergy medicines
- An eye injury or other problem with your eyes or eyelids (like a drooping eyelid or bulging eyes)

How to Minister: (All commands done in Jesus' name).
1. Command any blockage or abnormality to be gone and healing to take place.
2. Command the glands to produce normal amounts of fluid to keep the eyes healthy.

DUCK FEET

Feet turned excessively outward.

How to Minister: (All commands done in Jesus' name).
1. Lead them in a prayer of repentance for generational curses.
2. Command the pelvic bones to adjust.
3. Command the hips, legs, and feet to return to normal position and be totally healed.

DYSLEXIA

Developmental Reading Disorder, also called Dyslexia, is a reading disability resulting from the inability to process graphic symbols. Developmental Reading Disorder (DRD) is not caused by vision problems, but rather is a problem involving higher brain processing of symbols. Children with DRD may have trouble rhyming and separating the sounds in spoken words. These abilities appear to be critical in the process of learning to read.

Most children with DRD have normal intelligence and many have above-average intelligence. The disorder is a specific information processing problem that is not connected with the ability to think or comprehend complex ideas.

It may appear in combination with developmental writing disorder and developmental arithmetic disorder. All of these processes involve the manipulation of symbols to convey information. These conditions may appear alone or in any combination.

How to Minister: (All commands done in Jesus' name).

1. Command the nerves of the eyes to function normally and to send proper messages to the brain.
2. Lead them in a prayer of repentance for generational curses.
3. Command the brain to interpret the signals received and allow complete understanding.

EAR INFECTION (See Otitis Media).

ECZEMA (Also see Dermatitis).

Eczema is a chronic skin disorder (a form of dermatitis) categorized by scaly and itching rashes. People with Eczema often have a family history of allergic conditions like asthma, hay fever, or Eczema. Most common in infants, at least half of those cases clear by age 36 months. In adults, it is generally a chronic or recurring condition.

A hypersensitivity reaction (similar to an allergy) occurs in the skin, causing chronic inflammation. The inflammation causes the skin to become itchy and scaly. Chronic irritation and scratching can cause the skin to thicken and become leathery-textured. Exposure to environmental irritants can worsen symptoms, as can dryness of the skin, exposure to water, temperature changes, and stress.

How to Minister: (All commands done in Jesus' name).

1. Cast out the spirit of Eczema.
2. Command the inflammation to go and curse the infirmity.
3. Lead them in a prayer of repentance for generational curses.
4. Command the cells that manufacture skin to replace the damaged tissues, and the skin to return to normal structure, function, and texture.
5. Command the itching to go.

EDEMA

Edema (or swelling) involves the enlargement of organs, skin, or other body structures. It is caused by excessive buildup of fluid in the tissues which can lead to a rapid increase in weight over a short period of time (days to weeks). Swelling can occur throughout the body (generalized) or it may be limited to a specific part of the body (localized).

Slight edema of the lower legs commonly occurs in warm summer months, especially if a person has been standing or walking a lot. Generalized swelling, or massive Edema is common in severely ill people. Although slight Edema may be difficult to detect, especially in an overweight person, massive Edema is very obvious.

Edema or swelling is a normal body response to sudden injury but should diminish as healing occurs (such as a sprained ankle). Edema can indicate a chronic and progressive medical illness such as Congestive Heart Failure.

Lymphedema is a persistent local tissue swelling, a form of edema resulting from the loss of normal lymph channel drainage of the affected part. It can occur as a result of a mastectomy (removal of a breast) when numerous lymph nodes are also removed. This interruption of the lymph drainage system causes a back up of lymph fluid into the arm which, in turn, causes a severely enlarged arm and hand. It can occur in all limbs, is difficult to treat and can be severely debilitating.

How to Minister: (All commands done in Jesus' name).

1. Command healing for any underlying disease.
2. Command that the involved organs or tissues be healed and function normally.
3. Command the fluid to pass out through the body.

4. Lead them in a prayer of repentance, if necessary.
5. Lead them in a prayer of repentance for generational curses.

EMPHYSEMA (Also see COPD)

Emphysema is a lung disease that involves damage to the air sacs. The air sacs are unable to completely deflate and are therefore unable to fill with fresh air to ensure adequate oxygen supply to the body. Cigarette smoking is the most common cause of emphysema. Tobacco smoke and other pollutants are thought to cause the release of chemicals from within the lungs that damage the walls of the air sacs. This damage becomes worse over time affecting the exchange of oxygen and carbon dioxide in the lungs.

How to Minister: (All commands done in Jesus' name).
1. Lead them in a prayer of repentance from smoking, if necessary. (See Addiction).
2. Command a creative miracle: "a new set of lungs".
3. Command other damaged body tissue to be healed and function normally.

ENCEPHALITIS

Encephalitis is an inflammation (irritation and swelling) of the brain, usually caused by one of many viral infections. Exposure to viruses can occur through insect bites, food or drink contamination or inhalation of respiratory droplets from an infected person, or skin contact. In rural areas, viruses carried by mosquitoes, ticks, or accidentally ingested are the most common causes.

How to Minister: (All commands done in Jesus' name).
1. Rebuke the infection.
2. Command the swelling to go and the brain to be healed, restored and function normally.

3. Pray for the neck to come into proper alignment
4. Command the blood to flow normally within the brain.

ENDOMETRIOSIS (See Female Problems).

END-STAGE RENAL DISEASE (Kidney Failure).

ENLARGED PROSTATE (See Prostate Problems).

EPILEPSY

Epilepsy is a brain disorder involving recurrent seizures. Seizures ("fits") are episodes of disturbed brain function that cause changes in attention and/or behavior. They are caused by abnormal electrical excitation in the brain and usually last short periods of time. Occasionally, they occur undetected.

Sometimes, seizures are related to a temporary condition, such as exposure to drugs, withdrawal from certain drugs, or abnormal levels of sodium or glucose in the blood. In such cases, repeated seizures may not recur once the underlying problem is corrected.

In other cases, injury to the brain (such as a stroke or head injury) causes brain tissue to be abnormally excitable. In some people, an inherited abnormality affects nerve cells in the brain, which leads to seizures. In some cases, no cause can be identified. Often, the condition can be triggered by flashing lights.

How to Minister: (All commands done in Jesus' name).

1. Cast out the spirit of epilepsy.
2. Command the electrical and magnetic frequencies to be in harmony and balance.
3. Lead them in a prayer of repentance when necessary.
4. Command new brain tissues to develop and work normally.

EPSTEIN-BARR (See Mononucleosis).

ESSENTIAL TREMOR (See Tremor).

FARSIGHTEDNESS

Farsightedness is difficulty seeing objects which are nearby and is the result of the visual image being focused behind rather than directly on the retina. It may be caused by the eyeball being too small or the focusing power being too weak.

It is often present from birth, but children can compensate with their stronger eye muscles. Most children outgrow the condition. As aging occurs, glasses or contact lenses may be required to correct the vision. If you have family members who are farsighted, you are likely to become farsighted also.

How to Minister: (All commands done in Jesus' name).

1. Lay hands on the eyes, commanding the lens, nerves, ligaments, and muscles to be adjusted and work properly.
2. Command the eyeballs to be restored to their perfect size and function normally.
3. Command perfect sight to be restored.
4. Lead them in a prayer of repentance for generational curses.

FEAR

This is an abnormal fright of normal situations, people and/or things.

How to Minister: (All commands done in Jesus' name).

1. If possible, identify how and when it started.
2. Lead them in a prayer of repentance or forgiveness when necessary.
3. Cast out the spirit of fear.

4. Lead them in a prayer to lay all cares, worries and fears on the Altar of God.
5. Speak peace to them.

FEET (Also see Bunions, Corns and Calluses and Gout).

Most foot problems are inherited or from an injury, however they can also be a birth defect such as club feet.

How to Minister: (All commands done in Jesus' name).
1. Command the twenty-six bones in each foot to go into proper position and be healed and strong.
2. Lead them in a prayer of repentance for generational curses.
3. Command any infection to go.
4. Command all injury/scarring to be healed.

FEMALE PROBLEMS

(Also see Endometriosis, Fibroid Tumors and PMS).

This includes any problem with the female reproductive organs of the body. It includes painful menstrual periods, PMS (Premenstrual Syndrome), endometriosis, amenorrhea (absence of periods for six months or longer) and prolapsed uterus.

How to Minister: (All commands done in Jesus' name).
1. Command all the tissues, nerves and vessels to function normally,
2. Command the pelvis to go into proper alignment. (Do the pelvis adjustment.)
3. Command the sacrum to rotate into correct position.
4. Command any infection or irritation to go.
5. Command any scar tissue, damaged or destroyed parts to be restored and function properly.
6. Command all hormones to be in balance.
7. Command the electrical and magnetic frequencies to be in harmony and balance.

Endometriosis

Endometriosis is a condition in which the endometrium, tissue that normally lines the uterus, grows in other areas of the body causing pain, irregular bleeding, and infertility. The tissue growth typically occurs in the pelvic area, outside of the uterus, on the ovaries, bowel, rectum, bladder, or the delicate lining of the pelvis, but it can occur in other areas of the body as well.

The cause of endometriosis is unknown. Once the endometrial cells implant in tissue outside of the uterus, they may cause scarring and adhesions in the tubes and ovaries. These adhesions can make transfer of an ovum from the ovary to the fallopian tube difficult or impossible. They can also stop passage of a fertilized egg down the fallopian tube to the uterus.

Endometriosis is a common problem. It occurs in an estimated 10% of women during their reproductive years. The prevalence may be as high as 35% among infertile women. Endometriosis is typically diagnosed between the ages of 25 and 35, but probably begins about the time that regular menstruation begins.

How to Minister: (All commands done in Jesus' name).

1. Lead them in a prayer of repentance for generational curses.
2. Command the female organs to function normally.
3. Command the pelvis to come into proper alignment.
4. Command the extra tissues and scarring to dissolve.

Fibroid Tumors

Fibroids are benign (not cancerous) tumors of the uterus. Unpredictable in size and behavior, fibroids can be as tiny as a pencil point or as large as a grapefruit, growing slowly or rapidly, either alone or in groups. When Fibroids are small, women usually don't notice them, but as the tumors grow, women experience some common symptoms:

- Prolonged and/or heavy menstrual periods
- Bleeding between periods
- Pelvic or abdominal pain and pressure
- Enlarged abdomen
- Bladder pressure plus incontinence, frequent urination or chronic urine retention
- Bowel pressure and constipation
- Backache or leg pains

Symptomatic fibroids can be disabling causing women to seek treatment which can range from medications to surgical removal.

How to Minister: (All commands done in Jesus' name).

1. Command the pain and cramping to cease.
2. Command the spirit causing the tumor(s) to go.
3. Command the tumor cells to die and dissolve.
4. Command the pelvis to come into proper alignment.
5. Command the tissues of the reproductive organs be restored to normal function and be totally healed.

Premenstrual Syndrome (PMS)

Premenstrual Syndrome (PMS) involves symptoms that occur in relation to the menstrual cycle and which can interfere with the woman's life. The symptoms usually begin 5 to 11 days before the start of menstruation and usually stop when menstruation begins, or shortly thereafter.

An exact cause of PMS has not been identified. However, it may be related to social, biological, cultural, or psychological factors. PMS can occur with apparently normal ovarian function.

PMS is estimated to affect up to 75% of women during their childbearing years. It occurs more often in women between their late 20s and early 40s, those with at least one child, those with a family history of a major depression disorder, or women with a past medical history of either Postpartum Depression or any mood disorder. As many as 50-60% of women suffer with severe PMS.

How to Minister: (All commands done in Jesus' name).
1. Lead them in a prayer of repentance for generational curses.
2. Command the hormones to be in balance.
3. Command the electrical and magnetic frequencies to be in harmony and balance.
4. Command the spirit of PMS to leave.

FIBROMYALGIA

Fibromyalgia is a common condition characterized by widespread pain in joints, muscles, tendons, and other soft tissues. Some other problems commonly linked to Fibromyalgia include fatigue, morning stiffness, sleep problems, headaches, numbness in hands and feet, depression, and anxiety. Fibromyalgia can develop on its own or secondary to other musculoskeletal conditions, such as rheumatoid arthritis, or systemic lupus.

Diagnosis of Fibromyalgia requires a history of at least three months of widespread pain, and pain and tenderness in at least eleven of eighteen tender-point sites. The overwhelming characteristic of Fibromyalgia is long-standing, body-wide pain with the defined tender points.

Fibromyalgia pain can mimic the pain that occurs with various types of arthritis. However, the significant swelling, destruction and deformity of joints seen in diseases such as rheumatoid arthritis do not occur with Fibromyalgia syndrome alone. The soft-tissue pain of Fibromyalgia is described as deep-aching, radiating, gnawing, shooting or burning, and ranges from mild to severe. Fibromyalgia sufferers tend to wake up with body aches and stiffness.

For some patients, pain improves during the day and increases again during the evening, though many patients with Fibromyalgia have day-long, unrelenting pain. Pain can increase with activity, cold or damp weather, anxiety, and stress. The cause of this disorder is unknown. Physical or emotional trauma may play a role in development of the syndrome.

How to Minister: (All commands done in Jesus' name).
1. Cast out the spirit of Fibromyalgia.
2. Command the aches, pains, and stiffness to disappear.
3. Command the electrical and magnetic frequencies to be in harmony and balance.
4. Lead them in a prayer of repentance when necessary.
5. Lead them in a prayer to lay all stress, cares, worries and fears on the Altar of God.

FISSURE, RECTAL

This is a crack or a tear in the rectum which is quite painful and makes evacuation of the large bowel very difficult and very uncomfortable.

How to Minister: (All commands done in Jesus' name).
1. Lay hands on the lower back and command the tissues to be healed and fissure to close.
2. Command the pain to go.

FLOATERS or "WEBBING"

Floaters appear as specks in the eye. The floating specks you sometimes see in front of your eyes are not on the surface of your eyes, but inside them.

These floaters are bits of cellular debris that come and go without treatment. To some people these "floaters" look like spots. To others, they look like tiny threads. Most of the time they are nothing to worry about, but sometimes they can be a symptom of a retinal tear.

How to Minister: (All commands done in Jesus' name).
1. Lay hands on the eyes, commanding the blood and fluid in the eyes to be restored to normal function and all foreign substances to dissolve and go.
2. Command perfect sight to be restored.
3. If necessary, lead them in a prayer of repentance.

FLU (See also Influenza).

The Flu is a contagious infection of the nose, throat, and lungs caused by the influenza virus. Common symptoms include a high fever (over 102 degrees Fahrenheit), flushed face, chills, sweats and severe fatigue. Some people have dizziness or vomiting. The virus can settle anywhere in the respiratory tract, producing symptoms of a cold, croup, sore throat, bronchitis, ear infection, or pneumonia. Cough and tiredness usually last for weeks after the rest of the illness is over.

The most common way to catch the Flu is by inhaling droplets from coughs or sneezes of an infected person. Less often, it is spread when you touch a surface such as a faucet handle or phone that has the virus on it, and then touch your own mouth, nose, or eyes. Because the Flu is airborne and very contagious, with a short incubation period, it often infects a community all at once. The Flu usually arrives in the winter months.

How to Minister: (All commands done in Jesus' name).
1. Rebuke the infection and curse the root of it.

2. Command the immune system to be strengthened and to function properly.
3. Command the electrical and magnetic frequencies to be in harmony and balance.
4. Command all pain and discomfort to disappear.
5. Command all affected tissues to be healed and function normally.

GALLSTONES

Gallstones are formed within the gallbladder, an organ that stores bile excreted from the liver. Bile is a solution of water, salts, lecithin, cholesterol, and other substances. If the concentration of these components changes, they may precipitate from solution and form gallstones. Gallstones may be as small as a grain of sand, or they may become as large as an inch in diameter, depending on how much time has elapsed from their initial formation.

Gallstones often have no symptoms and are usually discovered incidentally by a routine x-ray. They are more common in women, native Americans, and people over the age of forty. Other risk factors include ethnic and hereditary factors, obesity, diabetes, liver cirrhosis and certain operations for peptic ulcers. If a Gallstone passes into the bile duct, it can trigger a gall bladder attack which is very painful and can cause complications with other organs of the body necessitating surgical removal.

How to Minister: (All commands done in Jesus' name).

1. Lay your hand over the area of the gall bladder, commanding the stones to dissolve.
2. Command the gall bladder to be healed and function normally.

GANGLION CYST

This is a hard, tumor-like swelling filled with fluid; usually found on the wrist around a tendon or joint.

How to Minister: (All commands done in Jesus' name).

1. Lay hands on the affected area, commanding the cyst to dissolve and fluid to reabsorb into the body.
2. Command the wrist structures, bones, muscles, and tendons to go back into normal position.
3. Command the joint lining to produce proper joint fluid and blood supply to be normal.
4. Command all pressure on the nerves to go back to normal.

GASTROESOPHAGEAL REFLUX DISEASE (GERD)

Gastroesophageal Reflux Disease (GERD) is a condition in which food or liquid travels from the stomach back up into the esophagus (the tube from the mouth to the stomach). This partially digested material is usually acidic and can irritate the esophagus, often causing heartburn and other symptoms.

This is a common condition that often occurs without symptoms after meals. In some people, the reflux is related to a problem with the lower esophageal sphincter, a band of muscle fibers that usually closes off the esophagus from the stomach. If this sphincter doesn't close properly, food and liquid can move backward into the esophagus and may cause the symptoms.

How to Minister: (All commands done in Jesus' name).

1. Command the muscles (sphincter) to function properly.
2. Lead them in the prayer to lay all cares, stress and worries on the Altar of God.
3. Lead them in a prayer of repentance for generational curses.

GINGIVITIS (See Gum Disease).

GLAUCOMA

Glaucoma involves increased fluid pressure inside the eye which damages the optic nerve and causes partial vision loss and can progress to blindness. Glaucoma is the third most common cause of blindness in the US.

All types of Glaucoma are characterized by increased pressure within the eyeball, and therefore all can cause progressive damage to the optic nerve. Increased pressure occurs when the fluid within the eye does not drain properly. The pressure pushes on the junction of the optic nerve and the retina at the back of the eye. This reduces the blood supply to the optic nerve, which carries visual information from the eye to the brain.

This loss of blood supply causes the individual nerve cells to progressively die. As the optic nerve deteriorates, blind spots develop in the field of vision. Peripheral (side) vision is affected first, followed by central (frontal) vision. Without treatment, glaucoma can eventually cause blindness.

How to Minister: (All commands done in Jesus' name).

1. Command the canals of the eyes to open and all pressure to normalize to allow fluid to flow normally.
2. Command any disease process or scar tissue to be healed and for the eyes to return to normal.
3. Command any damaged nerve cells to be healed.

GLUTTONY (See Addictions and Obesity).

GOITER (Also see Thyroid).

A Goiter is an enlargement of the thyroid gland that is NOT associated with inflammation or cancer. A simple Goiter usually occurs when the thyroid gland is not able to produce enough thyroid hormone to meet the body's requirements. The thyroid gland compensates by enlarging, which usually overcomes mild deficiencies of thyroid hormone. Iodine is vital to the formation of the thyroid hormone. The modern use of iodized table salt in the U.S. prevents this deficiency; however, it is still common in central Asia and central Africa.

In most cases of a sporadic Goiter the cause is unknown. Occasionally, certain medications can cause a nontoxic Goiter. Risk factors for the development of a Goiter include family history, female sex, age over forty years, or an inadequate dietary intake of iodine.

How to Minister: (All commands done in Jesus' name).

1. Lead them in a prayer of repentance for generational curses.
2. Lay hands on the goiter and command it to dissolve.
3. Command the electrical and magnetic frequencies to be in harmony and balance.
4. Command a new thyroid gland that will function normally.

GOUT

Gout is a disease involving uric acid deposits in the joints. The disorder causes pain, especially in the joints of the feet and legs. Patients with chronic gout have repeated episodes of joint pain.

Gout is caused by an overproduction of uric acid or a reduced ability of the kidney to eliminate uric acid. The exact cause is unknown. It is more common in males, postmenopausal women, and people with high blood pressure. Heavy alcohol use, diabetes, obesity, sickle cell anemia, and kidney disease also increases the risk. The condition may also develop in people who take drugs which interfere with uric acid excretion.

How to Minister: (All commands done in Jesus' name).

1. Lay hands on the affected area and command the crystals to dissolve and tissues and bones to be healed.
2. Command the body to produce only a normal amount of uric acid.
3. Lead them in a prayer of repentance for generational curses.

GUILLAIN-BARRé SYNDROME (Also known as GBS).

Guillain-Barré Syndrome is a disorder caused by nerve inflammation which causes progressive muscle weakness or paralysis. The inflammation damages portions of the nerve cell, resulting in muscle weakness or paralysis and sensory loss. The damage can permanently affect nerve function.

The exact cause of this disorder is unknown. It may occur at any age but is most common in people of either sex between the ages of thirty and fifty. Guillain-Barré Syndrome may occur in association with viral infections such as mononucleosis, AIDS and herpes simplex, after bacterial infections and some types of diarrhea.

How to Minister: (All commands done in Jesus' name).

1. Rebuke the infection and command the spirit to go.
2. Lay hands on the person and command the nervous system to be restored and function perfectly.
3. Command any other structures that have been damaged by the paralysis to become whole.
4. Lead them in a prayer of repentance if necessary.

GUM DISEASE (Also see Periodontitis).

Bleeding from the gums is mainly due to inadequate plaque removal from the teeth at the gum line. This will lead to a condition called gingivitis or inflamed gums. If plaque is not removed through regular brushing of the teeth and dental appointments, it will harden into what is known as tartar. Ultimately, this will lead to increased bleeding and a more advanced form of gum and jawbone disease known as periodontitis. It is important to follow the instructions from your dentist in order to maintain healthy gums. Improper brushing and flossing technique may actually irritate or traumatize the gum tissue.

How to Minister: (All commands done in Jesus' name).
1. Rebuke the infection.
2. Lay hands on the jawbone, commanding the tissues of the mouth to be healed and function normally.
3. Lead them in a prayer of repentance for personal dental care, if necessary.
4. Lead them in a prayer of repentance to break word curses.

HAIR LOSS (See Baldness).

HAMMER TOES

A Hammer Toe is a deformity of the toe in which the end of the toe is bent downward. Hammer Toe usually affects the second toe, although it may also affect the other toes. The toe assumes a claw-like position. The condition may occur as a result of pressure from a bunion. Often, a corn on the top of a toe and a callus on the sole of the foot develop, which makes walking painful. The condition may be congenital (present at birth) or acquired by wearing ill-fitting footwear.

How to Minister: (All commands done in Jesus' name).
1. Command all 26 bones in the foot to return to their normal position.

2. Command all tendons, ligaments and muscles to return to their normal length and strength.
3. Grow out the legs and command the nerves to be restored in the spinal column.
4. Lead them in a prayer of repentance, if necessary.

HANDS (See Arms and Hands).

HAY FEVER (See Allergies).

HEADACHES, CLUSTER

Cluster Headaches are a fairly common form of chronic, recurrent headache. Cluster Headaches affect one side of the head and may be associated with tearing of the eyes and nasal congestion. They occur in clusters, happening repeatedly every day at the same time for several weeks and then stopping. Unlike migraines, they affect men more often than women. They can affect people of any age but are most common between adolescence and middle age.

A Cluster Headache begins as a severe headache with a sudden onset. No specific cause has been found for the disorder. It happens most commonly during the dreaming phase of sleep. Cluster headaches may occur daily for months, alternating with periods without headaches (episodic), or they can recur for a year or more without stopping (chronic). A person may experience alternating chronic and episodic phases.

Some people who experience Cluster Headaches are heavy smokers. Alcohol use, glare, stress, or certain foods may trigger an attack.

How to Minister: (All commands done in Jesus' name).

1. Command the histamines and the serotonin levels to be normal and in balance.

2. Lead them in a prayer of repentance when necessary.
3. Lead them in a prayer to of repentance to break word curses
4. Command the pain to go and blood to flow properly.
5. Lead them in a prayer to lay all cares, stress and worries on the Altar of God.
6. Command the blood to come into proper pH balance.

HEADACHES, MIGRAINE

Migraine Headaches are a type of severe headache that some people get repeatedly over time. Migraines are different from other headaches because they occur with symptoms such as nausea, vomiting, or sensitivity to light. Some people who get migraines have warning symptoms, called an aura, before the actual headache begins. Most people, however, do not have such warning symptoms.

Many people get migraines -- about 11 out of 100. The headaches tend to start between the ages of 10 and 46, may run in families, and occur in women more often than men.

A Migraine Headache is caused by abnormal brain activity, which is triggered by stress, food, or some other factor. The exact chain of events is not known. However, it seems to involve various nerve pathways and chemicals in the brain. The changes affect blood flow in the brain and surrounding membranes. Migraine attacks may be triggered by:

- Allergic reactions
- Bright lights, loud noises, and certain odors or perfumes
- Physical or emotional stress
- Changes in sleep patterns
- Smoking or exposure to smoke

- Skipping meals
- Alcohol or caffeine
- Menstrual cycle fluctuations, birth control pills
- Tension headaches
- Foods containing tyramine (red wine, aged cheese, smoked fish, chicken livers, figs, and some beans), monosodium glutamate (MSG), or nitrates (like bacon, hot dogs, and salami)
- Other foods such as chocolate, nuts, peanut butter, avocado, banana, citrus, onions, dairy products, and fermented or pickled foods

How to Minister: (All commands done in Jesus' name).

1. Lead them in a prayer of repentance for generational curses.
2. Command the spirit of migraines to go.
3. Command the blood to flow properly to the brain.
4. Command the hormones to be in balance.
5. Lead them in a prayer of repentance to break word curses.
6. Command the pain to go.
7. Command the blood to come into proper pH balance.

HEADACHE, TENSION

A Headache is pain or discomfort in the head, scalp, or neck. Serious causes of Headaches are extremely rare. Most people with Headaches can feel much better by making lifestyle changes, learning ways to relax, and occasionally by taking medications.

Tension Headaches are due to tight, contracted muscles in your shoulders, neck, scalp, and jaw. They are often related to stress, depression, or anxiety. Overworking, not getting enough sleep, missing meals, and using alcohol or street drugs can make you more susceptible to them. Headaches can be triggered by chocolate, cheese, and monosodium glutamate (MSG). People who drink caffeine can have headaches when they don't get their usual daily amount.

Other common causes include: holding your head in one position for a long time, like at a computer, microscope, or typewriter, poor sleep position, overexerting yourself, clenching or grinding your teeth.

Tension Headaches tend to be on both sides of your head. They often start at the back of your head and spread forward. The pain may feel dull or squeezing, like a tight band or vice. Your shoulders, neck, or jaw may feel tight and sore

How to Minister: (All commands done in Jesus' name).

1. Command the neck to come into alignment.
2. Command the blood to flow normally and spasms of the vessels to release.
3. Cast out the spirit of headache, if necessary.
4. Lead them in a prayer of repentance, if necessary.
5. Lead them in a prayer of repentance for generational curses.
6. Lead them in a prayer to lay all cares, stress and worries on the Altar of God.
7. Command the blood to come into proper pH balance.

HEART

This includes any problem involving the heart.

Heart Arrhythmia

An Arrhythmia is any disorder of heart rate or rhythm or heartbeat pattern. The heartbeat can be too slow, too fast, have extra beats, skip a beat, or otherwise beat irregularly.

There are numerous causes; however, they all are related to an electrical dysfunction of the heart. Names of the more common specific rhythms are: Atrial Fibrillation, Bradycardia, PAT (Paroxysmal Atrial Tachycardia or PSVT), Ventricular Tachycardia, “skipped beats”, Heart Block, or “Wolf-Parkinson-White”.

Causes of Arrhythmias range from Heart Attacks, metabolic imbalance, medication side effects, lack of oxygen, high blood pressure, congenital heart defects, abnormal heart valves, lung diseases, heart stimulants such as caffeine, tobacco or alcohol, stress or viral infections, Coronary Artery Disease, to Arteriosclerosis.

Some people have no outward symptoms. Others complain about fast or slow heart beats (palpitations), skipping beats, fainting, light-headedness, dizziness, chest pain, shortness of breath, paleness, sweating, changes in the rate, rhythm, or pattern of the pulse.

Complications are serious and can be life-threatening: Angina (chest pain caused by imbalance of supply and demand for oxygen in the heart muscle), Heart Attack, Heart Failure, Stroke and sudden death.

Heart Attack

A Heart Attack (myocardial infarction) occurs when an area of heart muscle dies or is permanently damaged because of an inadequate supply of oxygen to that area.

Most Heart Attacks are caused by a clot that blocks one of the coronary arteries (the blood vessels that bring blood and oxygen to the heart muscle). The clot usually forms in a coronary artery that has been previously narrowed from changes related to Atherosclerosis. The atherosclerotic plaque (buildup) inside the arterial wall sometimes cracks, and this triggers the formation of a clot, also called a thrombus.

A clot in the coronary artery interrupts the flow of blood and oxygen to the heart muscle leading to the death of heart cells in that area. The damaged heart muscle loses its ability to contract, and the remaining heart muscle needs to compensate for that weakened area. Occasionally, sudden overwhelming stress can trigger a Heart Attack.

Heart, Congenital Heart Defects

This refers to any defect of the heart present at birth. Some involve holes in the heart muscle that either should not occur or that should close with time but don't. Others involve problems with the heart valves. These defects can cause numerous complications and are very often life-threatening to a baby. They need a new heart.

Heart Disease

Heart Disease includes any disorder that affects the heart's ability to function normally. The most common cause of Heart Disease is narrowing or blockage of the coronary arteries, which supply blood to the heart itself. This happens slowly over time. Some Heart Diseases can be present at birth (congenital heart diseases).

Other causes include: hypertension, abnormal function of the heart valves, abnormal electrical rhythm of the heart, or weakening of the heart's pumping function caused by infection or toxins

Heart Failure

Also called Congestive Heart Failure, Heart Failure is a disorder in which the heart loses its ability to pump blood efficiently throughout the body. The heart is unable to supply the vital organs of the body with enough blood (carrying nutrition and oxygen) to meet the body's demands. Fluid then backs up into the lungs and causes breathing problems. It can also back up into other areas of the body such as causing swelling (edema) of the lower legs.

The term "Heart Failure" should not be confused with cardiac arrest, a situation in which the heart actually stops beating. Heart Failure is almost always a chronic, long-term condition, although it can sometimes develop suddenly.

Heart, Valvular Heart Disease

Valvular Heart Disease refers to any condition of the four heart valves: the mitral valve, aortic valve, tricuspid valve and pulmonic valve. Such conditions include valvular regurgitation (closes improperly allowing leakage of blood) and stenosis (narrowing or stiffening of a valve restricting flow of blood). Surgical replacement is often necessary. These problems can be caused by infection or other disease processes. Numerous other body functions are affected by Valvular Heart Disease. It can lead to Congestive Heart Failure, Arrhythmias, Endocarditis (inflammation of the heart tissue), Pulmonary Edema, and cardiac arrest (heart stops beating leading to death)..

How to Minister: (All commands done in Jesus' name).

1. Command a creative miracle or "a new heart" into the body.
2. Cast out the spirit of death.
3. Command the electrical and magnetic frequencies to be in harmony and balance.
4. Command all the excess fluid to leave the body and breathing be normal.

5. Lead them in a prayer of repentance for lifestyle or diet, if necessary.
6. Lead them in a prayer of repentance for generational curses.
7. Command other body parts that have been affected by the heart disease/damage to be healed and function normally.
8. Lead them in a prayer of repentance to break word curses.

HEMORRHOIDS

Hemorrhoids are painful, swollen veins in the lower portion of the rectum or anus. This condition is very common, especially during pregnancy and after childbirth. Hemorrhoids result from increased pressure in the veins of the area. The pressure causes the veins to bulge and expand, making them painful, particularly when you are sitting or passing stool.

The most common cause is straining during bowel movements. Hemorrhoids may result from constipation, sitting for long periods of time, and anal infections. In some cases they may be caused by other diseases, such as liver cirrhosis. Internal hemorrhoids occur just inside the anus, at the beginning of the rectum. External hemorrhoids occur at the anal opening and may hang outside the anus.

How to Minister: (All commands done in Jesus' name).

1. Place hands on the lower back and command the hemorrhoids to be healed.
2. Command the blood vessels to shrink to normal size and function.
3. Rebuke pain.
4. Adjust the pelvis into proper alignment.
5. Command the nerves and muscles to be relaxed and normal.

6. Lead them in a prayer of repentance for diet, if necessary.

HEPATITIS C

Hepatitis C is an inflammation of the liver caused by infection with the Hepatitis C virus. The prevalence of Hepatitis C infection is approximately 4 million people in the United States or about 1 in 70 to 100 people.

Many people who are infected with the Hepatitis C virus do not have symptoms. Hepatitis C is often detected during blood tests for a routine physical or other medical procedure. If the infection has been present for many years, the liver may be permanently scarred -- a condition called cirrhosis. In many cases, there may be no symptoms of the disease until cirrhosis has developed.

How to Minister: (All commands done in Jesus' name).

1. Curse the virus and command the spirit to leave.
2. Lead them in a prayer of repentance, if necessary.
3. Command a creative miracle of a new liver if it is damaged.
4. Command the electrical and magnetic frequencies to be in harmony and in balance.

HERNIA

A hernia occurs when parts of an organ (usually the intestines) protrudes through a weak point or tear in the muscular wall that holds the abdominal organs in place. It appears as a soft swelling in the area. Usually, there is no obvious cause of a hernia, although they are sometimes associated with heavy lifting.

There are several types of hernias, based on where they occur.

- **Inguinal hernia** -- appears as a bulge in the groin or scrotum. This type is more common in men than women.
- **Femoral hernia** -- appears as a bulge in the upper thigh. This type is more common in women than in men.
- **Incisional hernia** -- can occur through a scar if you have had abdominal surgery.
- **Umbilical hernia** -- a bulge around the belly button or umbilicus. of the navel (umbilicus). This type of hernia occurs most often in infants, but it may also occur in adults, especially in pregnant women. Treatment for adults typically is surgery, especially if the hernia enlarges and causes pain.

Hernias rarely go away without treatment. Occasionally, the protruding abdominal tissue becomes trapped (incarcerated) and can no longer be pushed back into the abdominal cavity. This reduces the blood supply to the section of trapped intestine and can lead to tissue death. If not relieved, the person may develop signs and symptoms of bowel obstruction which include abdominal cramps, bloating and vomiting. Emergency surgery may be required.

Hiatal Hernia - This is a protruding of the stomach above the diaphragm leading to pain, indigestion, and swallowing difficulties. Food can get trapped in this pocket and cause severe pain as well as spontaneous vomiting. Symptoms may be similar to GERDS.

How to Minister: (All commands done in Jesus' name).

1. Grow out the arms.
2. Grow out the legs.

3. Command the hernia to disappear; muscles, nerves, tendons, ligaments and tissues to be healed and restored to proper alignment, strength, and function.
4. Command the pelvis to come into proper alignment.
5. Lead them in a prayer of repentance for generational curses.

HERPES

Herpes is a viral infection affecting various parts of the body.

Herpes Simplex HSV 1 (Cold Sore)

Herpes Simplex is an infection caused by Herpes Simplex virus 1 and is commonly called a Cold Sore. It primarily affects the areas of the lips, mouth, and face often causing lesions inside the mouth such as cold sores (fever blisters) and is transmitted by contact with infected saliva. Usually acquired in childhood, by adulthood, up to 90% of individuals will have antibodies to HSV-1.

How to Minister: (All commands done in Jesus' name).
1. Curse the root of the virus and command the spirit to leave.
2. Lead them in a prayer of repentance for generational curses.
3. Command healing in the affected areas and all affected tissues to be restored.
4. Command the electrical and magnetic frequencies to be in harmony and balance.

Herpes Simplex HSV-2 (Genital Herpes)

Genital Herpes is a sexually transmitted viral infection that is characterized by repeated eruptions of small, painful blisters, ulcers or sores on the genitals or adjacent areas of skin.

Herpes is caused by two viruses -- herpes simplex virus type 1 (HSV-1), and herpes simplex virus type 2 (HSV-2). While statistics vary, research shows that 90% of the population has been exposed to HSV-1, "oral herpes," and 25% of the population aged 25-45 years old in the United States has been exposed to infection with HSV-2, "genital herpes." Individuals may, however, harbor HSV-2 and not have developed any symptoms. Up to 30% of U.S. adults have antibodies against HSV-2. Cross-infection of type 1 and 2 viruses may occur from oral-genital contact.

How to Minister: (All commands done in Jesus' name).
1. Curse the root of the virus and command the spirit to leave.
2. Lead them in a prayer of repentance for generational curses.
3. Command healing in the affected areas and all affected tissues to be restored.
4. Command the electrical and magnetic frequencies to be in harmony and balance.
5. Lead them in a prayer of repentance, if necessary.
6. Command the immune system to be strong and function properly.

Herpes Zoster (Shingles).

Herpes Zoster is an acute, localized infection with varicella-zoster virus, which causes a painful, blistering rash. Herpes Zoster, or Shingles, is caused by the same virus that causes chickenpox. After an episode of chickenpox, the virus becomes dormant in the body. Herpes Zoster occurs as a result of the virus re-emerging after many years.

The cause of the re-activation is usually unknown, but seems to be linked to aging, stress or an impaired immune system. Often only one attack occurs, without recurrence.

How to Minister: (All commands done in Jesus' name).

1. Curse the root of the virus and command the spirit to leave.
2. Lead them in a prayer of repentance for generational curses.
3. Command healing in the affected areas and all affected tissues to be restored.
4. Command the electrical and magnetic frequencies to be in harmony and balance.
5. Lead them in a prayer to lay all their cares, worries and stress on the Altar of God.
6. Command the immune system to be strong and function properly.

HICCUPS (Also known as Hiccoughs).

A Hiccup is an involuntary movement (spasm) of the diaphragm, the muscle at the base of the lungs. The spasm is followed by rapid closure of the vocal cords, which produces a distinctive sound.

Hiccups often start for no apparent reason and usually disappear after a few minutes. Rarely, Hiccups can persist for days, weeks, or months. Hiccups are common and normal in newborns and infants.

How to Minister: (All commands done in Jesus' name).

1. Command the diaphragm to be at peace and the spasms to stop.

HIGH CHOLESTEROL (See Cholesterol, High).

HIV/AIDS (See AIDS).

HOMOSEXUALITY / LESBIANISM

Individuals who prefer intimate relationships with others of the same sex; the term homosexual refers to males, lesbian refers to females. The individual must want to be free from the desire before they can be delivered and healed from this condition.

How to Minister: (All commands done in Jesus' name).
1. Lead them in a prayer of repentance of idolatry.
2. Have them repent of sexual sins, if necessary (no details need to be spoken)
3. Lead them in the prayer to break ungodly covenants.
4. Cast out the spirit of homosexuality/lesbianism.
5. Lead them in a prayer of repentance to break word curses.
6. Minister to the emptiness in their heart. Speak peace to them.

HUNTINGTON'S CHOREA

Huntington's Chorea is an inherited disease characterized by involuntary abnormal quick, jerky, incessant body movements, dementia, and emotional disturbances. Huntington's disease is a progressive disorder involving wasting (degeneration) of nerve cells in the brain and is inherited as a single faulty gene on chromosome #4.

Symptoms do not usually appear until adulthood, typically between 35 and 50 years of age but it may also appear in younger people. In children it may appear to be Parkinson's disease with rigidity, slow movements, and tremor. There is progressive loss of mental function, including personality changes, and loss of cognitive functions such as judgment, and speech. There is no cure.

How to Minister: (All commands done in Jesus' name).
1. Lead them in a prayer of repentance for generational curses.
2. Cast out the spirits of Huntington's disease.
3. Command all the chromosomes to become normal.
4. Command any effected organs to be restored.

HYPERLIPIDEMIA (See Cholesterol, High).

HYPERTENSION (High Blood Pressure or HTN)

Hypertension generally means the systolic is consistently over 140 and diastolic blood pressure is consistently over 90. Blood pressure is determined by the amount of blood pumped by the heart as well as the size and condition of the arteries.

Many other factors can affect blood pressure, including volume of water in the body; salt content of the body; condition of the kidneys, nervous system, or blood vessels; arteriosclerosis and levels of various hormones in the body.

Complications of Hypertension include kidney damage, stroke, heart attack, visual disturbances, congestive heart disease, and chest pain (angina).

How to Minister: (All commands done in Jesus' name).

1. Lead them in a prayer of repentance for generational curses.
2. Command the entire vascular system to operate normally and vessels to return to normal elasticity.
3. Command the blood pressure to return to normal and to remain normal.
4. Lead them in prayer to lay all their stress, cares and worries on the Altar of God.

HYPOGLYCEMIA (Low Blood Sugar).

Hypoglycemia occurs when your body's blood sugar, or glucose, is abnormally low. Hypoglycemia develops when the body's glucose is used up too rapidly, when glucose is released into the bloodstream more slowly than is needed by your body, or when excessive insulin is released into the bloodstream. Insulin is a hormone that reduces blood glucose. It is produced by the pancreas in response to increased glucose levels in the blood. Hypoglycemia is relatively common in diabetics. It occurs when too much insulin or oral antidiabetic medication is taken, not enough food is eaten, or from a sudden increase in the amount of exercise without an increase in food intake. The term insulin shock is used to describe severe hypoglycemia that results in unconsciousness. If blood sugar levels continue to fall, seizures and death can occur.

How to Minister: (All commands done in Jesus' name).
1. Lead them in a prayer of repentance for generational curses.
2. Command the spirit of hypoglycemia to go.
3. Command a new pancreas to maintain blood sugar at normal levels.

IBS (See Irritable Bowel Syndrome).

IMMUNE SYSTEM

The immune response is how your body recognizes and defends itself against bacteria, viruses, and substances that appear foreign and harmful to the body.

The immune system protects the body from potentially harmful substances by recognizing and responding to so-called antigens. Antigens are large molecules (usually proteins) on the surface of cells, viruses, fungi, or bacteria. Non-living substances such as toxins, chemicals, drugs, and foreign particles (such as a splinter) can be antigens. Substances that contain these antigens are recognized and destroyed by the immune system. Even your own body cells have proteins that are antigens (these include a group of antigens called HLA antigens). Your immune system learns to see these antigens as "normal" and does not usually react against them.

Your immune system includes barriers that keep harmful materials from entering your body. These barriers form the first line of defense in the immune response. Some of these barriers are the skin, stomach acid, mucus (which traps bacteria and small particles), the cough reflex, and enzymes in tears and skin oils. If an antigen gets past the external barriers, it is attacked and destroyed by other parts of the immune system. Immunity also includes those things that make humans resistant to many of the diseases of animals.

The immune system includes certain types of white blood cells. It also includes chemicals and proteins in the blood. Some of these directly attack foreign substances in the body, and others work together to help the immune system cells.

How to Minister: (All commands done in Jesus' name).

1. Command the immune system to be restored completely.
2. Command it to stop all disease and viruses from infecting the body.
3. Command the electrical and magnetic frequencies to be in harmony and balance.
4. Lead them in a prayer of repentance, if necessary.

INCONTINENCE

Urinary Incontinence is the inability to control the passage of urine out of the body. This can range from an occasional leakage of urine, to a complete inability to hold any urine. There are two main types of urinary incontinence.

Stress incontinence occurs during certain activities like coughing, sneezing, laughing, or exercise.

Urge incontinence involves a strong, sudden need to urinate followed by instant bladder contraction and involuntary loss of urine.

Incontinence is most common among the elderly. Women are more likely than men to have urinary incontinence especially after bearing several children which causes stretching of the muscles of the pelvic floor. Loss of control can also be caused by loss of function following spinal injury, brain injury, back surgery, stroke or prostate surgery.

Bowel Incontinence is the loss of bowel control resulting in involuntary passage of stool. This can range from an occasional leakage of stool with the passage of gas to a complete loss of control of bowel movements.

Among people over the age of 65, women more frequently experience Bowel Incontinence, with 13 out of every 1,000 women reporting loss of bowel control. The most common cause of bowel incontinence, ironically, is constipation. Constipation causes the muscles of the anus and intestines to stretch and weaken. The weakened muscles will prevent the rectal sphincter from closing tightly thus resulting in leakage of stool. Weakened intestinal muscles will further slow down the transit time of the bowels, making it difficult to pass stools and further worsening the constipation. Chronic stretching of the anal and intestinal muscles can also make the nerves of the anus and rectum less responsive to the presence of stool in the rectum.

Loss of control can also be caused by loss of function following spinal injury, brain injury, back surgery or stroke.

How to Minister: (All commands done in Jesus' name).

1. Command the nerves and muscles in the effected area to operate properly.
2. Command any irritation/infection to leave.
3. Lead them in prayer to lay stress, cares and worries on the Altar of God.

INCURABLE DISEASES

This includes any disease in which doctors cannot find the cure.

How to Minister: (All commands done in Jesus' name).
1. Cast out the spirit of whatever disease is involved.
2. Speak healing or new parts into the body.
3. Lead them in a prayer of repentance, if necessary.
4. Lead them in a prayer of repentance to break word curses.

INDIGESTION (See GERDS).

INFECTION

Any infection caused by numerous organisms (such as bacteria, viruses, fungi or parasites).

How to Minister: (All commands done in Jesus' name).
1. Rebuke the infection.
2. Command the body to be healed and restored to normal condition and function.
3. Command the immune system to work properly.
4. Lead them in a prayer of repentance, if necessary.
5. Command the electrical and magnetic frequencies to be in harmony and balance.

INFERTILITY

Infertility is the inability to achieve a pregnancy after twelve months of unprotected intercourse. Primary infertility describes a couple that has never been able to conceive a pregnancy. The term secondary Infertility describes couples who have previously been pregnant at least once, but have not been able to achieve another pregnancy.

Causes of Infertility include a wide range of physical as well as emotional factors. Approximately 30% to 40% of all Infertility is due to a "male" factor, such as retrograde ejaculation, impotence, hormone deficiency, environmental pollutants, scarring from sexually transmitted disease, or decreased sperm count. Some factors affecting sperm count are heavy marijuana use or use of prescription drugs such as cimetidine, spironolactone, and nitrofurantoin.

A "female" factor is responsible for 40% to 50% of Infertility in couples. This can be scarring from sexually transmitted disease or endometriosis, ovulation dysfunction, poor nutrition, hormone imbalance, ovarian cysts, pelvic infection, tumor, or a transport system abnormality from the cervix through the fallopian tubes. The remaining 10% to 30% may be caused by contributing factors from both partners, or by no cause that can be identified.

How to Minister: (All commands done in Jesus' name).
**Before praying, confirm they are married.

1. Command the pelvis to be adjusted.
2. Command the reproductive system to function normally.
3. Lead them in a prayer of repentance for generational curses.
4. Lead them in a prayer for ungodly covenants.
5. Say, "Father, Your Word says the womb of Your children shall not be barren, and You will make the barren woman the joyful mother of many children."

INFLUENZA (See Flu).

INSOMNIA (See also Sleep Disorders).

Sleeping problems, called Insomnia, can take several forms:

- Difficulty falling asleep when you first go to bed at night
- Waking up too early in the morning
- Waking up frequently throughout the night

All types of Insomnia can lead to daytime drowsiness, poor concentration, and the inability to feel refreshed and rested in the morning. Everyone has an occasional sleepless night which is not a problem for most people. However, as many as 25% of Americans report occasional sleeping problems, and Insomnia is a chronic problem for about 10% of the population. In these cases, the lack of restful sleep impairs the person's ability to carry out daily responsibilities because they are too tired or they have trouble concentrating.

Most adults do best with about eight hours of sleep each night until age sixty, after which six hours may be adequate. Even though the elderly need less sleep, almost one half of people over sixty experience some degree of insomnia. The best measure of the amount of sleep needed is how you feel. If you awaken feeling refreshed, you are getting enough sleep.

Using long-acting or high-dose sedatives as a "cure" for Insomnia can make the problem worse, not better, over time. Antihistamines (the main ingredient in over-the-counter sleeping pills) can lead to similar difficulties. Using antihistamines over time may also lead to reversible memory impairment.

Strong, prescription sedatives do not produce a natural, restful sleep. In addition, you can develop tolerance or dependence on these drugs. In this case, the same dose of the drug no longer produces sleep, which may lead you to try a higher dose. The circular situation becomes worse. Higher doses worsen the chance of dependence, tolerance, and side effects. Stopping these medications can cause a rebound insomnia and withdrawal.

How to Minister: (All commands done in Jesus' name).

1. Lead them in a prayer of repentance, if necessary.

2. Command the sleep center of the brain to operate normally.
3. Lead them in a prayer to lay all cares, stress and worries on the Altar of God.
4. Repent for not taking a Sabbath's days rest, if necessary.

IRRITABLE BOWEL SYNDROME (IBS)

Irritable Bowel Syndrome refers to a complex disorder of the lower intestinal tract which is often worsened by emotional stress. The condition involves hypersensitivity to pain in the gut, combined with altered bowel habits resulting in gas, bloating, and alternating bouts of diarrhea and constipation.

Irritable Bowel Syndrome (IBS) can occur at any age, but often begins in adolescence or early adulthood. It is more common in women. The exact cause is uncertain. Predisposing factors may include a low-fiber diet, emotional stress, use of laxatives, a bout of infectious diarrhea, or other temporary bowel inflammation.

How to Minister: (All commands done in Jesus' name).
1. Command the intestines to be at peace and all irritation to leave.
2. Command the intestines to function normally.
3. Lead them in a prayer of repentance, if necessary.
4. Lead them in prayer to lay all stress, cares, and worries on the Altar of God.

JAW (Dislocated, Fractured or Broken Jaw):

Broken or dislocated jaw is a facial injury that results in the jaw bone breaking or moving out of position.

How to Minister: (All commands done in Jesus' name).
1. Command the joint with its cartilage, ligaments, tendons, and tissues to be healed and work normally.
2. If a bone is out of joint, command it to go back into the socket and stay there.
3. Lead them in a prayer for repentance to break word curses.
4. Command the neck to come into alignment.

KELOIDS (See Scars, Keloids and Adhesions).

KIDNEY DISEASE

Kidney Disease is classified as any disease or disorder that affects the function of the kidneys.

How to Minister: (All commands done in Jesus' name).
1. Command a new pair of kidneys to operate and function normally.
2. Command healing for underlying causes such as disease, high blood pressure, diabetes or infections.
3. Command any pain or discomfort to leave.
4. Command the pelvis to come into alignment.

Kidney Stones

Kidney Stones is a condition in which one or more stones are present in the pelvis or center of the kidney or in the ureter (tube leading from kidney to bladder to pass urine out of the body).

Kidney Stone formation may result when the urine becomes overly concentrated with certain substances. Kidney Stones are common. About 5% of women and 10% of men will have at least one episode by age seventy. Kidney Stones affect about two out of every thousand people. Recurrence is common, and the risk of recurrence is greater if two or more episodes of kidney stones occur. Kidney stones are common in premature infants. A personal or family history of stones is associated with increased risk of stone formation.

How to Minister: (All commands done in Jesus' name).

1. Lead them in a prayer of repentance for generational curses.
2. Command the stones to dissolve and pass out of the body.
3. Command the pain to go.
4. Command the kidneys and all damaged tissues to be healed and restored to normal function.

Kidney Failure (Also called End-Stage Renal Disease or Renal Failure).

Acute renal failure is a sudden loss of the ability of the kidneys to function normally; however it may be reversible. Chronic renal failure is a gradual and progressive loss of the ability of the kidneys to excrete wastes, concentrate urine, and conserve electrolytes. Chronic renal failure often leads to End Stage Renal Disease which affects more than 2 out of 1,000 people in the United States. Diabetes and hypertension are the two most common causes and account for approximately two thirds of the cases of chronic renal failure and ESRD (End-Stage Renal Disease).

Numerous serious complications result from this condition. Dialysis is the immediate treatment with kidney transplant as a possible necessity.

How to Minister: (All commands done in Jesus' name).

1. Command a creative miracle or "new kidneys" into the body.
2. Cast out the spirit of death.
3. Command the electrical and magnetic frequencies to be in harmony and balance.

4. Command all the excess fluid and impurities to leave the body.
5. Lead them in a prayer of repentance for generational curses.
6. Command other body parts that have been affected by the kidney disease/damage to be healed and function normally.

KNEECAP PROBLEMS

These problems can be caused by disease, trauma or developmental problems. A dislocated Kneecap is when the triangular bone covering the knee (patella) moves or slides out of place (displacement) usually towards the outside of the leg.

Dislocated Kneecaps most often occur in women with certain anatomic features of the knee, which predispose them to this condition. It is usually a result of sudden directional changes while running which puts the knee under stress. Dislocation may also occur as a direct result of injury.

How to Minister: (All commands done in Jesus' name).

1. Where arthritis is involved, cast out the spirit of arthritis.
2. Lay hands on the affected area, commanding all the tendons, ligaments, muscles, cartilage and tissues, to be healed; the blood and fluid to lubricate the area to be restored.
3. Command a new Kneecap, if needed.
4. Lead them in a prayer of repentance for generational curses.

KNOCK-KNEED

When a person is Knock-kneed, the lower legs are at an outward angle, the knees are touching, and the ankles are separated.

Most children develop a slight Knock-kneed stance by the time they are two or three years of age, often with significant separation at the ankles when the knees are touching. This is part of normal development and often persists through age five or six, at which time the legs begin to straighten fully. By puberty, most children can stand with the knees and ankles touching (without forcing the position).

How to Minister: (All commands done in Jesus' name).

1. Commanding the pelvic bone to rotate outward, do the pelvis adjustment.
2. Grow out the legs.
3. Command the legs and knees to straighten.
4. Lead them in a prayer of repentance for generational curses.

LARYNGITIS

Laryngitis is an inflammation of your voice box (larynx) due to overuse, irritation or infection. Inside the larynx are your vocal cords which normally open and close smoothly forming sounds through their movement and vibration. But when your vocal cords become inflamed or irritated, they swell, causing distortion of the sounds produced by air passing over them. As a result, your voice sounds hoarse. In some cases, your voice can become so faint as to be undetectable. Laryngitis may be short-lived (acute) or long-lasting (chronic). Although acute Laryngitis usually is nothing more than an irritation, persistent hoarseness can signal a more serious problem.

Laryngitis often makes you feel the need to constantly clear your throat. Other signs and symptoms may include: hoarseness, weak voice, tickling sensation and rawness of your throat, sore or dry throat. Usually, a viral infection causes acute laryngitis, however, a bacterial infection also may be the cause,.

Acute laryngitis may also occur during the course of or after another illness, such as a cold, flu or pneumonia.

Common causes of chronic Laryngitis include constant irritation from excessive alcohol, heavy smoking or reflux of stomach acid into the esophagus and throat, a condition called Gastroesophageal Reflux Disease. The following factors place you at greater risk of developing laryngitis:

- Having a respiratory infection, such as a cold, influenza, bronchitis or sinusitis.
- Exposure to irritating substances, such as cigarette smoke, excessive alcohol, stomach acid or workplace chemicals.
- Overusing your voice, by speaking too much, speaking too loudly, shouting or singing over an extended period of time.

How to Minister: (All commands done in Jesus' name).

1. Curse the root of any viral or bacterial infection.
2. Lead them in a prayer of repentance to break word curses.
3. Command the inflammation or irritation to go.
4. Command all the tissues of the throat to function normally and be totally healed.

LAZY EYE (See Amblyopia).

LEUKEMIA

Leukemia is not one disease but actually a group of closely-related diseases that all affect bone marrow cells and its function. Since blood is manufactured within the bone marrow, Leukemia affects our blood cell production. These diseases can cause varying symptoms and manifestations. Treatments can be tailored for the characteristics of the Leukemia. Different types of Leukemia have different prognoses. It can occur at any age.

It is considered to be a type of cancer in which white blood cells displace normal blood. This leads to infection, shortage of red blood cells (anemia), bleeding, and other disorders, and often proves fatal.

Acute Leukemia causes an abnormal buildup of immature cells in the bone marrow. This condition lowers a patient's red blood count and can cause symptoms such as: fever, infections, fatigue, shortness of breath and/or bleeding. Often the immature cells in the bone marrow can enter the bloodstream and elevate the white blood count. Once acute Leukemia is diagnosed, it usually requires prompt treatment. If left untreated, acute Leukemia can be fatal in a matter of weeks or months, depending on the patient's situation. However, advances in treatment during the past 40 years have shown that acute Leukemia is treatable and often curable.

How to Minister: (All commands done in Jesus' name).

1. Curse the root of the Leukemia and cast out the spirit of death.
2. Lead them in a prayer of repentance for generational curses.
3. Lead them in a prayer of repentance for bitterness or unforgiveness, if necessary.
4. Command electrical and magnetic frequencies to be in harmony and balance.
5. Curse any prions and command them to dissolve and be discarded.
6. Command the marrow to make the proper amount of white blood cells.

LIGAMENTS (Torn or Damaged)

Ligaments connect bones or cartilage at a joint or support an organ, muscle or other body part. Since ligaments are located throughout the body, this type of injury can be located anywhere; however, the most common sites of injury are the joints of the arms, legs, shoulders, hips or back. This condition is usually caused by twisting, excessive stretching or some form of trauma.

How to Minister: (All commands done in Jesus' name).
1. Rebuke any infection or inflammation.
2. Do the adjustment necessary: grow out the arms or legs; adjust the neck, back and / or pelvis.
3. Lead them in a prayer of repentance, if necessary.
4. Command the ligaments to be healed and restored to normal function.

LIGHTHEADEDNESS (See Dizziness, Vertigo).

LOU GEHRIG'S DISEASE
(See Amyotrophic Lateral Sclerosis. Also called ALS.)

LUMPS (Also see Tumors)
Abnormal growths found in or on the body.

How to Minister: (All commands done in Jesus' name).
1. Curse the core, root, and cause of the lump.
2. Lay hands on the affected area commanding the lump to dissolve and disappear.
3. Command all tissues to be healed and restored.
4. Lead them in a prayer of repentance, if necessary.

LUNG DISEASE
(Also see Asthma, Emphysema, COPD, Pleurisy, and Pneumonia)

Lung Disease is any disease or disorder where lung function is impaired. There are three major physiologic categories of lung diseases:

1. Obstructive lung disease -- a decrease in the exhaled air flow caused by a narrowing or

blockage of the airways, such as with asthma, emphysema, COPD and Chronic Bronchitis.
2. Restrictive lung disease -- a decrease in the total volume of air that the lungs are able to hold. Often, this is due to a decrease in the elasticity of the lungs themselves or caused by a problem related to the expansion of the chest wall during inhalation.
3. A defect in the ability of the lung's air sac tissue to move oxygen into a person's blood.

Most Lung Diseases actually involve a combination of these categories, such as Emphysema, which involves both airflow obstruction and oxygenation problems.

How to Minister: (All commands done in Jesus' name).
1. Command new lungs and new organs that may have been damaged.
2. Command the air sacs to open, excess fluid to dry up, or whatever symptoms that need healing.
3. Lead them in a prayer for repentance, if necessary.
4. Command the electrical and magnetic frequencies to be in harmony and balance.

LUPUS ERYTHEMATOSUS

With Lupus the body attacks itself and can affect many organs in the body including the skin, kidneys, and joints. Systemic Lupus Erythematosus (SLE) is a chronic, inflammatory autoimmune disorder. It may affect many organ systems including the skin, joints, and internal organs.

Normally, the immune system controls the body's defenses against infection. In SLE and other autoimmune diseases, these defenses are turned against the body and rogue immune cells attack tissues. Antibodies may be produced that can react against the body's blood cells, organs and tissues. These lead immune cells to attack the affected systems, producing a chronic (long-term) disease.

The mechanism or cause of autoimmune diseases is not fully known, but many researchers suspect it occurs following infection with an organism that looks similar to particular proteins in the body, which are later mistaken for the organism and wrongly targeted for attack.

The disease affects nine times as many women as men. It may occur at any age, but appears most often in people between ten and fifty years of age.

How to Minister: (All commands done in Jesus' name).

1. Cast out the spirit of Lupus.
2. Command the immune system and all affected organs to be healed and to function normally.
3. Lead them in a prayer of repentance for generational curses.
4. Command the electrical and magnetic frequencies to be in harmony and in balance.

LYMPHEDEMA (See Edema).

MACULAR DEGENERATION

Macular Degeneration is a disorder that affects the macula (the central part of the retina of the eye) causing decreased visual acuity and possible loss of central vision. The macula is the part of the retina that allows the eye to see fine details at the center of the field of vision.

This disorder results in the loss of central vision only while peripheral fields are maintained. Although loss of ability to read and drive may be caused by Macular Degeneration, the disease does not lead to complete blindness.

The disease becomes increasingly common among people over fifty years of age. By age 75, almost 15% of men and women have this condition. Other risk factors are family history, cigarette smoking, and being Caucasian.

How to Minister: (All commands done in Jesus' name).
1. Lay hands over the eyes. Speak a creative miracle and command a new retina and the macula to be totally restored.
2. Lead in the prayer of repentance for generational curses.
3. Command the blood filters in the eyes to work properly.

MARRIAGE PROBLEMS

Marriage problems include but are not limited to: a lack of sexual intimacy, exploding during an argument, getting too emotional and letting your temper get the best of you, being selfish, being dishonest, excessive teasing, not respecting your spouse, not being attentive to your spouse, not listening to your spouse, infidelity, breakdown in communications, abuse and / or financial difficulties.

How to Minister: (All commands done in Jesus' name).
1. Have each one cancel the debt the other owes them.
2. Lead them in prayers of forgiveness.
3. Have each one offer their heart without conditions.
4. Instruct them to seek Godly counsel from Christians with successful marriages.

MASTITIS (See Cystic Disease).

MENIERE'S DISEASE (Also see Dizziness and Vertigo).

Meniere's Disease is a disorder of the inner ear affecting balance and hearing, characterized by sudden abnormal sensation of movement (vertigo) lasting thirty minutes or longer, dizziness, fluctuating hearing loss, or fullness in one or both ears, and noises such as buzzing or ringing in the ear (tinnitus).

The fluid-filled semicircular canals of the inner ear, in conjunction with the cranial nerve VIII, control balance and sense of body position. Meniere's Disease involves a swelling of part of the canal. The exact cause of Meniere's Disease is unknown. In some cases, it may be related to middle ear infection, syphilis, head injury, viral illness, respiratory infection, stress, fatigue, use of prescription or nonprescription drugs including aspirin, a history of allergies, smoking, or alcohol use. There may be genetic risk factors as well.

How to Minister: (All commands done in Jesus' name).
1. Cast out the spirit of Meniere's Disease.
2. Command the inner ear to be healed, the nerves and blood flow to the inner ear to be normal, normal hearing to return and all dizziness stop.

MENOPAUSE

Menopause is the transition period in a woman's life when her ovaries stop producing eggs, her body produces less estrogen and progesterone, and menstruation becomes less frequent, eventually stopping altogether. Menopause is a natural event that normally occurs between the ages of 45 and 55. Once Menopause is complete (called postmenopausal), a woman can no longer become pregnant.

The symptoms of Menopause are caused by changes in estrogen and progesterone levels. As the ovaries become less functional, they produce less of these hormones and the body responds accordingly. The specific symptoms a woman will experience and how significant (mild, moderate, or severe) varies from woman to woman.

In some women, menstrual flow comes to a sudden halt. More commonly, it tapers off. During this time, menstrual periods generally become irregular. This irregularity may last for one to three years before Menstruation finally ends completely. A gradual decrease of estrogen generally allows the body to slowly adjust to the hormonal changes. When estrogen drops suddenly, as is seen when the ovaries are removed surgically (called surgical menopause), symptoms can be more severe.

How to Minister: (All commands done in Jesus' name).

1. Command all the symptoms (hot flashes, sweats, etc.) to go.
2. Command the hormones to be in balance.
3. Command the electrical and magnetic frequencies to be in harmony and balance.
4. Lead them in a prayer of repentance for generational curses.
5. Command the pelvis to come into alignment.

MENSTRUAL PAIN (Dysmenorrhea).

Painful Menstruation is when menstrual periods are accompanied by either sharp, intermittent or dull, aching pain usually in the pelvis or lower abdomen. Painful Menstruation affects many women. For a small number of women, such discomfort makes it next to impossible to perform normal household, job, or school-related activities for a few days during each menstrual cycle. Painful Menstruation is the leading cause of lost time from school and work among women in their teens and 20's.

Although some discomfort during Menstruation is normal, excessive pain is not. Dysmenorrhea refers to Menstrual Pain severe enough to limit normal activities or require medication. It may be accompanied by nausea, vomiting, constipation or diarrhea. There are two general types of dysmenorrhea:

- Primary dysmenorrhea refers to Menstrual Pain that occurs in otherwise healthy women and is not related to any specific problems with the uterus or other pelvic organs.
- Secondary dysmenorrhea is Menstrual Pain that is attributed to some underlying disease process or structural abnormality either within or outside the uterus.

Activity of the hormone prostaglandin, produced in the uterus, is thought to be a factor in primary dysmenorrhea. This hormone causes contraction of the uterus and levels tend to be much higher in women with severe Menstrual Pain than in women who experience mild or no Menstrual Pain.

How to Minister: (All commands done in Jesus' name).

1. Lead them in a prayer of repentance for generational curses.
2. Command the pelvis to go into alignment.
3. Command the hormones to be in balance.
4. Command all pain to leave.

MENTAL ILLNESS (Also see Depression, Schizophrenia, Bipolar Disorder, and Psychosis).

Mental Illness refers to the presence of a severe psychiatric disorder that causes untypical behavior (including but not limited to schizophrenia, dementia, major depression, and bipolar disorder) accompanied by significant functional impairment, disruption of normal life tasks, periods of hospitalization to total disability. It can affect men and women of all ages, races and socio-economic levels. Although the exact cause of most mental illnesses is not known, it is becoming clear through research that many of these conditions are caused by a combination of genetic, biological, psychological and environmental factors. With proper treatment, affected people can still lead normal lives.

How to Minister: (All commands done in Jesus' name).
1. Command the spirit of Mental Illness to come out.
2. Lead them in a prayer of repentance for generational curses.
3. If caused by an accident or injury, command new nerves and a new brain that will function perfectly.
4. If a chemical disorder, command the production of proper chemicals in normal amounts.
5. Curse any prions. Command them to be dissolved.
6. Command the electrical and magnetic frequencies to be in harmony and balance.

MIGRAINE (See Headaches).

MONGOLISM (See Down Syndrome).

MONONUCLEOSIS (Also called "Kissing Disease").

Infectious Mononucleosis (mono) or glandular fever is often called the kissing disease because kissing can spread the virus that causes this disease, but more commonly coughing, sneezing, or sharing a glass or cup transmits Mononucleosis. It's not highly contagious. Mononucleosis is caused by the Epstein-Barr virus. Full-blown Mononucleosis is most common in adolescents and young adults.

Symptoms include a severe sore throat, painful swallowing, fatigue, weakness, swollen lymph nodes, headache, fever, and tender spleen.

Mono usually isn't very serious, although the virus remains in your body for life. Most people have been exposed to the Epstein-Barr virus by the time they are 35 years of age and have built up antibodies. They're immune and won't get Mononucleosis again; however, the lasting effects of exhaustion can remain for months.

Mononucleosis can also result in complications such as Anemia, inflammation of the heart, Meningitis, Encephalitis, Seizures, Bell's palsy, Guillain-Barré Syndrome and swollen tonsils leading to obstructed breathing.

How to Minister: (All commands done in Jesus' name).

1. Command the virus and all the symptoms to go.
2. Command the immune system to function normally.
3. Command the electrical and magnetic frequencies to be in harmony and balance.
4. Command all body systems to return to normal including all circulation, nerve function, muscle strength and endurance levels.

MOTION SICKNESS

Motion Sickness (also known as car sickness, sea sickness, or air sickness) occurs when two "motion messages" to the brain conflict. One "motion message" comes from the inner ear that controls balance and another "motion message" comes from the eyes. During changes in position caused by travel, these two "motion messages" conflict thereby causing Motion Sickness. Motion Sickness is usually caused by riding in a car, boat, airplane or any other passive locomotion. Motion Sickness can also be caused by motion in the visual surroundings while standing still (viewing a large screen movie that contains significant motion). It can strike suddenly, progressing from a feeling of restlessness to a cold sweat, dizziness, vertigo and then vomiting.

How to Minister: (All commands done in Jesus' name).

1. Lead them in a prayer of repentance for generational curses.
2. Command the inner ear to adjust to movements.
3. Command the nerve messages from the eyes and ears to be in balance.
4. Command the dizziness and/or vertigo to go.

MULTIPLE SCLEROSIS (MS)

Multiple Sclerosis is a disorder of the brain and spinal cord (central nervous system) caused by progressive damage to the outer covering of nerve cells. This results in decreased nerve functioning, which can lead to a variety of symptoms including extreme weakness with increasing loss of control of muscles and other bodily functions.

The cause of MS is unknown. The disease involves repeated episodes of inflammation of nervous tissue in any area of the brain and spinal cord. These episodes occur when the body's immune cells attack the nervous system. The location of the inflamed areas varies from person to person and from episode to episode. The inflammation destroys the covering of the nerve cells in that area, leaving multiple areas of scar tissue (sclerosis). This results in slowing or blocking of the transmission of nerve impulses in that area, leading to the symptoms of MS. An increase in the number of immune cells in the body of a person with MS indicates that there may be a type of immune response that triggers the disorder.

How to Minister: (All commands done in Jesus' name).

1. Cast out the spirit of Multiple Sclerosis
2. Lead them in a prayer of repentance for generational curses.
3. Command the immune system to react normally.

4. Command healing and normal function to all parts of the body that have been affected by the disease.
5. Command the electrical and magnetic frequencies to be in harmony and balance.

MUSCULAR DYSTROPHY (MD)

Muscular Dystrophy is a group of disorders characterized by progressive muscle weakness and loss of muscle tissue leading to total disability and loss of function of most bodily functions.

These disorders are distinguished from each other by the type of inheritance (sex-linked, dominant gene, recessive gene), the age when symptoms appear, and the types of symptoms that develop. Because these are inherited disorders, risks include a family history of Muscular Dystrophy.

How to Minister: (All commands done in Jesus' name).
1. Cast out the spirit of Muscular Dystrophy.
2. Lead them in a prayer of repentance for generational curses.
3. Command the electrical and magnetic frequencies to be in harmony and balance.
4. Command all the muscles to return to normal and all damaged affected tissues to be healed.

MYASTHENIA GRAVIS

Myasthenia Gravis is a neuromuscular disorder characterized by variable weakness of voluntary muscles, which often improves with rest and worsens with activity. The condition is caused by an abnormal immune response. In Myasthenia Gravis, weakness occurs when the nerve impulse to initiate or sustain movement does not adequately reach the muscle cells.

This is caused when immune cells target and attack the body's own cells (an autoimmune response). This immune response produces antibodies that attach to affected areas, preventing muscle cells from receiving chemical messages (neurotransmitters) from the nerve cell.

The cause of autoimmune disorders such as Myasthenia Gravis is unknown. In some cases, Myasthenia Gravis may be associated with tumors of the thymus (an organ of the immune system).

How to Minister: (All commands done in Jesus' name).
1. Cast out the spirit of Myasthenia Gravis.
2. Command the nerve receptors on the muscles to be healed and function normally.
3. Command the immune system to be restored and function normally.
4. Command the electrical and magnetic frequencies to be in harmony and balance.

MYOPIA (See Nearsightedness).

NAIL BITING

Onychophagia is the clinical term for chronic nail biting. This behavior (habit) often starts in childhood and can be exacerbated by stress.

How to Minister: (All commands done in Jesus' name).
1. Lead them in a prayer of repentance for generational curses.
2. Lead in a prayer to lay all cares, stress and worries on the Altar of God.
3. Instruct them to break the habit by repeating (each time they want to start biting their nails) "I will not participate in onychophagia." (on-i-ko-FAY-jee-uh)

NARCOLEPSY (See Sleep Disorders).

NASAL CONGESTION (See Nose).

NEARSIGHTEDNESS (Also known as Myopia).

Nearsightedness is an error of visual focusing that makes distant objects appear blurred. A nearsighted person sees near objects clearly, while objects in the distance are blurred. As a result, someone with Myopia tends to squint when viewing far away objects.

It occurs when the physical length of the eye is greater than the optical length. For this reason, Nearsightedness often develops in the rapidly growing school-aged child or teenager and progresses during the growth years, requiring frequent changes in glasses or contact lenses. It usually stops progressing as growth is completed in the early twenties.

Nearsightedness affects males and females equally, and those with a family history of Nearsightedness are more likely to develop it.

How to Minister: (All commands done in Jesus' name).

1. Lay hands on the eyes, commanding the lens, nerves, ligaments and muscles to be adjusted and work properly.
2. Command perfect sight to be restored.
3. Lead them in a prayer of repentance, if necessary.

NECK PAIN

Neck Pain may originate from any of the structures in the neck. These include muscles and nerves as well as spinal vertebrae and the cushioning discs in between the vertebrae. Neck pain may also come from regions near the neck, like the shoulder, jaw, head, and upper arms.

When your neck is sore, you may have difficulty moving it, especially to one side. Many people describe this as having a stiff neck. If Neck Pain involves nerves (for example, a significant muscle spasm pinching on a nerve or a slipped disc pressing on a nerve), numbness, tingling, or weakness in the arm, hand, or elsewhere may be felt.

Common Neck Pain is from muscle strain or tension. Usually, everyday activities are responsible. Such activities include bending over a desk for hours, having poor posture while watching TV or reading, placing a computer monitor too high or too low, sleeping in an uncomfortable position, or twisting and turning the neck in a jarring manner while exercising.

Traumatic accidents or falls can cause severe neck injuries like vertebral fractures, whiplash, blood vessel destruction, and even paralysis. Other causes include a herniated disc, Fibromyalgia (pain syndrome throughout the body), and Arthritis. Meningitis, although much less common, can cause significant neck stiffness.

How to Minister: (All commands done in Jesus' name).

1. Command the neck to come into alignment.
2. Command vertebrae, discs, muscles, ligaments, nerves, and tendons to be healed and to go back into normal position.
3. Lead them in a prayer to lay cares, worries and stress on the Altar of God.

NERVOUSNESS (See Fear and Anxiety).

NIGHTMARES

A nightmare is a dream occurring during rapid eye movement (REM) sleep that brings out feelings of strong, inescapable fear, terror, distress, or extreme anxiety. They typically occur in the latter part of the night and usually awaken the sleeper, who is able to recall the content of the dream.

Nightmares tend to be more common among children and decrease in frequency toward adulthood. About 50% of adults experience occasional nightmares, women more often than men. They can stem from previous severe trauma or abuse.

How to Minister: (All commands done in Jesus' name).

1. Lead them in a prayer of repentance for generational curses.
2. Lead them in a prayer of repentance for demonic entertainment, TV, and/or movies.
3. Speak peace to them.

NOSE PROBLEMS (Also see Colds, Allergies, Flu and Sinus Problems).

This includes all problems with the nose including nasal congestion; congested sinuses, or a runny nose. Many people think that a nose gets congested (stuffy) from too much thick mucus. Actually, a congested nose develops when the membranes lining the nose become swollen from inflamed blood vessels. Congestion is often a symptom of colds, allergies, sinus infections, and the flu. Overuse of some nasal sprays or drops can also lead to congestion.

How to Minister: (All commands done in Jesus' name).

1. Lead them in a prayer of repentance for generational curses.
2. Curse the root cause (allergies, chronic infection, etc.) and command healing of the affected areas.
3. Command the nasal passages to remain open and to drain properly.
4. Command the immune system to work properly.

Nose Injury

A nose fracture is a break in the bone over the bridge of the nose. The most common facial fracture, it usually results from a blunt injury and is often associated with other facial fractures. The bruised appearance usually disappears after two weeks.

Sometimes, as a result of a blunt injury, the septum (wall dividing the nostrils) can separate. The symptoms may be the same as a fractured nose. Injury to the nose can also leave a deviated septum which makes one air passage larger than the other. In some cases, this can cause problems with breathing normally through the nose. Nose injuries and neck injuries are often seen together because a blow that is forceful enough to injure the nose may be hard enough to injure the neck.

How to Minister: (All commands done in Jesus' name).

1. Lay your finger on the nose and gently run it down the crest, commanding it to be straight, structures to be regenerated and to function normally.
2. Do the neck adjustment.
3. Cast out the spirit of fear, if necessary

NUMBNESS

Numbness and tingling are abnormal sensations that can occur anywhere in the body, but most often affect the hands, feet, arms or legs.

There are many possible causes:

- Remaining in the same seated or standing position for a long time.
- Injuring a nerve supplying the body part where the sensation occurs. With a neck injury, for example, the sensation may be felt anywhere along the arm or hand. Similarly, a low back injury can cause sciatica -- a sensation of numbness or tingling down the back of a leg.
- Lack of blood supply to the area. For example, plaque buildup from atherosclerosis in the legs can cause pain, numbness, and tingling while walking.
- Pressure on the spinal nerves from a herniated disk.

- Carpal tunnel syndrome which can cause numbness or tingling in your wrist, fingers, hand, or forearm.
- Certain medical conditions including diabetes, underactive thyroid, multiple sclerosis, seizures, or migraine headaches.
- Abnormal levels of calcium, potassium, or sodium in your body.
- Vitamin B-12 deficiency.
- Transient Ischemic Attack (TIA) or stroke (CVA)
- Certain medications.
- Toxic action on nerves from chemicals such as lead, alcohol or tobacco.
- Radiation therapy.

How to Minister: (All commands done in Jesus' name).

1. Command any disease process to go.
2. Command the discs and vertebrae of the back to return to normal position, pressure on the nerves to be released, and the nerves to function normally.
3. Command the electrical and chemical functions of the nervous system to function normally.
4. Command the blood to flow normally throughout the body.
5. Command the electrical and magnetic frequencies to be in harmony and balance.
6. Command all numbness and tingling to go.

OBESITY

More than half of the U.S. population is overweight. But being obese is different from being overweight. An adult male is considered obese when his weight is 20% or more over the maximum desirable for their height; a woman is considered obese at 25% or more than this maximum weight. Anyone more than 100 pounds overweight is considered morbidly obese.

Obesity increases a person's risk of illness and death due to diabetes, stroke, coronary artery disease, hypertension, high cholesterol, and kidney and gallbladder disorders. Obesity may increase the risk for some types of cancer. It is also a risk factor for the development of osteoarthritis and sleep apnea.

Genetic factors play some part in the development of Obesity. Children of obese parents are ten times more likely to be obese than children with parents of normal weight.

How to Minister: (All commands done in Jesus' name).

1. Lead them in a prayer of repentance for generational curses.
2. Lead them in a prayer of repentance for lifestyle or diet, if necessary.
3. Command healing of thyroid or other responsible organ.
4. Lay hands on the head and command the "Appestat" (appetite control center) to be readjusted to the normal level and the weight to return to a correct and healthy range.
5. Lead them in a prayer to lay all cares, stress and worries on the Altar of God.
6. Command the metabolism to function normally and the person's weight to be within healthy boundaries.

OBSESSIVE-COMPULSIVE DISORDER (OCD)

Obsessive-Compulsive Disorder is an anxiety disorder characterized by obsessions or compulsions. Having one or both is sufficient for the diagnosis. Obsessions are unwanted intrusive thoughts, ideas, doubts, or impulses that seem inappropriate or senseless yet cause intense distress. Compulsions are urges to repeat behaviors or have certain thoughts in order to decrease anxiety created by obsessions.

Examples of obsessions include:

- Exaggerated fears of contamination from contact with people or everyday items such as door handles or money
- Nagging doubts about having turned off the stove, iron or other appliances
- Overwhelming fears of having made terrible mistakes
- Intrusive thoughts that you did not do enough to prevent something terrible
- Unwanted senseless thoughts about harmful, violent, sexually inappropriate, immoral things
- Persistent feelings that things need to be arranged "just right"
- Persistent fears of throwing away unneeded items (such as bags, junk mail) away

Examples of compulsions include:

- Excessive hand washing, showering, or cleaning with antibacterial products
- Frequent checking of locks, lights, electrical outlets, etc.
- Repeating activities such as writing checks or going through a doorway
- Excessive praying to ensure that one will not commit an unacceptable or immoral action
- Continually seeking assurance from others
- Excessive rearranging
- Repeating special words or phrases to neutralize unacceptable thoughts

The exact cause of OCD is unknown, but several factors play a role. Changes in brain serotonin levels (chemical messengers) and other areas in the brain are thought to contribute to this disorder. Family history and genetic inheritance have been linked to OCD. Stress caused by a serious loss, difficult relationship, job change, financial problem or any other stressful situation can trigger or worsen symptoms.

Childhood infection, such as strep throat, has been associated with OCD in children. Research is ongoing to determine if there is a definite link. Learned habits, such as using compulsive behavior to cope with obsessional fears, is also thought by researchers to play a role in OCD.

How to Minister: (All commands done in Jesus' name).
1. Lead them in a prayer of repentance for generational curses.
2. Cast out the spirit of OCD.
3. Lead them in a prayer of repentance and / or forgiveness, if necessary.
4. Command the prions to dissolve and leave the body.
5. Command the electrical and magnetic frequencies to be in harmony and balance.
6. Lead them in a prayer to lay all cares, stress and worries on the Altar of God.
7. Speak peace to them.

OCCUPATIONAL LUNG DISEASE
(See Chronic Obstructive Pulmonary disease / COPD).

OSTEOARTHRITIS
(Also called Degenerative Joint Disease or DJD)

Osteoarthritis is a chronic disease causing gradual deterioration of the joint cartilage (the softer parts of bones, which cushion their connections to each other) and the formation of new bone (bone spurs) at the margins of the joints.

For most people, the cause of Osteoarthritis is unknown, but metabolic, genetic, chemical, and mechanical factors play a role in its development. It is associated with the aging process and is the most common form of Arthritis. Usually appearing in the mid-fifties, almost everyone has it by the time they reach seventy years of age.

The cartilage of the affected joint is roughened and becomes worn down. As the disease progresses, the cartilage becomes completely worn down and the bone rubs on bone. Bone spurs usually develop around the joints. The joints of the hands and fingers, hips, knees, big toe, and cervical and lumbar spine are commonly affected. The degeneration of the joint may begin as a result of trauma to the joint, occupational overuse, obesity, or mal-alignment of the joints (for example being bow-legged or knock-kneed).

Osteoarthritis can cause mild discomfort to severe debilitating pain with mobility of the joints becoming progressively limited.

How to Minister: (All commands done in Jesus' name).

1. Lead them in a prayer of repentance for generational curses.
2. Cast out the spirit of Osteoarthritis.
3. Command the cartilage to be restored and the joint to be healed.
4. Lead them in a prayer of forgiveness.
5. Command the electrical and magnetic frequencies to be in harmony and balance.

OSTEOPOROSIS

Osteoporosis is the thinning of bone and loss of bone density over time. Osteoporosis is the most common type of bone disease.

Osteoporosis occurs when the body fails to form enough new bone, or when too much old bone is reabsorbed by the body, or both. Calcium and phosphate are two minerals that are essential for normal bone formation. Throughout youth, the body uses these minerals to produce bones. If calcium intake is not sufficient, or if the body does not absorb enough calcium from the diet, bone production and bone tissue may suffer.

The leading causes are a drop in estrogen in women at the time of menopause, and a drop in testosterone in men. Women, especially those over the age of 50, get Osteoporosis more often than men. Other causes include corticosteroid excess from Cushing's Syndrome, hyperthyroidism, hyperparathyroidism, being confined to a bed, and bone cancers.

Researchers estimate that about 20% of American women over the age of 50 have osteoporosis. In addition, another 30% of them have Osteopenia, which is abnormally low bone density that may eventually deteriorate into Osteoporosis, if not treated. Dowager's Hump, (a marked abnormal curving of the spine around the area of the shoulder blade) is due to Osteoporosis changes in the thoracic spine. It may affect men or women. Like most osteoporotic changes, it is often preventable.

How to Minister: (All commands done in Jesus' name).

1. Lead in a prayer of repentance for generational curses.
2. Cast out the spirit of Osteoporosis.
3. Command the body to absorb calcium and other necessary minerals in the body to regenerate new, strong bones.
4. Command the back and sacrum to straighten and all the bones to strengthen.
5. Lead them in a prayer of repentance for forgiveness or to break word curses as needed.
6. Command the pain to go.

OTITIS MEDIA

Otitis Media is an inflammation or infection of the middle ear. Chronic indicates that the symptoms are recurring or persistent. Inflammation or infection of the middle ear occurs when the Eustachian tube to that ear is blocked. The Eustachian tube is the passage from the back of the throat to the middle ear. Chronic Otitis Media occurs when the Eustachian tube becomes blocked repeatedly (or remains blocked for long periods) due to allergies, multiple infections, ear trauma, or swelling of the adenoids.

When the middle ear is actually infected with bacteria (or occasionally, viruses) rather than just inflamed, it is more serious. A chronic ear infection may be the result of an acute ear infection that does not clear completely, or the result of recurrent ear infections. The infection may spread into the mastoid bone behind the ear (mastoiditis), or pressure from fluid build-up may rupture the eardrum or damage the bones of the middle ear.

Ear infections are more common in children because their Eustachian tubes are shorter, narrower, and more horizontal than in adults.

How to Minister: (All commands done in Jesus' name).

1. Rebuke the fungus or infection in the ear.
2. Command the tubes to open and fluid to flow normally.
3. Pray for the neck to go into proper alignment.
4. Command the blood to flow into the inner ear and remove impurities.
5. Lead them in a prayer of repentance for generational curses.
2. Command pain to go, and hearing to return to normal.
4. Command the immune system to work properly.

PALSY (See Parkinson's, Cerebral Palsy, Bell's Palsy).

PANCREATITIS

Pancreatitis is an inflammation (irritation and swelling) or infection of the pancreas which secretes digestive enzymes and the hormones insulin and glucagons.

The various types of Pancreatitis involve irritation, inflammation, and infection of the pancreas. The disorders differ according to whether symptoms develop suddenly or slowly. It usually occurs as a result of alcohol abuse or bile duct obstruction. Viral infection, traumatic injury, pancreatic or common bile duct surgical procedures and certain medications are other causes. Acute Pancreatitis may also be caused by abnormal anatomy of the pancreas, genetic factors, high lipid levels in the blood, and complications of cystic fibrosis.

How to Minister: (All commands done in Jesus' name).

1. Curse the root of any viral or bacterial infection.
2. Lead them in a prayer of repentance to break word curses.
3. Command the pain, inflammation and irritation to go.
4. Command all damaged cells to be healed and normal function returned.

PANIC ATTACKS (Also called Panic Disorder).

Panic Disorder involves repeated, unpredictable attacks of intense fear accompanied by severe anxiety that may last from minutes to hours.

The exact cause of Panic Disorder is unknown. There is an influence of heredity. In addition, Panic Disorder has environmental and learning influences, as it often occurs in family members who are not genetically related to each other. A person with Panic Disorder often lives in fear of another attack and may be reluctant to be alone or to be far from medical assistance.

Symptoms usually begin before the age of 25. Although Panic Disorder may occur in children, it is often not diagnosed until the person is older. People with this condition often undergo medical evaluations for symptoms related to heart attack or other conditions before the diagnosis of Panic Disorder is made.

With Panic Disorder, at least four of the following symptoms abruptly occur within ten minutes and attacks may be followed by at least a month of persistent fear of having another attack.

- Sensation of shortness of breath or smothering
- Dizziness or faintness
- Palpitations or pounding heart
- Trembling or shaking
- Sweating, chills or hot flashes
- Feeling of choking
- Nausea or upset stomach
- Numbness or tingling
- Chest pain or discomfort
- Fear of dying
- Fear of losing control
- Feelings of unreality
- Feelings of detachment

There are often extreme changes in behavior -- at home, school, work, or with family. People with the disorder often worry about the significance of their Panic Attacks - they may think they are "going crazy" or having a heart attack.

How to Minister: (All commands done in Jesus' name).

1. Lead them in a prayer of repentance for generational curses.
2. If possible, find out when it first started and what happened during this time. Minister to the cause.
3. Command the hormones to be in balance and vitamin and mineral absorption to be normal.

4. Lead them in a prayer of repentance, if necessary.
5. Lead them in a prayer to lay all cares, stress, fears and worries on the Altar of God

PARANOID PERSONALITY DISORDER

Paranoid Personality Disorder is a psychiatric condition characterized by extreme distrust and suspicion of others.

Paranoid Personality Disorders are chronic patterns of behavior that cause lasting problems with work and relationships. The cause of Paranoid Personality Disorder is unknown, but it appears to be more common in families with psychotic disorders such as schizophrenia and delusional disorder which suggests a genetic influence.

People with Paranoid Personality Disorder are highly suspicious of other people. They are usually unable to acknowledge their own negative feelings towards other people. Other common symptoms include: concerns that other people have hidden motives, expects others to exploit them, poor self-image, social isolation, detachment and hostility.

How to Minister: (All commands done in Jesus' name).

1. Lead them in a prayer of repentance for generational curses.
2. Cast out the spirit of PPD.
3. Command peace to the brain and to the heart.
4. Command the electrical and magnetic frequencies to be in harmony and balance.
5. Lead them in a prayer to lay all cares, stress, fears and worries on the Altar of God

PARKINSON'S DISEASE

Parkinson's disease is a disorder of the brain characterized by uncontrollable shaking (tremors) and difficulty with walking, movement, and coordination.

The disease is associated with damage to a part of the brain that is involved with movement. It was once called Palsy. Another medical name is Paralysis Agitans.

Parkinsonism may be caused by other disorders or by external factors like certain medications used to treat schizophrenia. Parkinson's Disease is caused by progressive deterioration of the nerve cells of the part of the brain that controls muscle movement. Dopamine, which is one of the substances used by cells to transmit impulses, is normally produced in this area. Deterioration of this area of the brain reduces the amount of dopamine available to the body. Without dopamine, the nerve cells cannot properly transmit messages and these results in the loss of muscle function.

In addition to the loss of muscle control, some people with Parkinson's Disease become severely depressed. This may be due to loss of dopamine in certain brain areas involved with pleasure and mood. Lack of dopamine can also affect motivation and the ability to initiate voluntary movements.

Although early loss of mental capacities is uncommon, with severe Parkinson's the person may exhibit overall mental deterioration.

How to Minister: (All commands done in Jesus' name).

1. Lead them in a prayer of repentance for generational curses.
2. Cast out the spirit of Parkinson's Disease.
3. Command a new brain and nerve tissue that will function normally and produce the correct amount of dopamine.
4. Command healing to all other affected parts of the body.

PERIODONTITIS (Also see Gum Disease).

Periodontitis is a dental disorder that results from progression of gingivitis, involving inflammation and infection of the ligaments and bones that support the teeth. Periodontitis occurs when inflammation or infection of the gums (gingivitis) goes untreated or treatment is delayed. Infection and inflammation spreads from the gums to the ligaments and bone that support the teeth. Loss of support causes the teeth to become loose and eventually fall out.

Periodontitis is the primary cause of tooth loss in adults. This disorder is uncommon in childhood but increases during adolescence. Plaque and tartar accumulate at the base of the teeth. Inflammation causes a pocket to develop between the gums and the teeth, which fills with plaque and tartar. Soft tissue swelling traps the plaque in the pocket. Continued inflammation eventually causes destruction of the tissues and bone surrounding the tooth. Because plaque contains bacteria, infection is likely and a tooth abscess may also develop, which increases the rate of bone destruction.

How to Minister: (All commands done in Jesus' name).
1. Command all infection to go.
2. Command the gums to be healed and tissues restored.
3. Lead them in a prayer or repentance to break word curses.

PHARYNGITIS (See Sore Throat)

PHLEBITIS

Phlebitis is an inflammation of a vein; thrombophlebitis is vein inflammation related to a blood clot within the vein. Risk factors include prolonged sitting and disorders related to blood clotting. Specific disorders associated with thrombophlebitis include superficial phlebitis (affects veins near the skin surface) and Deep Venous Thrombosis (See DVT).

How to Minister: (All commands done in Jesus' name).
1. Command blood clot to dissolve.
2. Command the infection and inflammation to leave and the blood to function normally.
3. Lead them in a prayer of repentance for generational curses.

PIGEON-TOED

This term describes a person with their feet/toes turned inward. It is also called In-toeing. This abnormality can be caused by a rotation of the feet, thigh bone or hip. Babies often appear to be Pigeon-Toed at birth due to their positioning in the womb. It is usually observed in small children who can grow out of it by school age.

How to Minister: (All commands done in Jesus' name).
1. Lead them in a prayer of repentance for generational curses.
2. Command the pelvic bones to rotate outward and into normal position and for the leg bones and foot bones to straighten and go into perfect alignment.

PITUITARY GLAND

The Pituitary Gland is a small growth-influencing gland at the base of the brain in vertebrates, producing hormones that control other glands and influence essential body processes including but not limited to growth of the bone structure, sexual maturing, and general metabolism.

The effects of underfunction of the anterior pituitary include growth retardation (dwarfism) in childhood and a decrease in other endocrine glands.

The results of overfunction of the anterior pituitary include overgrowth (gigantism) in children and a condition called acromegaly in adults. The posterior pituitary secretes the hormone which increases uterine contractions and antidiuretic hormone which increases reabsorption of water by the kidney.

Tumors (overwhelmingly benign), inflammation, infections and injury can cause the gland to malfunction, as well as cancer or spread of other tumors to the pituitary. Radiation therapy to the brain can also cause normal pituitary glands to malfunction Autopsy reports and radiologic and MRI evidence from around the globe indicate that one out of every five people worldwide has a pituitary tumor but are not diagnosed until symptoms occur. There are more than a dozen very different disorders that result from pituitary tumors and disease including but not limited to Cushing's Disease and Addison's Disease.

Pituitary Infarction is the death of an area of tissue in the Pituitary Gland and is most commonly caused by bleeding from a benign tumor on the pituitary which kills an area of tissue.

How to Minister: (All commands done in Jesus' name).

1. If cause is known, minister to the cause.
2. Lay hands on head and command the pituitary gland to function properly and produce normal amounts of hormones.
3. Command all other affected body parts to be healed and function normally.

PLEURISY

Pleurisy is an inflammation of the pleura, the lining surrounding the lungs and may develop in the presence of lung inflammation (pneumonia, flu, tuberculosis), rheumatic diseases, lupus, chest trauma, certain forms of cancer, asbestos-related disease, pancreatitis, blood clot in the lung, trauma to the chest or after heart surgery.

The primary symptom is pain over the chest wall at the site of the inflammation during breathing, coughing, and chest movement. Occasionally, the pain may be felt in the shoulder. Fluid often accumulates at the site of pleural inflammation. A localized collection of fluid separates the lung pleura from the chest wall pleura, causing the chest pain to disappear even though the illness may be worsening. The fluid buildup can interfere with breathing.

How to Minister: (All commands done in Jesus' name).

1. Curse the inflammation and command it to go.
2. Command the fluid to return to normal levels.
3. Command the pain to go and scar tissue to be healed and return to normal tissue.
4. Lead them in a prayer of repentance, if necessary.

PMS (Premenstrual Syndrome) (See Female Problems).

PNEUMONIA

Pneumonia is an inflammation of the lungs caused by an infection. Many different organisms can cause it including bacteria, viruses and fungi. It is a common illness that affects millions of people each year in the United States and more than 60,000 Americans die of Pneumonia every year. The severity depends on the type of organism causing the Pneumonia as well as age and underlying health condition of the person. Pneumonia is a particular concern for older adults and people with chronic illnesses or impaired immune systems, but it also can strike young, healthy people. Worldwide, it's a leading cause of death in children, many of them younger than a year old.

How to Minister: (All commands done in Jesus' name).

1. Curse the infection and command the virus or bacteria to die.
2. Command healing and clearing of the lungs of any excess fluid.
3. Command all scarring to be healed.
4. Lead them in a prayer of repentance, if necessary.
5. Command the electrical and magnetic frequencies to be in harmony and balance.

POLIO, POLIOMYELITIS

Poliomyelitis is a disorder caused by a viral infection (poliovirus) that can affect the whole body, including muscles and nerves leading to loss of voluntary movement and muscular wasting. Severe cases may cause permanent paralysis or death.

Poliomyelitis is a communicable disease caused by infection with the poliovirus. Transmission of the virus occurs by direct person-to-person contact, by contact with infected secretions from the nose or mouth, or by contact with infected feces. The virus enters through the mouth and nose, multiplies in the throat and intestinal tract, and then is absorbed and spread through the blood and lymph system.

In 1979 the last case of Polio occurred in the United States. Today, despite a concerted global eradication campaign, Polio continues to afflict children and adults in other parts of the world, especially west and central Africa as well as India. Precautions are advisable before traveling to certain parts of the world.

Post-polio Syndrome

Affecting people who have recovered from Polio, Post-Polio Syndrome is a cluster of disabling signs and symptoms that appear between 10 and 40 years after the initial illness. Common signs and symptoms include:

- New muscle weakness in limbs that may have been originally affected or in limbs that didn't seem to have been affected at the time
- General fatigue and exhaustion with minimal activity
- Muscle and joint pain
- Breathing or swallowing problems
- Sleep-related breathing disorders, such as sleep apnea
- Decreased tolerance of cold temperatures

How to Minister: (All commands done in Jesus' name).

1. Cast out the spirit of Polio.
2. Command creative miracle to the spinal cord and its damaged nerves, muscles, ligaments, tissues, and tendons to be healed, strengthened, and function normally.

POLYMYOSITIS

Polymyositis is a systemic connective tissue disease characterized by inflammation and degeneration of the muscles especially in the muscles closest to your trunk, such as your shoulder and hip muscles.

The cause of this disorder is unknown. It is thought that an autoimmune reaction or a viral infection of the skeletal muscle may cause the disease. It can affect people at any age, affects women twice as often as men, and more common in black than white people. Polymyositis is rarely fatal, but it can be disabling in its more severe forms.

How to Minister: (All commands done in Jesus' name).

1. Command the immune system to strengthen and function normally.

2. Command new muscles into the body.
3. Command electrical and magnetic frequencies to be in harmony and balance.
4. Lead them in a prayer of forgiveness, if necessary.

POSTPARTUM DEPRESSION (See also Depression).

The first month after birth (the postpartum period) is a time of major change for a new mother. Hormones and weight are rapidly readjusting. Changes in relationships with other children, the father of the baby, parents and in-laws, colleagues at work, and friends are very stressful. The newborn baby's needs often result in mom's sleep deprivation. All of these factors can contribute to postpartum mood swings.

If the moodiness only lasts 2 -3 weeks, it is commonly called the "baby blues" and is experienced by more than half of new mothers. However, if the feelings of depression or anxiety continue more than three weeks, a more serious condition called Post-Partum Depression may exist. About 10% of women experience significant depression after a pregnancy.

How to Minister: (All commands done in Jesus' name).
1. Command the hormones to come into balance.
2. Command the electrical and magnetic frequencies to be in harmony and balance.
3. Lead them in a prayer or repentance to break word curses.
4. Command the spirit of depression to go.
5. Speak peace to them.

POST-TRAUMATIC STRESS DISORDER (PTSD)

Post-Traumatic Stress Disorder is a psychiatric illness that can occur following a traumatic event in which there was threat of injury or death to you or someone else. PTSD may occur soon after a major trauma, or can be delayed for more than six months after the event. When it occurs soon after the trauma it usually resolves after three months, but some people experience a longer-term form of the condition, which can last for many years. PTSD can follow a natural disaster such as flood or fire, or events such as war or imprisonment, assault, domestic abuse, or rape.

The cause of PTSD is unknown but genetic, psychological, physical, and social factors are involved. PTSD alters the body's response to stress by affecting stress hormones and neurotransmitters (chemicals that transmit information between our nerves).

The severity of the traumatic event and how long the event lasted appear to be factors in the development of this disorder. Other factors that may increase the likelihood of developing Post-Traumatic Stress Disorder include:

- A previous history of depression or other emotional disorder
- A previous history of physical or sexual abuse
- A family history of anxiety
- Early separation from parents
- Being part of a dysfunctional family
- Alcohol abuse
- Drug abuse

Having Post-Traumatic Stress Disorder may place a person at a higher risk of:

- Depression which has many of the same signs and symptoms as Post-Traumatic Stress Disorder
- Drug abuse
- Alcohol abuse
- Eating disorders
- Divorce

How to Minister: (All commands done in Jesus' name).

1. Cast out the spirit of fear.

2. Minister to the cause through prayers for repentance, forgiveness and to break word curses.
3. Command the hormones to be in balance.
4. Command the electrical and magnetic frequencies to be in harmony and in balance.
5. Speak peace to them.

PREMENSTRUAL SYNDROME (PMS) (See Female Problems).

PROLAPSED UTERUS

Falling or sliding of the uterus from its normal position in the pelvic cavity into the vaginal canal is called a Prolapsed Uterus. The uterus is normally supported by the pelvic muscle and held in position by special ligaments. Weakening of these tissues allows the uterus to descend into the vaginal canal.

The loss of muscle tone and the relaxation of muscles, which are both associated with normal aging and a reduction in the female hormone estrogen, are also thought to play an important role in the development of Uterine Prolapse. Uterine Prolapse occurs most commonly in women who have had one or more vaginal births.

Obesity places additional strain on the supportive muscles of the pelvis, as does excessive coughing caused by lung conditions such as chronic Bronchitis and Asthma. Chronic constipation and the bearing down associated with it causes weakness in these muscles also.

How to Minister: (All commands done in Jesus' name).
1. Command the muscles and ligaments around the uterus to strengthen, the uterus to go back into place and function normally.
2. Command the pelvis to go into alignment.
3. Command the hormones to be in balance.

4. Lead them in a prayer for repentance, if necessary.

PROSTATE PROBLEMS

The prostate gland produces the fluid that carries sperm during ejaculation.

Prostate enlargement is often called Benign Prostatic Hypertrophy or hyperplasia (BPH). It is not cancerous and it does not put you at increased risk for prostate cancer. The actual cause of prostate enlargement is unknown. In addition to age, overgrowth of the prostate seems to inhibit normal function of the testicles, which produce testosterone.

As the prostate enlarges, which happens to most men as they get older, it can press on the urethra (the tube that empties urine from the bladder) causing problems with urination. The likelihood of developing an enlarged prostate increases with age. A small amount of prostate enlargement is present in many men over age forty and more than 90% of men over age eighty.

How to Minister: (All commands done in Jesus' name).

1. Grow out the legs.
2. Curse the cause of the enlargement.
3. Command the prostate gland to shrink to normal size and to function normally.
4. Command a new prostate when necessary.
5. Command the hormones to be in balance.
6. Command the nerves to work and blood to flow normally.

PSORIASIS

Psoriasis is a common skin inflammation (irritation and swelling) characterized by frequent episodes of redness, itching, and thick, dry, silvery scales on the skin. Psoriasis seems to be an inherited disorder, probably related to an inflammatory response in which the immune system accidentally targets the body's own cells.

Psoriasis may be aggravated by injury or irritation (such as cuts, burns, rashes, insect bites). It may be severe in immunosuppressed people (like those with AIDS or undergoing chemotherapy for cancer), or those who have other autoimmune disorders (such as rheumatoid arthritis).

Medications, viral or bacterial infections, excessive alcohol consumption, obesity, lack of sunlight, sunburn, stress, general poor health, cold climate, and frequent friction on the skin are also associated with flare-ups. The condition is not contagious.

How to Minister: (All commands done in Jesus' name).

1. Lead them in a prayer of repentance for generational curses.
2. Cast out the spirit of Psoriasis.
3. Rebuke the inflammation, itching, and scaling.
4. Lay hands on the affected areas, commanding healthy new skin cells to replace the affected tissues.

PSYCHOSIS

Psychosis is a loss of contact with reality, typically including delusions (false ideas about what is taking place or who one is) and hallucinations (seeing or hearing things which aren't there).

Psychosis is a severe mental condition characterized by a loss of contact with reality. There are numerous potential causes:

- Alcohol and certain drugs can induce Psychosis
- Bipolar disorder (manic depression)
- Brain tumors
- Epilepsy

- Psychotic depression
- Schizophrenia
- Dementia (Alzheimer's and other degenerative brain disorders)
- Stroke, TIA or CVA

How to Minister: (All commands done in Jesus' name).

1. Cast out the spirit of Psychosis.
2. Lead them in a prayer of repentance for idolatry.
3. Command the chemicals and hormones to be in balance.
4. Command any damaged tissues or organs to be healed and function normally.
5. Speak peace to them.

PULMONARY EDEMA

Pulmonary Edema involves fluid accumulation and swelling in the lungs. Pulmonary Edema is usually caused by Congestive Heart Failure that results in increased pressure in the pulmonary (lung) veins. However, problems within the lungs themselves can also result in fluid accumulation.

Pulmonary edema can also be caused by direct lung injury from toxins including heat and poisonous gas, severe infection, or an excess of body fluid as seen in kidney failure.

Common symptoms include severe shortness of breath or difficulty breathing, feeling of suffocating or drowning, wheezing or gasping for breath, and frothy sputum which may be tinged with blood. Drug-induced pulmonary edema is a frequent cause of death in people who abuse narcotics. When not treated, acute Pulmonary Edema can be fatal.

How to Minister: (All commands done in Jesus' name).

1. Command all excessive fluid to leave the lungs.

2. Command the heart and lungs to be strong and healthy.
3. Command any infections to go and any injured tissues to be restored to normal function.
4. Command new lungs and other organs, if necessary.
5. Command the electrical and magnetic frequencies to be in harmony and balance.

RECTAL PROLAPSE

Rectal Prolapse is the abnormal protrusion of the rectal mucosa down to or through the anal opening. When protruding through the anus, prolapse appears as a red mass that may be several inches long. The rectal mucosa is visible and may bleed slightly. Rectal Prolapse occurs predominantly in children under age 6 and in the elderly, especially women. Fecal (stool) incontinence may be the first symptom of Rectal Prolapse.

Many conditions increase the possibility of developing Rectal Prolapse. Risk factors for children include having certain health problems, such as cystic fibrosis, malnutrition, deformities or physical development problems, straining during bowel movements, and infections. Among the risk factors for adults are straining because of constipation, the effects of surgery or childbirth, structural conditions they were born with, and age-related weakness of the pelvic floor.

How to Minister: (All commands done in Jesus' name).

1. Command the muscles and tendons of the pelvic floor and surrounding structures to strengthen and for the colon to return to its proper position and function.
2. Lead them in a prayer of repentance, if necessary.

RESPIRATORY DISEASE (See Lungs).

RESTLESS LEG SYNDROME

Restless Leg Syndrome is characterized by uncomfortable sensations in the legs that occurs when a person is relaxed, lying down or sitting for an extended period of time such as in a car, airplane or movie theater. The uncomfortable sensation is relieved when the legs are moved by stretching, jiggling the limb, exercising or walking. Symptoms are more noticeable during the night because it usually causes Insomnia and, thus, may cause daytime sleepiness.

Restless Leg Syndrome is associated with Periodic Limb Movement Disorder. With this condition, a person involuntarily flexes and extends the legs while sleeping often resulting in a restless night's sleep for the person and their bed partner. Hundreds of these twitching or kicking movements occur throughout the night. These involuntary kicking movements may also occur while awake.

Restless Leg Syndrome can develop at any age. No known cause has been identified; however stress generally worsens the syndrome.

How to Minister: (All commands done in Jesus' name).

1. Lead them in a prayer of repentance for generational curses.
2. Curse the spirit and command it to go.
3. Command the electrical and magnetic frequencies to be in harmony and balance and function normally.
4. Command the nerves and blood circulation to operate normally.
5. Lead them in a prayer to lay all cares, stress and worries on the Altar of God.

RETARDATION

Generally related to significant central nervous system damage or abnormality, motormental

Retardation is described as delayed or decreased development of both mental and motor skills. The term refers specifically to delayed development of cognitive skills (such as speech) and delayed development of motor skills (such as walking).

There can be various degrees of mental Retardation, which include failure to meet certain normal developmental milestones. Infants can be born with conditions that cause mental retardation and delayed or absent motor development.

Motormental Retardation may also develop after birth with deterioration of both mental and motor function related to disease or accident.

How to Minister: (All commands done in Jesus' name).
1. Lead them in a prayer of repentance for generational curses.
2. Lay hands on the head, commanding a new brain with normal intelligence.
3. Command the spirit of Retardation to go.

RETINITIS PIGMENTOSA

Retinitis Pigmentosa is a progressive degeneration of the retina (part of the eye) which affects night vision and peripheral vision.

It commonly runs in families. The disorder can be caused by defects in a number of different genes. The cells controlling night vision, called rods, are most likely to be affected. However, in some cases, retinal cone cells are most damaged. The hallmark of the disease is the presence of dark pigmented spots in the retina. As the disease progresses, peripheral vision is gradually lost leaving only "tunnel vision".

How to Minister: (All commands done in Jesus' name).
1. Lead them in a prayer of repentance for generational curses.

2. Lay hands on the eyes, commanding a creative miracle to the eye for a new retina and perfect vision.
3. Lead them in a prayer of repentance, if necessary.

RHEUMATIC FEVER

Rheumatic Fever is an inflammatory disease which may develop after an infection with streptococcus bacteria (such as strep throat or scarlet fever) and can involve the heart, joints, skin, and/or brain.

Rheumatic Fever is common worldwide and is responsible for many cases of damaged heart valves which can lead to further heart disease. While it is far less common in the U.S. since the beginning of the 20th century, there have been a few outbreaks since the 1980s. Rheumatic fever primarily affects children between ages of six and fifteen and occurs approximately 20 days after strep throat or scarlet fever. In up to one-third of the identified cases, the underlying strep infection may not have caused any symptoms.

The rate of development of Rheumatic Fever in individuals with untreated strep infection is estimated to be 3%. Persons who have suffered a case of Rheumatic Fever tend to experience periodic strep infections.

How to Minister: (All commands done in Jesus' name).

1. Rebuke the infectious process.
2. Command the joints, heart, and other tissues of the body to be healed and function normally.
3. Command any damaged organs to be healed and function properly.
4. Lead them in a prayer of repentance, if necessary.

RHEUMATOID ARTHRITIS

Rheumatoid Arthritis is a chronic (long-term) inflammatory disease that primarily affects the joints and surrounding tissues, but can also affect other organ systems. The cause of Rheumatoid Arthritis (RA) is unknown. However, RA involves an attack on the body by its own immune cells (auto-immune disease). Different cases may have different causes. Infectious, genetic, and hormonal factors may play a role.

The disease usually begins gradually, with fatigue, morning stiffness (lasting more than one hour), diffuse muscle aches, loss of appetite, and weakness. Eventually, joint pain appears, with warmth, swelling, tenderness, and stiffness of the joint after inactivity. RA usually affects joints on both sides of the body equally. Wrists, fingers, knees, feet, and ankles are the most commonly affected.

When the synovium (the lining of the joint) becomes inflamed, it secretes more fluid and the joint becomes swollen. Later, the cartilage becomes rough and pitted. The underlying bone is eventually affected. Joint destruction may begin, often within one to two years after the appearance of the disease. Deformities of the joints result from cartilage destruction, bone erosions, and tendon inflammation and rupture. It can become seriously debilitating as deformities worsen.

How to Minister: (All commands done in Jesus' name).

1. Cast out the spirit of Rheumatoid Arthritis.
2. Command all inflammation and swelling to be healed and pain to go.
3. Command the cartilage to be restored to normal and all deformities to disappear.
4. Lead them in the prayer of forgiveness.
5. Command the immune system to function properly.

RHINITIS (Also see Allergies and Influenza).

Rhinitis is a nonspecific term that covers infections, allergies, and other disorders of the nose. Rhinitis occurs when the lining of the nose becomes inflamed (red and swollen). The mucous membranes become infected or irritated, producing a discharge, congestion, and swelling of the tissues. People with this condition usually complain of an itchy, stuffy, or drippy nose, a scratchy throat and coughing. Symptoms can also include nasal obstruction, red itchy eyes, difficulty breathing and sleeping, and headaches.

The nose makes thin, clear, liquid called mucus on the inside lining of the nose to help trap airborne dust, germs (bacteria, viruses), and pollen breathed in through the nose and prevent them from getting into the lungs. This thin mucus, along with the waste, normally drains down the back of the throat and into the stomach. It is usually in such small amounts that it goes unnoticed and causes no harm to the body. When the inside of the nose becomes inflamed, it creates more mucus which often becomes thicker and pale yellow in color. It also becomes more noticeable as it drains down the throat (Postnasal Drip), causing coughing. Some of this extra mucus may also drain out of the front of the nose.

The most widespread form of infectious Rhinitis is the common cold. Another common cause includes environmental allergies such as hay fever.

How to Minister: (All commands done in Jesus' name).
1. Curse the root of the infection or inflammation and command it to go.
2. Command healing to the lining of the nose, sinuses and for the mucus to drain normally.
3. Lead them in a prayer for repentance, if necessary.

RINGING IN THE EARS (See Tinnitus).

ROTATOR CUFF

The Rotator Cuff is a group of muscles and tendons that form a cuff over the shoulder. These muscles and tendons hold the arm in its "ball and socket" joint and help the shoulder to rotate. The role of these tendons is to hold the powerful shoulder muscles to the shoulder and arm bones. The Rotator Cuff is one of the most important parts of the shoulder because it allows a person to lift their arms and reach up.

The tendons can be torn from overuse or injury. An injury to the Rotator Cuff, such as a tear, may happen suddenly when falling on an outstretched hand or develop over time due to repetitive activities. Chronic inflammation or injury can cause the tendons of the Rotator Cuff to tear. Rotator Cuff tears can also occur due to aging.

The most common symptoms of a rotator cuff tear may include:

- Recurrent pain, especially with certain activities
- Pain that prevents sleeping on the injured side
- Grating or cracking sounds when moving the arm
- Limited ability to move arm
- Muscle weakness

The risk factors include being over age forty and/or participation in sports or exercise that involves repetitive arm motion over the head (such as baseball). A complete separation (or tear) usually requires surgical repair.

How to Minister: (All commands done in Jesus' name).

1. Command the muscles, tendons and ligaments to strengthen and go back to their normal length and strength.

2. Command the Rotator Cuff to be healed and all infection and inflammation to leave.
3. Command the socket to be well lubricated and the cartilage to be restored.
4. Cast out the spirit of Arthritis, if necessary.
5. Grow out the arms.
6. Command the pain to go and command full mobility to be restored.

SALIVARY GLANDS

The Salivary Glands produce saliva, which moistens food to aid chewing and swallowing. Saliva contains enzymes that begin the digestion process. Saliva also cleans the mouth by washing away bacteria and food particles. Saliva keeps the mouth moist and helps to keep dentures or orthodontic appliances (such as retainers) in place.

There are three pairs of salivary glands:

- The two largest are the parotid glands, one in each cheek in front of the ears.
- Two submandibular glands are at the back of the mouth on both sides of the jaw.
- Two sublingual glands are under the floor of the mouth.

All of the Salivary Glands empty saliva into the mouth through ducts that open at various locations in the mouth.

The Salivary Glands may become inflamed (irritated) because of infection, tumors, or stones. Mumps is an inflammation of the parotid glands.

How to Minister: (All commands done in Jesus' name).

1. Command any infection, tumor or stones to leave.
2. Command new salivary glands.
3. Lead them in a prayer of repentance to break word curses.

SCARS, KELOIDS, ADHESIONS

A Scar is a mark left on the skin after a wound, burn or sore has healed over. They often fade over time. Keloids are an abnormal overgrowth of scar tissue at the site of skin injuries such as surgical incisions, traumatic wounds, vaccination sites, burns, chickenpox, acne, or even minor scratches. Most Keloids will flatten and become less noticeable over a period of several years. They may become irritated from rubbing on clothing or other forms of friction. Extensive Keloids may become binding, limiting mobility. They may cause cosmetic changes and affect the appearance.

Adhesions are an abnormal joining of normally unconnected body parts by bands of fibrous tissue and/or organs inside the body; usually following surgery or an injury. Inflammation, surgery, or injury can cause tissues to bond to other tissue or organs, much like the process of forming scar tissue. Abdominal surgery, endometriosis, attacks of appendicitis, or pelvic inflammatory disease (PID) can also cause adhesions within the abdomen.

Depending on the tissues involved, Adhesions can cause various disorders. In the eye, Adhesion of the iris to the lens can lead to glaucoma. In the intestines, Adhesions can cause partial or complete bowel obstruction necessitating emergency surgery. Pelvic Adhesions can lead to Infertility and reproductive problems.

How to Minister: (All commands done in Jesus' name).

1. Command the scar tissue to be dissolved.
2. Command all organs and structures to be healed and to function normally.

SCHIZOPHRENIA

Schizophrenia is a serious psychiatric disorder with symptoms of emotional instability, detachment from reality, often with delusions, hallucinations, and withdrawal. It is difficult for the person to tell the difference between real and unreal experiences, to think logically, to have normal emotional responses to others, or to behave normally in social situations.

Experts in the field are not exactly sure what causes it. Genetic factors appear to play a role. The level of social and familial support appears to influence the course of illness and may be protective against relapse.

There are five recognized types of Schizophrenia: catatonic, paranoid, disorganized, undifferentiated, and residual. The psychotic symptoms include: delusions, hallucinations, disordered thinking, catatonic behavior, or flat affect.

Features of Schizophrenia include its typical onset before the age of 45, continuous presence of symptoms for six months or more, and deterioration from a prior level of social and occupational functioning.

How to Minister: (All commands done in Jesus' name).

1. Lead them in a prayer of repentance for generational curses.
2. Command all the chemicals and hormones in the body to be in balance.
3. Command the brain to process information properly.
4. Command a new brain.
5. Lead them in a prayer of repentance, if necessary.

SCIATICA

Sciatica is a condition involving pain, weakness, numbness, or tingling in the leg. It is caused by injury to or compression of the sciatic nerve and occurs when there is damage to the sciatic nerve which is located in the back of the leg. This nerve controls the muscles on the back of the knee and lower leg and provides sensation to the back of the thigh, part of the lower leg and the sole of the foot. Partial damage to the sciatic nerve may appear identical to damage to one of the branches of the sciatic nerve.

The sciatic nerve is commonly injured by fractures of the pelvis, or other trauma to the buttocks or thigh. Prolonged sitting or lying with pressure on the buttocks may also injure it. Systemic diseases, such as diabetes, can typically damage many different nerves, including the sciatic nerve. The sciatic nerve may also be harmed by pressure from masses such as a tumor or abscess, or by bleeding in the pelvis. In many cases, no cause can be identified.

Note: A ruptured lumbar disc in the spine may cause symptoms very similar to the symptoms of sciatic nerve dysfunction.

How to Minister: (All commands done in Jesus' name).

1. Grow out the legs.
2. Command the lumbar vertebra and sacrum to return to normal alignment and the supporting muscles to strengthen.
3. Command all the discs to go back into place and relieve all pressure on the nerves.
4. Command the spirit of Sciatica to go and the nerve to be released.
5. Lead them in a prayer of repentance, if necessary.

SCLERODERMA (Also called Systemic Sclerosis).

Scleroderma is a debilitating disease in which the skin becomes progressively hard and thickened. Scleroderma is a diffuse connective tissue disease characterized by changes in the skin, blood vessels, skeletal muscles, and internal organs. Excess collagen deposits in the skin and other organs produce the symptoms. Damage to small blood vessels within the skin and affected organs also occurs. In the skin, ulceration, calcification, and changes in pigmentation may occur. Systemic features may include fibrosis and degeneration of the heart, lungs, kidneys and gastrointestinal tract.

The disease usually affects people 30 to 50 years of age. Women are affected more often than men. Risk factors are occupational exposure to silica dust and polyvinyl chloride. The cause of Scleroderma is unknown. The course and severity of the disease varies widely in those affected.

How to Minister: (All commands done in Jesus' name).

1. Cast out the spirit of Scleroderma.
2. Command the immune system to be healed and return to normal function.
3. Command new tissue to replace the damaged areas of the skin and all affected internal organs.
4. Command the electrical and magnetic frequencies to come into harmony and balance.

SCOLIOSIS

Scoliosis is a sideways curvature of the spine. There are three general causes of scoliosis: congenital, usually related to a problem with the formation of vertebrae or fused ribs during prenatal development; neuromuscular (poor muscle control or muscular weakness or paralysis due to diseases like cerebral palsy, muscular dystrophy, spinal deformities and polio); and idiopathic (of unknown cause), which appears in a previously straight spine.

The idiopathic form in adolescents is the most common and may have a genetic predisposition. Most cases occur in girls and curves generally worsen during growth spurts. There are also infantile and juvenile forms that are less common and affect a similar number of boys and girls.

Scoliosis may be suspected when one shoulder appears to be higher than the other or the pelvis appears to be tilted.

How to Minister: (All commands done in Jesus' name).

1. Lead them in a prayer of repentance for generational curses.
2. Cast out the spirit of Scoliosis.
3. Command the bones in the back, the ribs, and supportive structures of the body to come into normal and perfect alignment.
4. Command the muscles, tendons and ligaments to strengthen.
5. Grow out the legs.
6. Grow out the arms.
7. Do the pelvic adjustment.

SEIZURES (Also see Epilepsy).

A Seizure is a sudden change in behavior due to excessive electrical activity in the brain. During normal waking and sleeping, your brain cells produce various electrical discharge patterns. If the electrical discharges by your brain cells become abnormally synchronized, a seizure or convulsion occurs. A convulsion is a violent shaking of the body or limbs caused by uncontrollable muscle contractions.

There are a wide variety of possible symptoms of seizures depending on what parts of the brain are affected. Many types of seizures cause loss of consciousness with twitching or shaking of the body. However, some seizures consist of staring spells that can easily go unnoticed. Occasionally, seizures can cause temporary abnormal sensations or visual disturbances.

Seizures can generally be classified as either "simple" (no change in level of consciousness) or "complex" (change in level of consciousness). Seizures may also be classified as generalized (whole body affected) or focal (only one part or side of the body is affected). Other types of seizures include petit mal (mild epilepsy) seizure and temporal lobe seizure.

Often, the cause of a seizure is unknown. Some of the known causes of seizures include:

- Metabolic disturbances. Diseases of the kidney or liver can cause chemical disturbances in your body, as can very low levels of sodium, calcium, magnesium or glucose (Insulin shock with Diabetes).
- Previous brain trauma. Traumatic head injuries, such as those sustained in automobile accidents or serious sports injuries, can cause seizures.
- Vascular system problems. Blood vessel disorders, such as a malformation of the brain blood vessels, and strokes.
- Toxic substances. Using drugs or other chemicals or withdrawing from addicting substances, especially alcohol.
- Infection. An inflammation of your brain, such as meningitis or encephalitis.
- Birth defects. Congenital malformations in the brain can be responsible for seizures in infants and young children.
- Brain tumor. Although a brain tumor is an uncommon cause, a seizure may be an indication of a brain tumor.

A typical Grand Mal Seizure starts with a loss of consciousness and falling down, loss of bowel or bladder control, and rhythmic convulsions. This is followed by a 15 to 20 second period with muscle rigidity and then a one to two minute period of violent, rhythmic convulsions. During a grand mal seizure, the person may take on a dusky appearance, resulting from decreased blood oxygen levels due to impaired breathing during the seizure.

Most Grand Mal Seizures last from thirty seconds to five minutes. After the seizure, there may be headache and drowsiness or confusion. Seizures often occur randomly, though in rare cases, stimulation by light, sound or touch can trigger a seizure in susceptible people. Sleep deprivation and excessive alcohol use also may trigger seizures.

Sometimes the Seizures involve only a few muscles, such as one side of the face or one arm or leg. This is called a focal seizure.

Epilepsy is a chronic disorder with recurrent seizure episodes. Some types of epilepsy are hereditary (run in families).

How to Minister: (All commands done in Jesus' name).

1. Lead them in a prayer of repentance for generational curses.
2. Curse the spirit and command it to go.
3. Command the electrical and magnetic frequencies to be in harmony and balance and function normally.
4. Command a new brain.

SHORT LEG

Unless there is a birth defect or bone loss, short legs are caused by a lower back problem that draws up the ligaments, muscles, and bones, making the leg appear to be "short".

How to Minister: (All commands done in Jesus' name).

1. Grow out the legs.
2. Command the back to be healed and muscles, tendons and ligaments to be their normal length and strength and to go into proper alignment.

3. If the leg is actually shorter or smaller, command a creative miracle. Command the leg to grow to normal length and size.

SICKLE CELL ANEMIA

Sickle Cell Anemia is an inherited disease in which the red blood cells, normally disc-shaped, become crescent shaped. As a result, they function abnormally and cause small blood clots. These clots give rise to recurrent painful episodes called "sickle cell pain crises."

Sickle Cell Anemia is caused by an abnormal type of hemoglobin (oxygen carrying molecule) called hemoglobin S. Approximately 8% of African Americans have the Sickle Cell trait. Someone with Sickle Cell trait or these forms of sickle cell disease will usually have no symptoms or only mild ones. However, some of these conditions can cause symptoms similar to Sickle Cell Anemia.

How to Minister: (All commands done in Jesus' name).

1. Lead in a prayer of repentance for generational curses.
2. Cast out the spirit of Sickle Cell Anemia.
3. Command the defective genes to be restored to normal.
4. Command the marrow to produce normal blood cells and the affected organs and tissues of the body to be healed.

SINUS PROBLEMS

Sinusitis refers to inflammation of the sinuses. This is generally caused by a viral, bacterial, or fungal infection and occurs in conjunction with Rhinitis.

The sinuses are air-filled spaces around the forehead, cheeks, and eyes that are lined with mucous membranes. When inflamed, the sinuses become blocked with mucus and can become infected. Sinusitis can occur from one of these conditions:

- The small openings from the sinuses to the nose become blocked from allergies, deviated nasal septum, or nasal polyps (growths).
- Small hairs in the sinuses, which help move the normally produced mucus out, are not working properly.
- Too much mucus is produced.

Sinusitis usually follows respiratory infections such as colds or an allergic reaction. Some people never get sinusitis and others develop sinusitis frequently. Though not everyone with a cold develops sinusitis, colds are the most common cause of acute sinusitis. It's estimated that more than 30 million Americans experience sinusitis every year. The blockages associated with sinusitis can become worse if you smoke or are exposed to air pollution, both of which can cause further irritation or inflammation.

How to Minister: (All commands done in Jesus' name).

1. Rebuke the infection and curse any allergies.
2. Lay hands on the face and command the sinuses to drain, open up, and be healed.
3. Grow out the arms.
4. Command the blood vessels to open and reduce swelling and inflammation of the areas.
5. Lead them in a prayer of repentance, if necessary.

SJOGREN'S SYNDROME

Sjogren's (SHOW-grins) Syndrome is a disorder of the immune system often defined by its two most common symptoms — dry eyes and a dry mouth and often accompanies other autoimmune disorders — rheumatoid arthritis, lupus and others. These rheumatic diseases are marked by inflammation of the connective tissues, and it is common for people with Sjogren's Syndrome to also have a connective tissue disorder.

In Sjogren's Syndrome, the immune system attacks healthy tissue. The mucous membranes and moisture-secreting glands of the eyes and mouth are usually affected first, resulting in decreased production of tears and saliva. This can lead to problems from difficulty swallowing to dental cavities to light-sensitive eyes to corneal ulcers. Sjogren's Syndrome can also result in damage to tissues of the lungs, kidneys and liver.

Although Sjogren's Syndrome can develop at any age, most people are older than 40 years of age when diagnosed. The condition is nine times as likely to occur in women as in men. There's no cure for Sjogren's Syndrome, but treatments can relieve many of the symptoms.

How to Minister: (All commands done in Jesus' name).
1. Rebuke the infectious process.
2. Command the all affected tissues of the body to be healed and function normally.
3. Command the immune system and any damaged organs to be healed and function properly.
4. Lead them in a prayer of repentance, if necessary.

SLEEP DISORDERS

(Also see Insomnia, Snoring and Restless Leg Syndrome).

Sleep Disorders involve any difficulties related to sleeping, including difficulty falling or staying asleep, falling asleep at inappropriate times, excessive total sleep time, or abnormal behaviors associated with sleep.

More than 100 different disorders of sleeping and waking have been identified. They can be grouped in four main categories:

- Problems with staying awake
- Problems with falling and staying asleep
- Problems with adhering to a regular sleep schedule
- Sleep-disruptive behaviors

Insomnia or Problems Falling and Staying Asleep

Insomnia includes any combination of difficulty with falling asleep, staying asleep, intermittent wakefulness and early-morning awakening. Episodes may be transient, short-term (lasting as long as 2 to 3 weeks), or chronic.

Common factors associated with insomnia include:

- Physical illness
- Depression
- Anxiety or stress
- Poor sleeping environment such as excessive noise or light
- Caffeine
- Alcohol or other drugs,
- Use of certain medications
- Heavy smoking
- Physical discomfort
- Daytime napping
- Counterproductive sleep habits

Narcolepsy

Narcolepsy is a chronic sleep disorder characterized by overwhelming daytime drowsiness and sudden sleep attacks. They fall asleep inappropriately without warning, anywhere and at any time regardless of the circumstances. They also exhibit other features that may include sleep paralysis and hallucinations.

The exact cause of Narcolepsy is unknown. The first symptoms usually appear between the ages of ten and twenty-five and affect males and females equally and occur in all racial and ethnic groups. The cause is unknown.

Narcolepsy can cause serious problems in both professional and personal lives. Sleep attacks may result in physical harm if they occur during many activities such as driving a car or using dangerous equipment. An attack while lighting a fire or cutting food can result in serious injuries.

Sleep Apnea

Sleep Apnea more commonly affects obese people, but it may affect anyone with a short neck or a small jaw, regardless of weight. The disorder causes breathing to stop intermittently during sleep, resulting in the person being awakened repeatedly. Loud snoring and labored breathing can occur. When complete blockage of the airway occurs, air cannot reach the lungs. People with Sleep Apnea have difficulty achieving prolonged deep restorative sleep. This results in excessive daytime sleepiness.

Older obese men seem to be at higher risk, though as many as 40% of people with obstructive Sleep Apnea are not obese. Nasal obstruction, a large tongue, a narrow airway and certain shapes of the palate and jaw seem also to increase the risk. A large neck or collar size is strongly associated with obstructive Sleep Apnea. Ingestion of alcohol or sedatives before sleep may predispose to episodes of Sleep Apnea. Because Sleep Apnea causes sudden drops in blood oxygen levels, people with Sleep Apnea are at risk for complications such as brain damage, stroke, high blood pressure, or sudden death. Children with Sleep Apnea may be hyperactive and may be diagnosed with ADHD. The most common cause of childhood Sleep Apnea is overgrown tonsils and adenoids.

Sleepwalking

Usually occurs during deep sleep, early in the night, and most often affects children between the ages of six and twelve. Episodes typically last less than thirty minutes, may be related to fatigue or anxiety and appear to run in families.

Sleepwalkers do more than just walk. They may change their clothes, move furniture or just sit up in bed. If the child turns up sleeping in an unusual place and cannot remember getting there, they may have been sleepwalking. Most children outgrow this by adolescence.

How to Minister: (All commands done in Jesus' name).

1. Lead them in a prayer of repentance for generational curses.
2. Lead them in a prayer to lay all cares, stress, fears and worries on the Altar of God.
3. Command all hormones to be in balance.
4. Command the electrical and magnetic frequencies to be in harmony and balance.
5. Command the neck to come into alignment and for all obstructions in the breathing pathways to be removed.
6. Command the muscles in the upper part of the throat to function normally during sleep.
7. Command any ungodly spirit to come out.
8. Speak a blessing of restful and restorative peaceful sleep.

SNORING (Also see Sleep Disorders).

Snoring is loud, hoarse, or harsh breathing sounds that happen while a person is asleep. It is a disruptive nuisance to the person as well as to others within hearing distance. It occurs when air flows past the relaxed tissues in the throat causing the tissues to vibrate as a breath is taken, creating hoarse or harsh sounds.

Snoring is common in adults and may possibly be an indication of an underlying disorder such as chronic nasal congestion, deviated nasal septum, sleep apnea, or enlarged tonsils or adenoids. Other contributing factors include being overweight; sleeping pills, antihistamines or alcohol at bedtime; or sleeping on the back.

How to Minister: (All commands done in Jesus' name).
1. Lead them in a prayer of repentance for generational curses.
2. Command the muscles and tissues of the upper throat to function normally during sleep.
3. Command any blockages in air pathways to be removed.

SORE THROAT (Also see Influenza, Cold, Laryngitis).

A Sore Throat causes discomfort, pain, or scratchiness in the throat and often makes it painful to swallow. A Sore Throat usually occurs in combination with other signs and symptoms of an upper respiratory infection, but can occur alone.

Like Colds, the vast majority of Sore Throats are caused by viral infections. Many people have a mild Sore Throat at the beginning of every Cold. When the nose or sinuses become infected, drainage can run down the back of the throat and irritate it, especially at night. Or, the throat itself can be infected.

Mononucleosis is a much longer-lived viral illness associated with a severe Sore Throat. Other viral illnesses which include a Sore Throat include measles, chickenpox and Croup.

Strep throat is the most common bacterial cause of Sore Throats. Bacterial infections associated with a Sore Throat also include strep throat, tonsillitis and diphtheria.

Still, not all Sore Throats result from viral or bacterial infections. Other common causes of Sore Throat include Allergies, excessively dry indoor air, breathing through your mouth (because of chronic nasal congestion), outdoor air pollution, inhaling tobacco smoke (primary or secondary), alcohol, spicy foods, muscle strain of the throat, Acid reflux (GERDS) or vomiting,

How to Minister: (All commands done in Jesus' name).

1. Curse the root of any viral or bacterial infection.
2. Lead them in a prayer of repentance for word curses.
3. Command the pain, inflammation or irritation to go.
4. Command any allergic reaction to disappear.
5. Command the electrical and magnetic frequencies to be in harmony and balance.

SPASTICITY

Spasticity is marked by stiff or rigid muscles and exaggerated, deep tendon reflexes. The condition can interfere with walking, movement or speech.

Spasticity generally results from damage to the motor area of the brain (the portion of the cerebral cortex that controls voluntary movement) and to any nerves traveling from brain down to the spinal cord. When control of the muscles from the central nervous system is damaged, muscle feedback pathways from the spinal cord produce symptoms such as exaggerated deep tendon reflexes (the knee-jerk reflex), scissoring (crossing of the legs as the tips of scissors would close), repetitive jerky motions, unusual posturing, and carrying the shoulder, arm, wrist, and finger at an abnormal angle.

Spasticity may also interfere with speech. Severe, long term Spasticity may lead to contracture of muscles causing joints to be bent at a fixed position.

It can be seen with any form of brain, spine or nerve damage including Multiple Sclerosis, or Cerebral Palsy

How to Minister: (All commands done in Jesus' name).

1. Command the nervous system to be healed, completely restored and function normally.
2. Speak a new brain, if necessary.
3. Command the hormones to be in balance.
4. Command the electrical and magnetic frequencies to be in harmony and balance.
5. Cast out the spirit of fear.
6. Lead them in a prayer of forgiveness, if necessary.

SPINA BIFIDA

Spina Bifida is a serious birth defect where the backbone and spinal canal do not close properly before birth. Spina Bifida includes any congenital defect involving insufficient closure of the spine. It is one of the more common birth defects in the USA.

There are three forms; however the most severe form is called Myelomeningocele or Open Spina Bifida. This can result in the spinal cord and its covering membranes to protrude from the infant's back. If a child is born with myelomeningocele, subsequent children in that family have a higher risk than the general population. The cause is unknown.

In most cases of Open Spina Bifida, the baby is prone to life-threatening infections such as meningitis. Other neurological impairments include paralysis, bowel and bladder problems, seizures, learning disabilities as well as other medical complications. It is more common among Hispanics and whites of European descent. Risk increases with the mother's history of diabetes and/or obesity.

How to Minister: (All commands done in Jesus' name).

1. Lead them in a prayer of repentance for generational curses.
2. Command the spine to close completely.
3. Command a new spine, if necessary.
4. Command any scarring from surgery to dissolve.
5. Command the brain and all nerve tissue and pathways to be totally healed and function normally.

SPRAIN (or STRAIN)

During physical activity, sudden pain and swelling around a joint or a muscle may occur when you stretch too far, change direction or slow down abruptly, land awkwardly, or collide with a solid object such as another player during a sporting event. The injury you have may be a Sprain or a Strain.

Sprains occur when a ligament is stretched too far or torn. Ligaments are bands of tough fibrous tissue that connect one bone to another and stabilize the joints. The common locations for a Sprain include the ankles, wrist or knees.

A Strain is a stretching or tearing of muscle tissue. People sometimes called this a "pulled muscle". Hamstring and back injuries are examples of common Strains.

Symptoms of an ankle injury, for example, vary and can range from mild tenderness or soreness to swelling, bruising, severe pain and an inability to walk. Since the symptoms are close to those from a fracture, often an x-ray is necessary to determine the extent and type of injury since it could be a Strain, Sprain or fracture.

How to Minister: (All commands done in Jesus' name).

1. Command the tendons, muscles and ligaments to be restored and strengthened.
2. Grow out the arms or the legs.
3. Command the pain and all inflammation to go.

STOMACH PROBLEM

This includes any problem associated with the stomach.

How to Minister: (All commands done in Jesus' name).

1. If possible, determine specific problem and command it to be healed or new part created and to function normally.
2. Lead them in a prayer to lay cares, stress and worries on the Altar of God.
3. Lead them in a prayer for repentance to break word curses.

STREP THROAT (See Sore Throat).

STRESS

Stress can come from any situation or thought that makes a person feel frustrated, angry, or anxious. What is stressful to one person is not necessarily stressful to another.

Stress is a normal part of life. In small quantities, stress is good because it can motivate and help a person be more productive. However, too much stress, or a strong response to stress, is harmful. It can exacerbate general poor health as well as specific physical or psychological illnesses like infection, heart disease, or depression.

Persistent and unrelenting Stress often leads to anxiety and unhealthy behaviors like overeating and abuse of alcohol or drugs. Anxiety is a feeling of fear or apprehension. The source of this uneasiness is not always known or recognized which can add to the distress (or Stress) that is felt.

Emotional problems such as grief or depression or health conditions such as an overactive thyroid, low blood sugar, or heart attack can also cause Stress.

How to Minister: (All commands done in Jesus' name).
1. Lead them in a prayer to lay all cares, stress, fears and worries on the Altar of God.
2. Command all chemicals and hormones to return to normal.
3. Lead them in a prayer of repentance, if necessary.
4. Speak peace to them.

STROKE (CVA – Cardiovascular Accident)

A stroke is an interruption of the blood supply to any part of the brain thus depriving the brain tissue of the oxygen and nutrients necessary to function properly. If the flow of blood supplying the brain is interrupted for longer than a few seconds, brain cells can die causing permanent damage. An interruption can be caused by either blood clots, bleeding into the brain or particles which block the blood flow. It is a leading cause of death in the USA as well as a leading cause of adult disability.

A common cause of a Stroke is atherosclerosis. Fatty deposits and blood platelets collect on the walls of the arteries, forming plaques. Over time, the plaques slowly begin to block the flow of blood. The plaque itself may block the artery enough to cause a Stroke or it causes the blood to flow abnormally slow, which leads to a blood clot. A clot can stay at the site of narrowing and prevent blood flow to all of the smaller arteries it supplies. In other cases, a clot formed elsewhere can travel and wedge into a smaller vessel.

The clot is commonly caused by Atrial Fibrillation of the heart.

Bleeding into the brain occurs if a blood vessel ruptures or there is a significant injury. This brain hemorrhage can result from uncontrolled high blood pressure (Hypertension) and weak spots in your blood vessel walls called Aneurysms.

Symptoms of an event and the after effects are often the same: numbness, weakness or paralysis on one side of the body, loss of speech, problems with vision, dizziness, loss of coordination, confusion and loss of memory. If severe, the Stroke can leave the person severely disabled and totally dependent on another person for all cares and movements.

A "mild stroke" or TIA is a temporary interruption of the blood flow to a part of the brain with symptoms that may last from a few minutes to a few days. It is a warning sign that a more serious blockage may occur later. A TIA usually disappears without leaving apparent permanent effects.

Risk factors include family history, age, sex, race, hypertension, high cholesterol, smoking, diabetes, obesity, cardiovascular disease, use of birth control pills, heavy drinking of alcohol and illicit drug use.

How to Minister: (All commands done in Jesus' name).

1. Cast out the spirit of death.
2. Command any blockage to dissolve and be removed.
3. Command all damaged tissue of the brain and other affected body parts be healed, restored and function normally.
4. Command a new brain, if necessary.
5. Command the communication from the brain to the body to be restored and function normally.

STUTTERING

Stuttering is a disorder that involves hesitation, repetition, or stumbling while speaking. Young children often go through a short period of stuttering, but this phase is very brief. For a small percentage (less than 1%), the stuttering progresses from simple repetition of consonants to repetition of words and phrases. Later, vocal spasms develop with a forced, almost explosive sound to the speech.

Stuttering tends to run in families, but it is unclear to what extent genetic factors are important. There is also evidence that Stuttering may be associated with some neurological deficits.

Surprisingly, people with significant speech difficulty often don't stutter when singing or when they are alone talking to themselves. Stuttering tends to persist into adulthood more frequently in males than females.

How to Minister: (All commands done in Jesus' name).

1. Lead them in a prayer of repentance for generational curses.
2. Command the nervous system to operate properly.
3. Command the spirit of fear to leave.

SUICIDE

Suicide is the act of deliberately taking one's own life. Suicidal behavior is any deliberate action with potentially life-threatening consequences, such as taking a drug overdose or deliberately crashing a car. Suicidal behaviors can accompany many emotional disturbances, including depression, bipolar disorder, and schizophrenia.

Suicidal behaviors often occur as a response to a situation that the person views as overwhelming, such as social isolation, death of a loved one, emotional trauma, serious physical illness, growing old, unemployment or financial problems, guilt feelings, and alcohol or other drug dependence.

Suicide attempts should always be taken seriously and help should be sought immediately. Dismissing them as attention-seeking can have devastating consequences. Relatives of people who seriously attempt or complete Suicide often blame themselves or become extremely angry, seeing the attempt or act as selfish.

However, when people are suicidal, they often mistakenly believe that they are doing their friends and relatives a favor by taking themselves out of the world. These irrational beliefs often drive their behavior.

How to Minister: (All commands done in Jesus' name).

1. Lead them in a prayer of repentance.
2. Command all chemicals and hormones to be in balance.
3. Lead them in a prayer of forgiveness and repentance to break word curses.
4. Cast out the spirit of Suicide.
5. Lead them in a prayer to lay all cares, stress and worries on the Altar of God.
6. Ask them to repeat the declaration "I choose life!" many times.

SWELLING (See Edema).

TAILBONE (Coccyx)

Tailbone trauma is an injury to the small bone at the lower tip of the spine. Actual fractures of the tailbone (coccyx) are infrequent. Tailbone trauma usually involves bruising of the bone or pulling of the ligaments. Backward falls onto a hard surface, such as a slippery floor or ice, are the most common cause of this injury. These injuries are painful and make sitting very uncomfortable.

How to Minister: (All commands done in Jesus' name).
1. Command the tailbone to go back into place.
2. Command any fractures, bruising or swelling to be healed.
3. Command all pain to go.

TEETH
(Also See Periodontitis, Gingivitis and Gum Disease).
Widely spaced or crooked teeth can be a temporary condition related to normal growth and the acquisition of adult teeth. It can also occur as a permanent condition in several diseases. Wide spacing can also result from abnormal continued growth of the maxilla or jaw.

Teeth - Overbite or Underbite
An Overbite is a faulty alignment of the teeth in which the upper front teeth project too far over the lower teeth when the mouth is closed. An Underbite indicates the lower teeth project further than the upper teeth. These both can be caused by a child sucking its thumb. These conditions can be caused by the jaw being out of place.

How to Minister: (All commands done in Jesus' name).
1. Lead them in a prayer of repentance for generational curses.
2. Lay hands on the jaw and command the jaw to be adjusted to allow enough space for the teeth to be in proper alignment.
3. Command the teeth to line up properly.

Teeth - Grinding (Also see TMJ).
Teeth grinding usually occurs at night while asleep. This condition affects both children and adults.

Some people unconsciously clench their teeth together during the day, often when they feel anxious or tense; however most grind or gnash their teeth during sleep. It can lead to jaw disorders (TMJ), headaches, damaged teeth and other problems.

Psychological factors may include anxiety, stress or tension, suppressed anger or frustration, aggressive, competitive or hyperactive personality type. In some children, it may be related to growth and development. It is common in children with cerebral palsy or severe mental retardation. It can be a complication of another disorder, such as Huntington's disease or Parkinson's disease.

How to Minister: (All commands done in Jesus' name).

1. Grow out the arms.
2. Command the affectred nerves to be released.
3. Lead them in a prayer of forgiveness, if necessary.
4. Lead them in a prayer to lay all cares, stress, fears and worries on the Altar of God.

Toothache / Tooth Decay

Toothache is pain in or around a tooth. A Toothache is generally the result of Tooth Decay or sometimes an infection. Tooth Decay is often caused by poor dental hygiene, although the tendency to get Tooth Decay is partly inherited. Sometimes, pain in other locations is perceived as occurring in the Teeth (this is called referred pain or radiating pain).

How to Minister: (All commands done in Jesus' name).

1. Curse the decay and command the pain to go.
2. Lay hands on the affected area and command the teeth to be restored.
3. Command new teeth.

TENDONITIS

Tendonitis is inflammation, irritation, and swelling of a tendon, which is the fibrous structure that joins muscle to bone. In many cases, tendonosis (tendon degeneration) is also present.

Tendonitis can occur as a result of injury, overuse, or with aging as the tendon loses elasticity. It can also be seen in systemic diseases such as rheumatoid arthritis or diabetes. Tendonitis can occur in any tendon, but some commonly affected sites are the shoulder, the wrist, the heel (Achilles tendonitis), and the elbow.

How to Minister: (All commands done in Jesus' name).

1. Rebuke the inflammation.
2. Grow out the arms or legs of the affected area.
3. Command the tendon and its surrounding tissues to be healed.
4. Command the pain, all swelling and irritation to go.
5. If worn out from use, then command new tendons and ligaments.

TENNIS ELBOW

Tennis Elbow is an inflammation, soreness, or pain on the outside of the upper arm near the elbow. There may be a partial tear of the tendon fibers, which connect muscle to bone, at or near their point of origin on the outside of the elbow.

This injury is caused by repetitively twisting the wrist or forearm. The injury is classically associated with tennis playing, hence the name "Tennis Elbow," but any activity that involves repetitive twisting of the wrist (like using a screwdriver) can lead to lateral epicondylitis or “Tennis Elbow.”

How to Minister: (All commands done in Jesus' name).

1. Command all inflammation and pain to go.
2. Command the muscles, tendons and ligaments to be healed and go back to their proper length and strength.
3. Lead them in a prayer of repentance if necessary.

THYROID DISEASE (Also see Goiter).

The thyroid gland is located in the base of the neck on both sides of the lower part of the larynx (voice box) and upper part of the trachea (wind pipe). The gland produces a thyroid hormone in response to stimulation by a hormone from the pituitary gland. The thyroid hormone acts throughout the body to regulate metabolism.

Thyroid diseases can be broadly divided into the following categories:

- Overproduction of the thyroid hormone (hyperthyroidism)
- Underproduction of the thyroid hormone (hypothyroidism)
- Benign (noncancerous) thyroid disease
- Thyroid cancer

How to Minister: (All commands done in Jesus' name).

1. Lead them in a prayer of repentance for generational curses.
2. Command a new thyroid that works properly.
3. Command any swelling to leave.
4. Command all hormones to be in balance.
5. Curse the root of cancer, if necessary.

TIC DOULOUREUX

Trigeminal Neuralgia (Tic Douloureux) is a very painful disorder of the fifth cranial nerve (trigeminal nerve) located in the face. Because the sudden, sharp pain often causes the individual to wince, the condition is also known as Tic Douloureux (in French) or Painful Twitch. Trigeminal Neuralgia occurs in two different forms. The typical form occurs almost exclusively in persons over the age of 50. It affects women more frequently than men. The symptomatic form can occur in any age group. It may be caused by a tumor of the trigeminal nerve or pressure on the nerve root by a blood vessel (vascular anomaly).

How to Minister: (All commands done in Jesus' name).

1. Lead them in a prayer of repentance for generational curses.
2. Command all the pressure on the nerves to be healed and all nerves to function normally.
3. Curse the disease and command the spirit to go.
4. Lead them in a prayer of repentance or forgiveness, if necessary.

TINNITUS

Tinnitus is the medical term for "hearing" noises in your ears when there is no outside source of the sounds. The noises you hear can be soft or loud. They may sound like ringing, blowing, roaring, buzzing, hissing, humming, whistling or sizzling. You may even think you are hearing air escaping, water running, the inside of a seashell or musical notes.

Tinnitus is common. Many people experience a mild form of Tinnitus occasionally that only lasts a few minutes. However, constant or recurring Tinnitus is stressful and can interfere with your ability to concentrate or sleep.

It is not known exactly what causes a person to "hear" sounds with no outside source of the noise. However, Tinnitus can be a symptom of almost any ear problem, including ear infections, foreign objects or wax in the ear, and injury from loud noises. Alcohol, caffeine, antibiotics, aspirin, or other drugs can also cause ear noises. Tinnitus may occur with hearing loss. Occasionally, it is a sign of high blood pressure, an allergy, or anemia.

How to Minister: (All commands done in Jesus' name).
1. Lead them in a prayer of repentance for generational curses.
2. Curse the root cause and command it to go.
3. Command the blood to flow through the ear canal properly.

TEMPOROMANDIBULAR JOINTS (TMJ)

The Temporomandibular Joints connect your lower jaw to your skull. There are two matching joints - one on each side of your head, located just in front of your ears. The abbreviation "TMJ" literally refers to the joint, but is often used to refer to any disorder or symptoms of this region. Such problems include popping sounds in the jaw, inability to fully open the mouth, jaw pain, headaches, earaches, toothaches and various other types of facial pain.

Many TMJ symptoms are caused by the effects of physical and emotional stress on the structures around the joint. These structures include the muscles of the jaw, face and neck; the teeth; the cartilage disc at the joint; and nearby ligaments, blood vessels and nerves.

For example, daily stress can lead you to clench and grind your teeth, both during the day and at night while you sleep. Clenching means you tightly clamp your top and bottom teeth together, especially the back teeth. The stressful force of clenching causes pressure on the muscles, tissues and other structures around your jaw.

How to Minister: (All commands done in Jesus' name).

1. Lead them in a prayer of repentance for generational curses.
2. Command the jaw to go back into place and pain to go.
3. Command the tissues, ligaments and cartilage to be healed and adjusted to the right alignment.
4. Lead them in a prayer of repentance to break word curses.

THROMBOPHLEBITIS (See Phlebitis and DVT).

TONSILLITIS

Tonsillitis is inflammation of the tonsils. The tonsils are lymph nodes in the back of the mouth and top of the throat. They normally help to filter out bacteria and other microorganisms to prevent infection in the body. They may become so overwhelmed by bacterial or viral infection that they swell and become inflamed, causing Tonsillitis. The infection may also be present in the throat and surrounding areas. Tonsillitis is extremely common, particularly in children.

How to Minister: (All commands done in Jesus' name).

1. Rebuke the infection and command it to be gone.
2. Command the tonsils to return to normal size and to function normally.
3. Command all pain to go.

TOOTHACHE / TOOTH DECAY (See Teeth).

TOURETTE SYNDROME

Gilles de la Tourette Syndrome, also called simply Tourette Syndrome, is a disorder characterized by multiple motor and vocal tics that begin before the age of 18. It is characterized by repeated and involuntary body movements (tics). A tic is a sudden, rapid, stereotyped motor movement or vocalization. Tics can include eye blinking, repeated throat clearing or sniffing, arm thrusting, kicking movements, shoulder shrugging or jumping.

Though a gene for Tourette syndrome has not yet been identified, there is strong evidence that it is an inherited disorder transmitted through one or more genes. It is an autosomal dominant trait. The most common initial symptom is a facial tic - other tics may follow. Contrary to popular belief, use of socially inappropriate words or phrases occurs in only a minority of patients.

Many patients explain that the tics are not totally involuntary, but that "things just would not feel right" if they did not do them. In this respect Tourette Syndrome differs from Obsessive-Compulsive Disorder, in which patients are compelled to do the behaviors out of fear of impending doom.

How to Minister: (All commands done in Jesus' name).
1. Lead them in a prayer of repentance for generational curses.
2. Command the spirit of Tourette Syndrome to go.
3. Command the electrical and magnetic frequencies to be in harmony and balance.
4. Lead them in a prayer of repentance, if necessary.

TRAUMATIC EVENT

A traumatic event is an experience that causes physical, emotional, psychological distress or harm. It is an event that is perceived and experienced as a threat to one's safety or to the stability of one's world.

A traumatic event may involve:

- Physical injury or illness

- Separation from parents (perceived abandonment)
- Death of a friend, family member, or pet
- Divorce
- Hospitalization
- A move to a new location
- Anxiety
- Fear
- Pain
- Loss of trust
- Violence or war
- Terrorism or mass disaster
- Loss of job
- Financial loss
- Car or other serious accident

At the time of a traumatic event, the person experiencing the event might feel numb and, therefore, not know how to respond. Later on, memories of the trauma can bring out feelings of helplessness, fear, or horror as if they are reliving the trauma all over again. To try to resolve such feelings and move forward after a trauma, it is helpful to discuss the events and feelings, especially with a child.

How to Minister: (All commands done in Jesus' name).

1. Command the spirit of fear to go.
2. Lead them in a prayer to lay all cares, stress, fears and worries on the Altar of God.
3. Lead them in a prayer of forgiveness or repentance.
4. Speak peace to them.

TREMOR, ESSENTIAL

Essential Tremor is a nerve disorder in which tremors (shakes) occur when a person is moving or trying to move purposefully. It occurs most often in the hands but can also affect the head or voice.

Essential Tremor is the most common form of abnormal tremors. Although the cause is unknown, research shows that one part of the brain does not appear to function properly. Stress, fatigue, anger, fear, caffeine, and cigarettes may temporarily worsen the condition.

How to Minister: (All commands done in Jesus' name).
1. Command the brain to function properly.
2. Command the electrical and magnetic frequencies to be in harmony and balance.
3. Command the hormones to be in balance.
4. Lead them in a prayer of repentance when necessary.
5. Lead them in a prayer to lay all cares, stress, fears and worries on the Altar of God.

TRIGEMINAL NEURALGIA (See Tic Douloureux).

TUMOR

A Tumor is a growth of tissue that forms an abnormal mass. Tumors generally provide no useful function and grow at the expense of healthy tissues. In general, Tumors appear to be caused by abnormal regulation of cell division.

If the balance of cell division and cell death is disturbed, a Tumor may form. Tumors are classified as either benign (slow-growing and often harmless depending on the location) or malignant (faster-growing and likely to spread to other parts of the body and cause problems). Malignant Tumors are called Cancer.

Abnormalities of the immune system, which usually detects and blocks abnormal growth, can lead to Tumors. Other causes include tobacco, obesity, sedentary lifestyle, excessive alcohol consumption, radiation, genetic abnormalities, excessive sunlight exposure, benzene and a number of other chemicals and toxins.

How to Minister: (All commands done in Jesus' name).

1. Curse the root of the Tumor and command it to dissolve.
2. Lead in repentance for bitterness or unforgiveness, if necessary.
3. Command electrical and magnetic frequencies to come into harmony and balance.
4. Curse any prions and command them to be discarded.
5. Command the immune system to operate properly.
6. Lead them in a prayer of repentance for lifestyle or diet, if necessary.

ULCER

An Ulcer is an open sore on a body surface and can appear on the skin or mucous membranes either inside or outside of the body. They may be caused by inflammation, infection (stomach ulcer), or malignant conditions (tumors); excessive stress, poor diet and sedentary lifestyle (decubitus or bed sores); medication side effects (peptic ulcer), drug or alcohol abuse (esophageal ulcers); smoking, stress; or pressure (bed sores). Many other diseases exacerbate Ulcer formation and make healing difficult such as Crohn's Disease, Herpes, Diabetes, or circulation problems.

How to Minister: (All commands done in Jesus' name).

1. Command all tissues in the affected area to be healed.
2. Command all underlying disease processes to cease and all body systems to function normally.
3. Lead them in a prayer to lay all cares, stress, and worries on the Altar of God.

4. Lead them in a prayer of repentance for diet or lifestyle, if necessary.

URINARY TRACT INFECTION (UTI)

A Urinary Tract Infection, or UTI, is an infection that can happen anywhere along the urinary tract including the kidneys, the ureters (the tubes that take urine from each kidney to the bladder), the bladder or the urethra (the tube that empties urine from the bladder to the outside).

Most Urinary Tract Infections are caused by bacteria entering the area from outside the body. A very common bacteria which causes a UTI is E Coli which comes from feces (stool). This leads to inflammation and infection in the lower urinary tract. The most common symptom is burning with urination Women tend to get them more often because their urethra is shorter and closer to the anus. Elderly people (especially those who have chronic incontinence) and people with diabetes also get more UTIs. Cystitis is the term to describe an inflammation of the urinary bladder.

How to Minister: (All commands done in Jesus' name).

1. Rebuke the infection and command it to go.
2. Command the kidneys, bladder and all the tissues and nerves to be restored to normal structure and function.
3. Lead them in a prayer of repentance, if necessary.

VARICOSE VEINS

Varicose Veins are large, twisted, and painful superficial veins resulting from poorly functioning valves. In normal veins, valves in the vein keep blood moving forward toward the heart. With varicose veins, the valves do not function properly, allowing blood to remain in the vein. This abnormal pooling of blood in a vein causes it to enlarge.

Causes include congenitally defective valves, thrombophlebitis and pregnancy. Prolonged standing and increased pressure within the abdomen may increase susceptibility to the development of varicose veins or aggravate the condition.

How to Minister: (All commands done in Jesus' name).
1. Lead them in a prayer of repentance for generational curses.
2. Command all affected valves to be healed.
3. Command all swollen veins to return to normal.

VENEREAL DISEASE (Also called VD or STDs).

STDs are among the most common infectious diseases. Sexually Transmitted Diseases are infections that are passed from person to person through sexual contact. Because sexual activity includes intimate contact, it provides an easy opportunity for organisms to spread from one person to another. A variety of infectious microorganisms can be spread by sexual contact.

Some diseases may be transmitted by kissing or by close body contact. Also, the organisms responsible for some STDs (for example, HIV and hepatitis viruses) can be transmitted through nonsexual means, such as from mother to child at birth or through breastfeeding or exposure to contaminated food, water, blood, medical instruments or needles.

How to Minister: (All commands done in Jesus' name).
1. Lead them in a prayer of repentance for ungodly covenants, if necessary.
2. Curse the root of the infection and / or virus and command it to go.

3. Command the immune system to function properly and be fully restored.
4. Command healing to any affected parts.
5. Lead them in a prayer of forgiveness, if necessary.
6. Lead them in a prayer to lay all cares, stress, and worries on the Altar of God.
7. Lead them in a prayer of repentance for diet or lifestyle, if necessary.

VERTIGO (See also Meniere's Disease).

Dizziness may be experienced as being unsteady, lightheadedness, feeling like you might faint, loss of balance or Vertigo (a feeling that you or the room is spinning or moving).

Most causes of dizziness are not serious and either quickly resolve on their own or are easily treated. However, dizziness can progress to Vertigo which can be disabling until symptoms resolve.

The most common causes of Vertigo are benign positional Vertigo and labyrinthitis (inflammation of the inner ear). Benign positional Vertigo happens when you change the position of your head. Labyrinthitis usually follows a cold or flu and is caused by a viral infection of the inner ear. Meniere's Disease is another common inner ear problem. It causes Vertigo, loss of balance, and ringing in the ears. It can accompany or be exacerbated by nausea, vomiting, and / or migraine headaches.

How to Minister: (All commands done in Jesus' name).

1. Lead in a prayer of repentance for generational curses.
2. Command the fluid in the ears to return to normal.
3. Command any infection to leave and the Vertigo to go and balance to return to normal.

WALLEYED (See Cross-eyed).

WARTS

Warts are small, usually painless growths on the skin caused by a virus. They are generally harmless. However, warts can be disfiguring embarrassing, and occasionally they itch or hurt (particularly on the feet). The different types of warts include:

Common warts: usually appear on the hands, but can appear anywhere.

Flat warts: generally found on the face and forehead.

Genital warts: usually found on the genitals, in the pubic area, and the area between the thighs, but can appear inside the vagina and anal canal.

Plantar warts: found on the soles of the feet.

Subungual and periungual warts: appear under and around the fingernails or toenails

Common warts tend to cause no discomfort unless they are in areas of repeated friction or pressure. Plantar warts, for example, can become extremely painful. Large numbers of plantar warts on the foot may cause difficulty running and walking.

How to Minister: (All commands done in Jesus' name).

1. Curse the seed of the root and command the wart to dry up and fall off.
2. Lead them in a prayer of repentance, if necessary.

WATER ON THE KNEE OR ELBOW (See Edema).

WEBBING (See Floaters).

WEST NILE VIRUS

West Nile Virus is transmitted by mosquitoes and causes an illness that ranges from mild to severe. The mild, flu-like form of the illness is often called West

Nile Fever. More severe forms of the disease, which can be life-threatening, may be called West Nile encephalitis or West Nile meningitis, depending on where it spreads.

West Nile Virus is a type of organism similar to many other mosquito-borne viruses, including Japanese encephalitis (which is found in Asia). Researchers believe the virus is spread when a mosquito bites an infected bird and then bites a person.

Although many people are bitten by mosquitoes that carry West Nile Virus, most do not know they have been exposed. Few people develop severe disease or even notice any symptoms at all.

How to Minister: (All commands done in Jesus' name).
1. Curse the root of the disease and command it to go.
2. Command all prions to be discarded.
3. Command new blood and organs, if necessary.

WHIPLASH

Whiplash is caused when the soft tissues of the neck are injured by a sudden jerking or "whipping" of the head. This type of motion strains the muscles and ligaments of the neck beyond their normal range of motion.

When a vehicle stops suddenly in a crash or is struck from behind, a seat belt will keep a person's body from being thrown forward. But the head may snap forward, then backward, causing Whiplash. In addition to car accidents, Whiplash can be caused by roller coasters and other amusement park rides, sports injuries, or by being punched or shaken. If seen in a young child, Abuse is the suspected cause.

How to Minister: (All commands done in Jesus' name).
1. Curse the pain and command it to go.
2. Command the neck to come into alignment.

3. Command any damaged disc, vertebrae, nerve, ligament, tendon or muscle to be healed.
4. Command the spirit of fear to leave, if necessary.

YEAST INFECTIONS (See Candida).

INDEX

Please Note: This Index is to assist you in finding specific conditions mentioned in Chapter 13. Items in all capital letters are major headings in Chapter 13 Prayers for Various Conditions. Items in upper and lower case are mentioned within other major headings.

A

B

C

D

E

F

G

H

I

T

U

V

W

Y

OTHER PRAYERS